BLACKLIGHT CHRONICLES
BOOK FIVE

STAR MAGE

JOHN FORRESTER

AMBER MUSE

ISBN-10: 150097692X

ISBN-13: 978-1500976927

Cover Design by Anca Gabriela Marginean

Visit: www.blacklightchronicles.com

1

Resurrection

The energy of the black crystal burned strong in Talis's body as he pressed his palms against the wet ground. He could feel the crystal still alive beneath the desolate wreckage of the destroyed Temple of the Sun. Although he possessed powerful crystals from the heart of Ghaelstrom, there was something special and serene about the feeling of the crystal that the Goddess Nacrea had given him. The Temple would be renewed. The land was still sacred.

A few paces away, the spring still bubbled cool water from deep within the earth and spilled into the stream that flowed down to the grassy field below the hill where the temple once stood. Blackened beams and broken stones were strewn across the old temple grounds. What a mess the Jiserians had made of the holy place. But Talis was determined to restore the Temple to its former glory.

He lifted his eyes to where a ray of light beamed down onto the burned and broken City of Naru. So much work remained to rebuild their once beautiful city. And only Master Goleth to help in the casting of the spells of building and creation. He had refused to teach Talis the spells, claiming that his vow to an unrevealed god prevented him from passing on the knowledge without the blessing of the masters of his Order.

Once in Naru, the Builder had seemed reluctant to help them beyond repairing the core structural damage to the larger buildings and temples. In the days that had passed since their return, Goleth's distracted face told Talis it was time for them to fly south and return the Builder to his family.

"We'll build a new temple to the Goddess Nacrea." Mara strode up alongside him and provided a pleasant interruption from his solitude in surveying the hillside. Her hopeful eyes studied him. *Should a new temple be constructed again so soon after they'd built the last Temple of the Sun, or should they wait and let the land rest?* He prayed to the Goddess that the new Temple would stand and remain strong and protect his city. *Unlike the last temple… Was it cursed as Master Viridian had said it would be?*

"And build stronger walls to protect her." Talis vowed to do whatever he could to prevent this kind of destruction against his city. Even if it meant forming an alliance with their once enemies in the Jiserian Empire. *Or seeking out and killing Rikar, wherever he decided to go and hide.* The Starwalkers would come for Rikar, Talis was certain of it. But would they also come and seek revenge against Nikulo for his slaying of the Starwalker known as Jeremiah? Talis doubted it.

5

"Master Goleth sent me to find you. He's insisting we leave today for Ishur," she said, her voice bitter at the Builder's refusal to aid them any longer in the restoration of Naru. "I sense some secret in the man, as if he's been contacted by his superiors in the Jiserian Empire. His eyes have completely changed these last few days. They're dull and distracted as if he's duty bound to obey his master in Ishur."

"Perhaps they've captured his wife and family and hold them hostage until he returns." Talis pictured the joy and appreciation on Goleth's face when Talis had insisted that the Builder return with them to their world.

"I've tried asking him if something is wrong, and each time he ignores my question and stares off to the south. I think he truly believes that his family was in a safe place when he left, and I am certain that his conviction has now been shattered."

"Let's go find out," Talis said, and changed into dragon form. Mara mounted on his back and with a quick flapping of his wings, rose high into the sky until the city sped by far below. Soon he landed at the grounds surrounding the Temple of Nestria, the Goddess of the Sky, and he changed forms after Mara had dismounted.

She pointed at a figure far off in the distance standing and studying the southern horizon. Master Goleth had chosen this spot to rest after long days spent reconstructing the critically damaged portions of the city. The first building Talis had asked Goleth to rebuild was the Temple of the Order of the Dawn, and the massive golden dome that was shattered after the assault on Naru by the Jiserians. Since the wizards of the Order had either fled or been killed after the last Jiserian assault, Talis decided to erase the tragedy of the past and start fresh with a new Temple. He planted one of the crystals from Ghaelstrom underneath the temple, and let it grow in girth and power once it was seeded deep in the earth. Now the temple rose some fifty-feet higher than before, and it towered over that part of the city.

Goleth ignored them as they approached, choosing instead to lock his gaze on a bank of black storm clouds off to the southeast. The man's voice was low and thoughtful as he spoke. "Will the storm affect our flight?"

"I've flown through far worse storms." Talis thought back to the vicious storm that assaulted them on the way to Ghaelstrom. "Shall we leave now, Master Builder?" He intentionally elongated the last word, hoping to prod the man's integrity at leaving without completely restoring Naru.

"I will return to Naru and help in your reconstruction once I know my family is safe." Goleth turned to fix fearful eyes on Talis. "By now you have likely guessed that something was amiss. They'll kill my family if I don't return within three days, starting with my eldest son first. I don't know how they've found them, I worked so hard to hide them and keep them safe. I must have been betrayed by the few souls that I trusted with my secret."

"Who is threatening your family?" Mara said, and could see Master Goleth struggle in his thoughts, as if uncertain whether to answer the question. After ten heartbeats the man opened his mouth to speak.

"I won't lie to you, but the truth will expose you to great danger. Are you sure you want to hear this?" The Builder narrowed his eyes in examination of Talis's reaction. "I was only going to ask for you to take me as far as a village northeast of Ishur, so as to guarantee your safety and keep a good distance from the danger within the walls of that great and terrible city. Those of Ishur leave Naru alone because they believe the city vanquished. If they were to discover otherwise, you'd once again face the wrath of their necromancers."

Talis scoffed, wondering why the man thought the Jiserians more of a threat, especially with Aurellia so far away from the world. Were the remnants of his followers any real threat? And hadn't Aurellia summoned his strongest supporters when Elder Raelles was sent here before the armada had left? Was there any real force of power remaining inside the Jiserian Empire?

"Don't believe this world is without danger, young mage, for you would be making a grave mistake. I heard the mocking tone from King Valeron in describing our planet. As if nothing of value exists here…" Master Goleth lifted the corners of his mouth in a wry smile. "It is better to promote such a myth and keep the seekers from our land.

Aurellia's master has done much to ensure that this is the case."

"Aurellia has a master here on this world?" Talis thought back to all the words Aurellia had spoken, trying to remember any hints of his having a master. But he found none in his mind. "How is that possible? All of his followers spoke of him as the Dark Lord."

Master Goleth issued a small, mocking laugh. "The *visible* Dark Lord to the sorcerers and necromancers of this world. But think about it, if darkness is hidden away in the shadows, then wouldn't the true master be invisible, concealed behind the curtains and orchestrating all the movement in one grand plan?"

At what must have been Talis's perplexed expression, Master Goleth leaned in and whispered in a serious tone. "The true master of Aurellia is talked about only in hushed tones by the most senior adherents. He is called the Unknowable, the Nameless, the Bane of Light. It is not even known if he exists in a corporeal state, and perhaps is he merely a being that lurks in the depths of some dark place. Where the Nameless exists in this world is not known to me. I cannot speak a word more of this, as I've already said too much. Though from your face I can see you will now heed my original warning. Do not underestimate the danger. You lack the power and knowledge and mental fortitude to withstand the forces of the Nameless."

Talis stiffened at the Builder's condescending tone, but held back a retort and instead considered the wisdom in

Master Goleth's words. If there were a Dark Lord still in the Jiserian Empire, the Nameless, as his followers called him, then perhaps Talis should fear the threat. Too often he had underestimated his enemies, and he wasn't about to do so again.

"What if we can help you ensure freedom for your family?" Mara said, and Talis was surprised at her willingness to help. He knew she was trying to appeal to the man's emotions.

"You simply don't stand a chance fighting against them. Take me to the village northeast of Ishur, that is all I ask of you. Any more would risk your lives and the lives of those in your city. Do you have much preparation needed for the journey?"

"Who said anything about fighting?" Talis sent the man a mischievous grin. "Call me your apprentice and let me search around for this master. If his followers are still as dangerous as you claim, then what other choice do I have? It seems like only a matter of time before the Jiserians discover that Naru is filled with living people and they'll return to conquer and destroy. Our only hope is to seek out this master in the purpose of either striking an alliance or somehow dissuading him from harming our city."

Master Goleth scoffed and shook his head dismissively. "You are so naive. Brave, but stupidly so. Are you so eager for your own death? Instead of rebuilding your beautiful city, my advice for you is to run and escape far from Jiserian lands. Go and find a nice quiet corner of the world to live and thrive and grow old in peace and die. In the south you'll find nothing but and darkness and torture and death."

"But is it feasible to pretend that I am your apprentice? Could you convince them?" Talis said, his voice insistent.

"It is possible…though unadvisable. I could claim you as a practitioner of magic from Vellia, a boy who begged to return with me and study under my tutelage. Your face is unknown in Ishur and likely the masters of my Order would believe me. And you *have* been craving to learn the spells of creation and elemental assembly. But I would warn you to speak nothing of what I have revealed to you…not once. And if trouble arises then escape and flee back to your city." *And not in dragon form*, Talis told himself, certain that a magical portal was the safest way out of Ishur.

"I'm coming also," Mara said, her eyes narrowed in a way that Talis knew was useless to argue against, though he hated the idea of her coming on such a dangerous journey into the heart of their enemies. "Don't shake your head, Master Goleth. I know girls are allowed in the Jiserian ranks. I've encountered more than a few sorceresses."

The Builder's face crinkled in confusion. "But I had assumed that you did not possess the magical gift?"

"Can't your magic be taught?" She retorted, a stubborn expression fixed on her face. Talis knew from experience that magic could be taught, but it had taken him many difficult years to cast spells outside training dreams. And he had only been admitted into the Order of the Dawn since the gift of magic existed in his family lineage.

"It is a difficult and painful thing to learn magic—at least the way we Jiserians teach the art." Master Goleth stared at the southern Nalgoran Desert, and Talis studied a look of expanding anguish forming on his face. *His lessons in magic must have been terrifying and agonizing.* "I would not wish such torture inflicted on one such as yourself."

"You think me a simple, weak girl?" Mara scowled at the Builder, her face tensed with some fantastic rage that surprised Talis. "You have no idea of what torture I've been through at the hands of Elder Relech. That monster forced me to kill countless innocent people and the gods only know what else he imparted inside my mind during his *lessons* as he called them. I know Princess Minoweth's dagger tainted me all the while, but I also know that through that experience something hardened inside of me and formed a deep well of strength in my heart."

Mara exhaled forcefully and clenched her face and a twist of harsh emotions seethed inside. "There is still magic inside of me from Elder Relech and the cursed dagger—I can feel it burning and itching and screaming to release from my fingers. I don't trust myself around blades because I see them and my hands crave to stab and cut and maim, as if some dark magic is waiting to release from each slash. I have no choice but to learn magic and tame whatever it is in that I'm feeling inside. Can you help me? Otherwise I'm afraid I'll lose my mind."

"Why didn't you talk to me about this before?" Talis said, his voice low and fearful.

She turned away from him to stare out at the Nalgoran Desert. "I didn't want you to worry about me or think me an evil person. I wanted you to believe me healed after separating from Princess Minoweth's dagger. But how can I ever truly be free of that curse? I remember everything, every feeling and dark desire. It's like the Princess is somehow inside of me still. I truly believe I need to channel that rage into something productive, like the learning of magic."

With an intense stare she fixed pleading eyes on Master Goleth. "I trust you and know you won't do anything to hurt me. Can you teach me of your magic? I'll gladly humble myself as your apprentice if you can assure me that I'll study under you and no one else. Will your Order allow this?"

"Only if you both swear a blood pact to our Order, and pledge your life in the defense of the Jiserian Empire and the Nameless, who is the Lord of All, and the true Emperor of the Dark. Only then will you be admitted into the Order of Rezel."

2

Nightmares

Nikulo had kept his distance from Talis and Mara over the last few days, hoping to avoid the inspecting eyes of his friends. He knew he couldn't keep the truth from them for long, especially from Mara, who had a keen sense of his moods. With the dark dreams that had plagued him since their return to Naru, he avoided family and friends, and anyone that knew him too well.

A mug of ale raised to his mouth provided him with temporary relief from the reality of his sleeplessness. A few more drinks and he'd pass out into a blissful, dreamless sleep. He glanced around the dark and dreary tavern, seeing drunk men living in a world of suffering and sadness. *Likely loved ones slain in the attack on the city,* Nikulo thought. He hadn't lost anyone in his family, so why was he suffering as them?

He wondered why the pain and the nightmares had struck him with such a torrential ferocity. Was there something different about Naru since the plague? Or a simpler explanation: there was something vastly different about himself since he'd returned? *And maybe that something still haunted his mind.* The voices and the eruption of many stabs of pain across his head, especially around his eyes and temples. Never in his life had he experienced such quick bursts of crippling agony.

Even with the ale the pain was still there lodged in the background, numbed but present and speaking dark words of malice. The feeling was like a musician playing a vengeful tune inside his skull, and the musician's instrument was a collection of sharp needles jabbing notes into his brain.

"Another ale for ya, sweetie?" The buxom barmaid bent over his table, revealing wrinkled, leathery cleavage that caused Nikulo to look away in disgust.

"I think I've had enough." Nikulo was sick of this filthy tavern and he slapped down a few copper coins and stood to leave. Why had he decided to come here in the first place? The fog over his mind cleared for a moment, and he remembered that this was the only tavern he had yet to visit, and likely the last place Talis and Mara would look to find him.

You can't hide from them forever, Nikulo thought. *Soon enough they'll find you and then what will you tell them?* Maybe he could just join a caravan and travel west to the Ursulan Coast. He could always claim he was going to help find Talis's family and let them know that Naru was safe for their return. *But would they ever be safe in Naru, so close to the Jiserian Empire?* The voices told him that they weren't sheltered. They droned endlessly about how exposed they were to more Jiserian attacks.

Nikulo staggered over to leave and paused awhile to rest against the wood until the dizziness went away. The world seemed to tip sideways and as he opened the door, the crisp, cold air invigorated his mind enough for him to make his way outside and down the dark alleyway. His bladder demanded immediate attention and he obeyed, relieving himself in a hurry.

"Ah, gods!" shouted a voice from below. "Why'd ya piss on my face?"

Blinking, Nikulo gaped down at the man sleeping in the darkness. He yanked up his trousers and fought to keep his balance. "Sssoo sssoorry." He reached into his coin purse and handed the pissed-on man a silver coin and hobbled away, mumbling slurred apologies along the alley until he reached a small square filled with chatting people.

His stomach complained as the smell of roasted meat wafted into his nostrils. He realized he hadn't eaten all day. *How the hell is that possible?* he asked himself. Perhaps some food would bring stability to his steps and get him home safely. Where was home these days? His befuddled brain refused to provide any insights. Was he staying with a brown-haired girl he'd met at a tavern, or with friends he'd gambled with, or perhaps an old witch who bartered in blood?

He slumped into a chair at a table serving slices of pork slathered in oil and herbs and stinking of garlic. A tall man with jutting bones and shifty eyes brought him a plate of meat and chunks of burned potatoes. Nikulo produced another silver and the man went to hand him change, but Nikulo shook his head and found the world spinning perilously in reaction to his movement. The man seized him by the shoulders to steady him.

"Eat up. Might want to slow down on the drink, young master." The man gave him a sad stare as he turned and strode over to another table. *Damn him*, thought Nikulo. *All he sees the one of the saviors of Naru all drunk and pathetic. What does he know of my torment?*

Then another voice spoke in Nikulo's mind, a sinister voice that sounded like one of the Naemarians. *"Kill him, kill the fool who dares look at you like that. Why are you still stuck in this city? Go west, go and find your power and free yourself from the pain; leave your family and friends. They'll never understand what you must become."*

He covered his ears in a lame attempt at stopping the voices, and found eyes staring at him as a yelp of pain escaped his mouth. His head lowered in shame. All he could do was to shove the roasted pork and potatoes into his mouth, wishing he had more ale to wash down the food. Each day since they'd returned, the pain had proved progressively worse, until now there seemed truly few reasons to stay. Would the pain really subside if he left Naru? The Naemarians promised him it would.

Off in his addled mind he heard a familiar voice, "At least he's not dead." He raised his eyes and squinted at

Talis and Mara staring down at him with concerned and troubled expressions on their faces. How were they able to look so kindly on him in such a horrible condition?

"Go away. I don't want you to see me like this." Nikulo lowered his eyes and returned to his food, and sighed malcontentedly when he heard them drag over chairs and sit next to him.

"We're leaving for Ishur with Master Goleth," Talis said, the tone of his voice sounding like their journey was a punishment. "We wanted to see if you'd join us."

Nikulo scoffed at that. "Fly down and visit with our enemies? Sounds like a perfect idea." He let out a wet belch that smelled like ale and garlic pork. "Count me out."

"What's happened to you?" Mara placed a hand on Nikulo's arm and he stiffened and found the urge to punch her in the face. "We've been looking everywhere for you. Where did you go? We haven't seen you in days and your parents are really worried about you. They said you had a fight and you stormed out and vowed never to return. What's going on with you?"

"I won't ever return. I have no need for parents anymore. Now leave me alone, I told you I don't want to see you."

"We're not leaving," Talis said, his voice low and determined. "Not even if you force us."

Nikulo shoved the table and sent the food flying, standing furious over them. "Can't you stop bothering me!" he shouted, and aimed a finger at Talis. "Go off south, go

18

on to Ishur, I don't care! Just leave me alone, will you? I'm tired and drunk and this pain is killing me." He seized his scalp and pressed his fingers hard until the agony subsided for a moment.

"You're gravely ill!" Mara came close and pressed a blissfully cool palm against his forehead. "When did the pain start?"

"The day after we returned. It woke me from the most hideous nightmare I've ever had and has never left me since." Nikulo pinched his eyes shut and seethed as a vast, jolting pain stabbed into his brain and caused his arms to tremble and shake. "I'm afraid it's slowly driving me insane…"

"Do you still hear the Naemarians inside your head?" Mara said.

Nikulo nodded, too tired to resist anymore. "But it's different this time, distant but more shrill, like the wailing of demons. I feel as if they're still trying to reach out to me— they crave the power of the fragment. I've been telling them over and over again that I don't have it. They just shriek and scream for me to steal it back. If I could only stop the pain and the voices…and sleep, sweet, wonderful sleep. Now do you know why I've hidden myself away from everyone?"

"Have you tried visiting the Temple of Tolexia? Perhaps the Goddess will heal you."

"I've tried everything and nothing helps. Don't you think I would have visited all the shrines and temples and priests in Naru? I've even drunk from the waters of the spring at the grounds of the destroyed Temple of the Sun. Nothing works. The Naemarians keep demanding that I leave Naru and go west and follow their commands. I have to obey them. They've promise the pain will pass once I leave Naru."

"So leave Naru with us," Mara said. "Come south and help us."

With a shake of Nikulo's head he staggered away and refused to answer their calls. He knew what he had to do. He would leave Naru tonight and join a caravan west, and find whatever the voices wanted him to find, and blissfully soon the pain would stop. At least he hoped and prayed to the gods that it would leave him...

3

Desert Flight

Talis woke early the next morning, hoping that his parents and sister were well protected along the western sea. After he'd healed the undead of the plague, he'd sent a messenger west to send word to his family that the city was once again safe. And now, as he gazed at the Nalgoran Desert from atop the city, he realized he wouldn't be able to see his parents and little sister for a long while until he returned. *If I ever return*, he told himself.

Master Goleth strode up alongside and together they silently studied the horizon. After yesterday's conversation, the Builder had assumed a serious demeanor in his role as their master. What bothered Talis the most about his agreement with the Builder was the fact that he'd have to swear a vow of traitorous protection to the Jiserian Empire, the very empire that had destroyed his city.

Mara snuck up to Talis and wrapped her small hands around his chest, joining him in gazing at the desert horizon. She leaned in and whispered something tender and undecipherable into his ear, and planted a kiss on his neck. He found a smile forming on his face at her touch, and glanced around to enjoy her mischievous eyes.

"When we arrive at the village," Master Goleth said, "you will follow my lead and remain quiet. Act as apprentices would act, respectful of their master and obedient. Do you understand? That's good, then it's all settled. Let's depart at once, as my masters await my return to Ishur. I have informed them that I will be arriving from the mountains. The very mountains that I had intended to keep my wife and family safe during my journey."

But things rarely go as planned, Talis thought, and he transformed himself into a dragon. He had rarely assumed the shape, shunning the stares and suspicion of the people of Naru. But here high on the temple grounds of the Goddess Nestria, the emptiness of the early morning air surrounded and invigorated him as he flapped his dragon wings.

Mara helped strap on a leather saddle fashioned by Master Goleth, a twin saddle fit to carry the Builder and Mara on their long journey south across the sands. Talis wasn't certain how long the trip might take, but with the Ghaelstrom crystal positioned in the saddlebags, the power of the stars flooded into his dragon heart and prepared him for the flight. *If only King Valeron had taught me more of the magic of dragons,* Talis thought.

On their long flight south across the vast Nalgoran Desert, Talis wondered about Nikulo and the voices that plagued him. Was there a way to heal his friend and keep him from going insane? He hated leaving Nikulo alone in his suffering, and worried that his friend might venture out west all alone. Were the voices truly the Naemarians or simply artifacts left in Nikulo's mind? Talis was determined to use the Surineda Map to track his friend's movement and ensure that he was all right. *But what could he do if Nikulo refused his help?*

After many longs hours, the day faded into twilight, and the shifting sands shimmered under the soft light of the sun. Talis relished in the feeling of the air striking his snout and the sensation of speed racing over the land. He swooped low and soared over the serpentine sand dunes. The taupe and onyx shadows provided a vivid contrast to the breathtaking burnt orange and gold of the dunes. With the wind whipping the sands in a harmonic fury, the undulating landscape brought a depth to Talis's flying meditation. The shapeless sands formed at once into a face, the harrowing eyes of a ghoul studying him.

Talis snapped his dragon eyes shut and back open, and instantly locked on a series of ruins in the desert. The feeling of awe and horror overtook his heart and compelled him to circle around the desert ruins, much to the protestation of Master Goleth. Talis spied the inky darkness of an entryway into a submerged sandstone building, and he dove down and landed.

"Why have you stopped here in the Ruins of Elmarr?" Master Goleth said, his face fearful as he glanced around at the structures jutting above the sands. "These ruins are forbidden to all citizens of the Jiserian Empire, and the skies are often patrolled by flying sorcerers. Change at once back to dragon form—we must leave here immediately!"

But Talis ignored the Builder's command, a powerful premonition pushing him on, and he carried the heavy saddle over to the dark opening of the largest building in the ruins. Mara jogged alongside, casting him worried glances, her eyes alert and scared as they entered the tunnel. Talis swore he could hear a low, raspy breathing coming from deep within the ruin. *Like the sound an ancient, slumbering dragon makes*, Talis thought, and sniffed for signs of sulfur but found only stale, putrid air. *Like the smell of old bones and decaying flesh.*

Every bit of sense in his mind shouted at him to flee this foul place and never return. He ignored the thoughts racing through his mind and instead focused on the rhythm of his pounding heart. *Who resides within these ancient halls, the dead or the tortured living?* Thump thump—whump—thump thump. His erratic heart seemed to battle against his mind. He pictured something pervasive and black, something greasy and hideous lurking down in the depths. *Or should I ask "what" resides within the ruin?* Talis told himself, and the words "*The Nameless*" entered his mind like the cold steel of a blade.

Someone seized his wrist and he jumped in fright, and realized that Mara was holding him from blindly striding down the tunnel like a thrall. "I don't want to go inside." Her voice was a terrified whisper.

24

A new, mesmerizing voice hissed and slithered into his mind. *Enter...enter my embrace. Another step, just one more foot inside. Come and claim your reward.*

Death awaited him inside and it was no reward, not after all he'd been through. He had the people of Naru who counted on him, and his family who would be returning soon. And Mara needed him. So with a surge of strength he forced himself away from the enticing tunnel, and strode back to the windswept desert, greeted by Master Goleth's confused and terrified face.

Talis changed back into dragon form and allowed the Builder to strap the saddle onto his back, and once again they took flight towards the craggy hills off to the southeast. Night was falling and as he flapped his wings and lifted higher and higher, he took one last glance at the Ruins of Elmarr and the hissing voice wailed in his mind.

Darkness fell and the stars flooded the shimmering sky, the air so clear and black, and swaths of diffused white and pink and blue arced across the sky as if painted by the Goddess Nestria. Soon he sniffed water from the ground far below and he circled and followed his nostrils to land near a small oasis of palms and sweet acacias scenting the air. Back in human form, Talis stretched his spine and strode with Mara over to where he heard a bubbling spring in the middle of a stand of palm trees.

He avoided eye contact with Master Goleth, and instead found a secluded place behind a palm and cuddled up with Mara to fight off the night chill. The Builder seemed to perceive his desire for privacy, as he had not followed them to their resting place. Talis unfurled the Surineda Map and checked for Master Goleth's location, and found him far back in the place where they had landed. A morbid curiosity caused him to check on Nikulo's location, and Talis's heart sank as he found his friend in the desert west of Naru. *Separate ways for old friends*, Talis thought.

"That's Nikulo, isn't it?" Mara's wistful voice whispered as she studied the map. "I hope he's ok. I'm really worried about him."

"First Rikar and now him. Too much strain and darkness." *And too much death.* Talis pictured the hordes of dead in the Underworld, and Zagros leading the fray.

"Why did you stop there in the ruins? That place freaked me out." A shiver went through her small frame and she seized his arm as if for protection. "There was something down there at the bottom of the tunnel, something alive and hideous."

"Maybe not alive, at least not like a human. Something else. Something Nameless." The hissing voice surged in his mind in frenzied excitement, *"Yes, yes, you will worship me and drink from the well of power."*

"The same being that Master Goleth talked about? You think the Nameless is there in the Ruins of Elmarr?" Her voice had turned cold and fearful and Talis caught her emotions. He wanted to feel the heat of a campfire on his skin.

"Let's collect some wood…I'm freezing." She joined him in scavenging fallen branches under the acacia trees and returned to the spring and assembled the wood. He released a wiry stream of flame from his palms and the wood ignited into a slow, soothing burn. The fragrant smell of the burning acacia intoxicated Talis's mind and caused him to lean back against the palm tree and enjoy the heat of the blaze.

"I do think the Nameless resides there in those ruins." Talis found Mara wiggling her way back into him, where she reclined against his chest. "I barely stopped myself from going inside. The power was so strong and seductive. I wonder if Aurellia stumbled upon those ruins and fell into that trap."

Mara bobbed her head as she nibbled on some dried meat. "Different." She finished chewing the meat and turned to look up at him. "Your heart is pure and filled with light, but his heart is obsessed by the darkness. That's why you could resist going in there."

"I can still hear its voice inside my head, like a hissing snake." He shivered at the memory of the sound and the feeling of the Nameless trying to writhe its way inside his brain. "If the masters of the Jiserian Empire worship that thing… Perhaps we've made a grave mistake in coming here with Master Goleth."

"We've not sworn any oath to him or to his Order. What's to prevent us from leaving him there in that village and exploring the City of Ishur on our own?"

"I don't know how much we'd learn as simple travelers to their realm. Besides, we know little of their culture and how to fit in to their society. We'd likely be suspected as spies or rejected as unwelcome strangers to their realm. And without caravan owners or ship captains to vouch for us, how would we say we arrived to Ishur? They might not believe me if I claimed I was a dragon."

She released a small laugh and glanced up at his eyes.

She looks so pretty tonight and smells of the roses from her mother's garden. He tried to concentrate on the problem at hand, but found her body pressed against him incredibly distracting. Out of habit, his mouth opened to speak, but she placed a finger against his lips to quiet him. She shook her head and smiled, a wild fascination dancing in her eyes. The four moon sisters were arrayed low in the sky and the hazy light illuminated Mara's face in a soft glow. Her hand snaked up behind his neck and she pulled him closer.

His speeding heart sent a quick rush racing through him. He held his breath and felt the tingling exhalation from her nostrils land on his chest as she nestled there and pressed her ear against his heart. Once he felt her breathing quicken, he wondered what was spinning in her mind. *Maybe we are thinking the same thing,* Talis thought, and for some reason a clear vision came to him of Mara laughing and twirling in a white dress, her enraptured eyes raised to the flittering rose petals he had thrown above her head. She was so beautiful. Why hadn't he ever told her so?

"Hey, where did you go?" Mara's voice was gravely, as if unused to speaking. "I could feel you'd drifted off someplace."

"I was picturing you in your mother's garden." He chuckled at the memory of how he'd tickled her after she'd raised her hands to catch the petals.

"When?" She pushed herself up and stared at him with insistent eyes.

"A long time ago, before we had tried to hunt a boar. It was late spring and the roses were in bloom. We had snuck out of some stupid royal ceremony and were running around in the gardens. You wore this white, lacy dress with embroidered patterns of the Goddess Nacrea."

Mara gave him this serious, entranced look and her eyes sparkled in the firelight. "You paid attention to what I wore all the way back then? And you never once told me? I hated that dress and thought for sure you'd make fun of me for wearing it. I remember that day in my mother's gardens, and you tickled me so long I almost peed myself. I was furious at you."

"But you were smiling the whole time," Talis said, and chuckled as Mara rolled her eyes. "Your face had this pretty combination of rage and delight. That's how I always picture you in my mind."

She went suddenly still and stared up at him. "You think I'm pretty?"

"No," he said, and paused to watch her face fall in disappointment. "I think you're beautiful."

4

The Twin Daggers

Mara felt herself go from heart-broken to heart pounding in an instant. *Talis thinks I'm beautiful?* They had always teased and flirted with each other, and were incredibly close—especially after their long journeys together—but to hear him tell her that he thought she was beautiful caused her mouth to gape in amazement. He must have noticed her stupid expression for his eyes twinkled mischievously and he let out a nervous laugh.

"I'm really happy to have you on this journey with me," Talis said, and paused as his face turned cloudy. "But I'm scared at the same time. A large part of me wanted to heed the Builder's words and go west with you to the Ursulan Coast. To be honest, I'm pretty confused and uncertain as to what path to take. I'm really not sure what we're doing here."

"You think I'm beautiful?" Mara felt her face flush after she was unable to stop herself from blurting out the words. *What's wrong with me that I can't hold my tongue?*

His face flowered to a broad smile filled with warmth and what Mara hoped was love. Did he feel the same way?

"I should have insisted we go west." He scooped her hands up and she shivered as the heat and electricity danced through her at his touch. "Of course I think you're beautiful, Mara. You're more than beautiful, you're literally everything that is important in my life. I realize that now and I wish I had before we'd agreed to go on this insane journey. I thought the people of Naru and my family were important, and keeping our city safe, but now I know I was really just trying to protect you and our home."

"Our home?" She pictured a mansion of their own rising high in the sky next to the temple of the Goddess Nestria, with Talis by his side as they stared east and watched the sun plummet beneath the Nalgoran Desert.

"Yes, our city and our home, the place we grew up together and where our family and our people live. If that's destroyed then what else do we have?"

We have each other, Mara thought, *no matter where in this world or another we find ourselves.* But she just gave him a reassuring smile and squeezed his hands, disappointed that he didn't yet share the same vision as she. *Maybe one day he will...*

The night mist fell and sent a cold chill shivering through her. She snuggled into Talis's arms and he wrapped her with a woolen blanket from his house. The familiar sweet smell of Talis's skin entered her nostrils and she held her breath, devouring every scent as if at any moment someone might take him away from her. Sleep came soon, and so did the nightmare.

The wind howled over a putrid plain stained with sulfuric-smelling ash. *And graves, and the shambling feet...* Hands seized her ankles and started pulling her under the ground as fibers wriggled around her body and searched for her mouth and ears and nostrils to invade and ingest her lifeblood. *Talis!* She screamed and shouted his name, and begged for him to save her. She spotted him off in the distance and shouted again for help, but he ignored her and sauntered off into the mist with that witch Lenora. His laughing eyes glanced back only once at Mara, and he was gone.

She found herself yanked down deep into the devouring earth, the hands still squeezing her ankles and tugging her down on the descent into darkness. Loamy soil no longer surrounded her, replaced instead with the cold air of a cavern. Out there in the vastness she sensed a malicious presence lingering in the inky blackness. She waited and waited in a tense, anxious silence, trying to spot the thing that was out there. But nothing ever came and the cold chilled her to the bone until her teeth started chattering.

"Why did you leave me?" she cried, the betrayal driving deep into her heart. The image of the beautiful and mysterious Lenora appeared in the cave, her laughing, sensuous eyes taunted her. How could Mara ever appeal to Talis the way she could? The stupid expression of lust on his face when he first saw the witch in that inn. *He desired her in a way that he's never desired you before,* a voice told her. *How can you ever believe that he'll want you like he wanted her? You lack the figure that boys crave,* the voice said, *but you can kill them all and keep his affection.*

Princess Minoweth's green dagger shone eerily in the blackness of the cave, and the blade stabbed over and over again into Lenora's white neck, causing beautiful bursts of brilliant red to explode and stain the air as if splashing onto a black canvas. *You're missing your dagger, dearest one,* the voice scolded, *would you like to feel it in your hand once again?*

Mara shook her head and shouted an agonizing "no" over and over, but the more she squirmed and fought the more she felt the power of the dagger blossom once again inside of her. She remembered the sickly strong feeling, the rage and the craving for blood, and the howling fury that seethed through her mind. The power possessed her as it did once before.

She flipped her eyes open and the brilliance of starlight caused her to wince in pain. Hands that held daggers covered the moons, shielding the blinding light from her face. *Why in the name of the gods are there daggers in my hands?* Mara found herself whimpering in horror, and she jolted up and glanced around, feeling comforted that Talis snored peacefully beside her, but she found herself terrified at the strange blades in her palms.

Lifting the daggers to her inspection under the bright light of the moons, her heart pounded inside her chest at recognizing the design. *But the dagger was destroyed in Vellia!* Here it was, though, and twins this time, twin replicas of Princess Minoweth's dagger. *The feeling of the dagger is the same, and the power stronger!* She dropped the daggers and they dug deep into the sandy soil, but eerie green filaments of light still poured through the air and into her palms. How could this be happening? Was she still having a nightmare?

"Talis," she hissed, and shook him hesitantly on the shoulder, half expecting him to open demonic eyes to stare at her.

He stirred groggily and groaned, then sighed and went back to sleep. *At least I know I'm not dreaming,* she told herself. But that knowledge made everything so much worse. How in the name of the gods did she acquire the daggers? From the nightmare? *The voice and the darkness, the Nameless.* Did the voice read her mind and cause the creation of the blades?

She thought of Master Goleth and his words about the Nameless. *The Bane of Light, the Unknowable...* Were all the practitioners of magic in the Jiserian Empire adherents of the Nameless Master? *And farther across the world, even to Darkov, perhaps?* How far did his power extend? All the way to Vellia now, with his apprentice Aurellia and his odd, heart-felt reunion with his brother? Was it all a ruse?

A fear seized her heart. Talis couldn't find out about the daggers. He would recognize the design and believe the curse returned to her. She had to hide them from him, stash them away deep in her backpack and never let him find them. *Why not leave them buried here in the desert,* she told herself, *and release yourself from the torment of livid power within the daggers.*

34

So she tried, and stood and separated herself from the blades, testing out distances farther and farther away until a pain grew in her womb and she gasped and collapsed to her knees as a burst of crippling agony surged through her. In quick response she crawled back to the daggers and found the feeling fading away. A low ache and a burn still buzzed in her belly, and she vowed to never again leave the daggers.

She shoved the blades into her pack and lay back down next to Talis, knowing that sleep would be difficult to find. In her memory she pictured Jeremiah the Starwalker stealing Princess Minoweth's dagger, and the feelings of rage that had possessed her. Nikulo had killed the Starwalker with the fragment and had caused her to sleep just as she was about to reclaim the dagger. *Did Nikulo steal the dagger?* But Talis had told her that the blade was vaporized by a blast from the fragment. *Maybe he lied, or maybe Nikulo fooled him?* But then why did she now possess twin blades of the same design? *The Nameless feeds off memories*, the same voice from her nightmare told her.

What if she controlled her mind and hid her memories from the voice? Would she save herself from the pain and torment? She winced at the flood of images pouring into her mind, of Elder Relech's cackling face, of stabbing and slicing innocents in the dark, of raging in jealousy over Lenora's ability to steal Talis's attention. It all tumbled inside in an uncontrollable torrent.

This Unknowable Master of Nightmares, this Order of Rezel that demanded vows of blood, they both conspired to weave a web of constriction and choke the life out of her. But she would not be defenseless, not with the daggers close to her side. And she would not be controlled by the blades again, not that she now understood the power and could name it rage and malice and jealousy. She would conquer those emotions and train herself in the ever-mindfulness of the observer.

Constant and consistent control she would learn from the masters of Ishur. She must contain the power and not allow it to rule her mind.

Even at the cost of her life.

5

The Caravan West

Nikulo followed the voices into the desert like a raving lunatic absent of memories and hope. He had killed the uncompliant caravan owner and turned his young wife into a slave—her weak mind failing to provide much resistance to the magic of his mental suggestions. The other slaves in the caravan barely raised an eye at the unexpected change in ownership. *Likely I'm their fourth or fifth master over the length of their bitter life,* Nikulo told himself, and found an unfamiliar laugh escape from his mouth.

The pain had left him immediately upon exiting the city. His bliss and wild fervor had been so great that he celebrated with a raging domination of the muscular caravan owner's mind. The man seemed gleeful as he sliced his own neck. His wife had tried to stem the flow of blood from her husband's gushing throat but she only managed to paint her white silk dress red. Nikulo's cruel thoughts came quickly into his corrupted mind. *Pretty little thing decided a wet rouge matched her ruddy cheeks…*

The voices inside gave clear instructions: *go west to Ursula and find a ship sailing to Carvina.* From Nikulo's recollection,

Carvina was the capitol of the Jiserian Empire, where the Emperor sat upon the Ebony Throne. Though Ishur was rumored the largest city in the Jiserian Empire, it was said that the Emperor preferred to keep a distance from the power of the various orders of magic housed inside Ishur.

Beyond those instructions the voices were unclear, instead showing him images of a vast body of water seated near a range of mountains. *Naemarians thrive in ancient water,* the voices chanted to him in unison, *as deep as the planet, and as old as the stars.* He realized they were taking him to drink once again from a spring where they thrived. The idea of regaining their power and knowledge both excited and terrified him at the same time.

Used to traveling at dragon speed, Nikulo found the slow life of the caravan tedious, and with the excess amount of free time he was left with many moments to contemplate his time back on Vellia. He wished he was able to remember the flying spell he'd cast from the Naemarian well of knowledge. But other than the voices commanding him on, they seemed unable to grant him powers or expertise. *They're only able to inflict horrific pain and mind-numbing words of repetition.* He'd trade his soul for a magic flying carpet.

He'd given up on trying to make conversation with the slaves, finding their terse, obedient responses tiresome. The caravan owner's wife was intoxicatingly beautiful, and her lissome figure provided adequate entertainment along the way. Once, in a fit of rapturous generosity, he had released the mental bond that held her will to his, and found a furious shriek spurting from her sweet mouth. He restored the bond and quickly bored of her beatific compliance.

Now the young woman stared euphorically at him, her doll-like eyes batting in rapt fascination in response to his noxious release of gas. "Gods, girl, you smile quite prettily after I fart. Could it conjure some fond memory in that simple mind of yours? Not a thought? How about you tell me your name?"

The girl was perhaps a year his senior, and no doubt taken as a wife in Naru in exchange for vows of protection. *Little good the caravan owner's massive muscles did her*, Nikulo mused. He studied as she struggled to express herself through the haze of his mental mastery. The crystal from Ghaelstrom provided him with vast quantities of power to sustain a spell that would have quickly tired him. *What will I do when I sleep?* he wondered. Something had to be done to encourage her acceptance of the fate she found herself living.

"My name is Callith," the girl said, her mouth moving as if in a great struggle.

"It's a pleasure to know your name, Callith. What do you say we call a truce and not have you scream when I release the magic from your mind? Would you be open to a bargain? How about I promise to allow your freedom when we arrive in Ursula? By owning such a large and prosperous caravan you could easily find another strong, horrible husband. Agreed?"

Her face darkened as his words seemed to sink down deep into the distant recesses of her brain. She nodded, the left side of her face twitching and marring her otherwise beautiful self. He gradually released the spell over her mind and winced, covering his ears as the scream came loud and swift from her mouth. Her eyes clenched shut as if refusing to glimpse some horror, and they opened again as if her mind played the image of the blood gushing from her handsome husband's throat. Soon she broke into sobbing, great convulsions wracking her fine figure in a fit of wretched beauty.

He distanced himself from her in preparation of a flurry of nails trying to claw at his face. None came and the sobs and tears degraded into a low, pitiful moaning, and she chewed the name of her dead husband in her mouth like a bitter herb. The scene was so touching that for a moment Nikulo felt a pang of guilt for causing the man to slit his own throat.

The guilt failed to last long as the ale swirling in his belly washed it all away. His mind and his morals told him he shouldn't slay innocent people like that, but then again, from his journey to the Underworld he knew that especially the innocent suffered the most. *I'll be joining you in hell,* Nikulo told the dead man and found a mug and raised it in respect to the wife's husband. *You should have listened when I asked you to relinquish the caravan and walk back to Naru. Would have extended your miserable life for a while.* At least until the

Jiserians returned to destroyed and dominate Naru once again.

Callith brought a slender hand across her tearful eyes and fixed a gaze on the mug of ale in Nikulo's grip.

"You want some of this, love?" He rummaged around in the back and found another mug, filling it from a barrel jostling about under the wagon's bouncy ride. She accepted the mug and tossed back her head and drank and drank until the glistening foam trailed down her pretty cheeks.

"Married in a day and widowed on the next day," Callith said, her voice raspy from all the screaming she'd released from her system. "He performed his duty with me all drunk and sloppy, and you finished where he left off, with a great deal more exuberance. I'm not sure what to think of it all..."

Nikulo grunted at the girl's wit. "I'm sorry your husband had to die." He found his eyes settling on the ground as he spoke. "He insisted on going to Ostreva and I have urgent business in Ursula. Your husband left me with no other option."

The girl sniffed and spoke with cutting tones, "I have no husband now. I've cried my just due tears for the man and have nothing left for him. Did you really mean your vow? Or do I have you to expect you as my new husband?"

He grimaced at the girl's bluntness. But her words spoke of her resilience and strength. "My vow holds true. When we arrive in Ursula the caravan is all yours. You are free to sell the wagons and goods and slaves, or find another man to lead your trading caravan. Suit yourself..."

"You're one of the heroes of Naru?" Callith's fiery hair danced as she shook her head in sudden stunned recognition. "Your friend Talis saved us from the plague that inflected our minds. I remember the crowds cheering in a chorus of laughter and singing songs to the gods. You were there in the background but your friend pulled you up to the front and raised your hand in victory. I remember your face now. You seemed so reluctant and resistant, and there was this pain that showed around your eyes as a wince. It's strange, I only remembered you just now."

"Perhaps because the pain is all gone now that I've left Naru." Nikulo filled his mug again and took another sip, scanning the shimmering sands that stretched across the horizon. "It's a curse to be famous and unable to disappear from curious eyes, though not as much as the curse that afflicts my mind."

"What happened to you? There were these rumors circling the city that you left through a portal. Some say you went to the Underworld, and others say you visited another world."

"Both true, though the trip to the Underworld happened long before we left this world—twice mind you, once to Haldrax and once to Vellia, the world of dragons and light."

A wry smile creased her full lips. "Now you're jesting with me. There's no such thing as dragons, everyone knows that."

"True enough for this planet. I've traveled far and wide across the world, to the northlands and Khael and over the Melovian Sea to the Island of Lorello. And in all my travels on this world I've never once encountered a dragon. Except of course if you count my friend Talis as a dragon, since he can change shape into one."

She laughed mirthfully at his words and her face flowered fetchingly and free for the first time. He admired her beauty and found himself staring at her blue, crystalline eyes that sparkled in the sunlight. She blushed and turned away to study the slaves trudging along in the sand.

"Why do you tease me with tall tales and your endless longing stares?" Her expression was one of forced annoyance, but her parted lips and expectant eyes told him another story.

He came closer and took her mug, refilling it with a grunt of satisfaction. "You've not enough ale in you to believe all the tales I hold in my mind. Drink more and let us enjoy the long ride. And you can tell me why you haven't tried to kill me."

She raised an eyebrow at that, her face thoughtful and wicked. "You haven't gone to sleep yet."

6

The Village of Farin

Talis gazed at the Village of Farin from the foothills overlooking the stone houses and wooden fences holding countless sheep and goats. Riders wheeled their horses around the flocks, driving them home for the night. They had flown all day and Talis tried to keep the worry and doubts from his mind, instead staring at the endless shifting desert sands and allowing the wind to push away his thoughts. Master Goleth had advised him to land far away from villager eyes, and they'd trekked for an hour down the mountain until the sun sank low beneath the ridgeline. Talis sensed something suspicious down in the village, and found his shoulders tensing as they neared the outskirts.

"Let me talk with them first," advised Master Goleth, his rugged face rigid as he squinted at the approaching riders. "And when they interrogate you, stay calm and answer their questions without flourish."

Interrogate us? Talis didn't like the idea of walking into a trap. He clenched his jaw as the riders circled around them, their eyes harsh and mistrustful. They barely glanced at

Master Goleth, and instead focused their attention on Mara.

"Who's the little tart, Master Goleth? I thought you swore to never take a female apprentice?" one of the riders said, his mean, chiseled face ogling Mara as he rode around them.

"My apprentices are none of your concern, Jahkel. We had a long and tiresome trip and Lord Aurellia has asked me return with these two. You will treat them with the upmost respect."

"You will go to hell, where you belong, *Builder*. All your buildings have burned and disintegrated back to dust. We've had enough of your promises of power and aid for Farin...we don't believe you anymore."

Master Goleth snapped a finger and two hands made of sand surged up from the ground and seized the front legs of the horse Jahkel was riding. The poor creature whinnied and bolted and sent the man crashing to the earth in a bone-snapping thump.

The Builder caused the sandstone hands to disintegrate and calmly approached the fallen man. His glance at the moaning and cursing Jahkel was brief, and he turned a challenging stare at the other riders.

"My how the minions turn sour like two-day old milk." The riders retreated from the Builder, their eyes flared in fear. "Our Lord Aurellia leaves on a mission and the hierarchy is already in disarray? Speak, minions! Tell me what has transpired in the empire since I've left."

A bulky man in stained leather pants opened his mouth to speak, but stopped when the Builder aimed a finger at him. "Go on, Biltis, speak. I won't harm you."

"Ishur is in chaos, Master Goleth." The man glanced from the Builder to the tense faces of his fellow riders, as if uncertain who would hurt him the most. "The various magical Orders have declared war on each other, with the Order of Rezel allying itself with the Order of the Dead.

Necromancers, Talis thought, and found a scowl forming on his face. Master Goleth swiveled around and studied his expression. Talis bowed his head in submission to the Builder.

"And Emperor Ghaalis? Is that fat drunk still whoring in Carvina?"

"The finest red wine in the capitol still flows freely, Master Builder." Biltis decided to take a stern tone and trotted closer to Goleth.

"I see, that is most unfortunate." The way the Builder said the words Talis was unsure if he was displeased that the Emperor still lived or that he was still drunk. "And now for the real question, which I'm sure you traitors are *most* eager to answer. Where are my wife and children?"

An ill-timed grunt of pain from the prostrated Jahkel caused Master Goleth to whirl around and fix a furious gaze on him. "You know of something, traitor? I trusted too many of you with my secret, thinking my family safe here from the frightfulness of our fetid empire. Speak quickly or discover how the desert can so easily swallow you up."

Jahkel's defiant eyes met Goleth's as his mouth trembled open and he spit stupidly at the Builder. Master Goleth flourished his hands in anger and the sand opened up underneath the screaming man and devoured his body in an instant. Mara let out a horrified yelp and seized Talis's arm as Jahkel was engulfed by the desert.

"I do not believe him the last traitor in our midst. Where are my allies and closest companions? The friends and families faithful to me over these long and troubled years. While the Empire saw war and bloodshed and famine, the Village of Farin enjoyed peace and prosperity and protection. You, Master Waynor? You knew of my family and had a cousin who'd joined the Order of the Dead. Did you spill my secret?"

The old, leather-skinned man leapt off his horse and the wind whipped up around his white robe as he locked tired eyes on Master Goleth. "Those of the Order of Rezel demanded answers to their questions. You were gone and we could not refuse. Call us traitorous, but if you were given the question by your masters, what would you have done? You answered Lord Aurellia's call to venture through the portal and help fight his war for him off on that other world. Would you have dared say no to him?"

Master Goleth narrowed his eyes at Waynor, a flicker of uncertainty and perhaps regret crossing his face. He steeled his gaze once again and spoke softer this time. "Just answer my question, where is my family?"

"They were taken by the Stelan Knights to Carvina." Waynor's voice was resigned as he spoke, but his eyes yielded nothing. They beamed with sanctimoniousness pride. *Carvina?* Talis thought, *Why would they take Master Goleth's family to the capitol? The Order of Rezel was located in Ishur, far from the Emperor.*

"Why would the Emperor want to hold my family?" For the first time, a confused and troubled expression crossed the Builder's face, and Talis shared in his bewilderment.

"Did your masters from the Order of Rezel contact you and tell you that they had your family?" Master Waynor scoffed, a grin forming on his grizzled face. "You almost fell into their trap, gullible Goleth. Nothing different than when you were a boy. Though back then you didn't kill falsely accused friends quite so easily." He stared at the ground where Jahkel's body had once been. At the Builder's exasperated expression, Master Waynor raised a placating hand and continued.

"The Emperor took your family to Carvina to keep them safe. This was no more than a few days after you left. Commander Safir of the Stelan Knights assured me that there would soon be disruption and chaos amongst the magical orders, and that the Emperor had heard word from Lord Aurellia himself to keep your family safe during the crisis. The Dark Lord named the upcoming period as the *Sieving Span.*"

Master Waynor glided up into the air and landed smoothly onto his horse. "Now do you regret killing your old friend Jahkel? Stay here a moment longer and you will answer for your crimes. Leave our village, and never return." He wheeled his horse around and trotted off, and the other riders followed, contempt and hatred thick in their eyes as they rode off towards Farin.

Defeat and self-loathing hung like a chain around Master Goleth's neck. All his certainty and righteous rage had vanished. He looked to Talis and Mara with expectant eyes, as if they knew the right course of action. Talis just shrugged and glanced around, and scoffed knowing the entire reason for agreeing to come with Master Goleth had evaporated.

"You were about to guide us into a trap," Mara said, and sent a derisive laugh at the Builder. "At least you had enough sense to come here first before taking us straight into the chaos of Ishur."

"And you dared to ask us to vow a blood-pact with the Order of Rezel? The very Order that now allies itself with the Necromancers?" Talis hated the irritated expression on the Builder's face and wanted to vaporize him with a blast of Light Magic. "The same hideous creatures who turned my entire city into a horde of undead!"

Talis sought agreement from Mara and was surprised to find her face fuming with fury. "The Order of the Dead calls Master Relech as their leader, I suppose? The same master who forced me to kill so many innocents over and over again. So much needless blood spilled... And all for what? To train me in the way of the assassin? Is this how your Order operates in Ishur? Twisting and warping the minds of the young for some nefarious purpose? You wanted us to swear a blood-pact to such an Order? Are you mad?"

Master Goleth looked genuinely ashamed of himself and injured by her outburst. His eyes now appeared desperate and placating as he faced them. "I believe I can still help you, help prevent unnecessary war and bloodshed from striking your city. Hear me out first before you leave." He sighed in frustration and ran a hand over the stubble of his bald head. "It's absolutely inevitable that the Order of the Dead will soon discover that Naru is not vanquished. And you know what will happen? Unless you want to stave off wave after wave of armies, undead and sorcerers and necromancers alike. How will you be able to protect your city? You are only one person—"

Mara huffed and interrupted him. "Don't be so dismissive of the girl! Why do boys and adults treat girls as if they don't matter?"

"I apologize for insulting you, it was not my intention to slight your ability to help defend your city." The Builder looked perplexed and studied Mara as if trying to ascertain the right moment to proceed. After her fuming subsided, he spread his hands wide in a gesture of acquiescence. "Listen to one final plea from me and I will not say another word. If there is any possibility of peace between Naru and the

Jiserian Empire it lies with Emperor Ghaalis. He is the only one who wields divine authority over the magical Orders of our Empire. And only I can make an introduction and open the Emperor's Court to you and your people."

7

The Emperor's Revenge

Much to Mara's disbelief, Talis agreed with Master Goleth's proposition. They didn't really fight about the decision, more like a disagreement over their next course of action. She wanted to immediately return home and seek out an official diplomatic engagement with the Emperor, while Talis felt it best to go to Carvina directly. In the end she agreed with Talis, realizing that likely no one in Naru had any leverage at the Emperor's Court.

The position of diplomat to the Jiserians had been held by her father, Viceroy Lei. Mother had remained quiet on the subject of her father's death, although rumor had it that the Viceroy was slain by wizards of the Order of the Dawn. Wizards that were now far from Naru.

After they had taken a count of the citizens still alive in Naru, the truth of the wizards' disappearance was clear. Talis had gone through the official list of wizards and witches of the Order and crossed off names slain by the war and added those names to prayer lists for the Rites of Zagros, ensuring their souls swift passage to the Fair Seas. *A grim task*, Mara told herself, remembering her dark and bitter mood at the performed ritual. Most of the original names of wizards belonging to the Order had been added to the prayer list. *So many men and women and children were slain senselessly in the war,* she had thought.

The few surviving wizards received a notation on the original list as to their current location. Talis had utilized the Surineda Map to plot their position in the world. Master Jai was west with Talis's family along the Ursulan Coast. Mistress Cavares had been located inside the City of Carvina, which at the time Talis had found incredibly strange, as he was both unwilling to believe his former runes master imprisoned or a traitor. The other remaining wizards and witches were scattered across the lands mainly to the west and northwest of Naru.

They followed the Builder's advice and took flight directly south to the sea until they reached a smuggler's cove, a pretty beach and humid hovel that dealt in illegal ore and gems from the mountains. There were only a few fishing boats bobbing in the bay, and the sleepy smugglers seemed uninterested at their arrival. When Master Goleth produced coin in exchange for room and lodging, and to secure passage on the next available vessel, the old hag baking octopus by the sea aimed a sagging arm at a dilapidated shack nestled amidst a stand of towering palm trees.

"It ain't pretty, but Hestor will gladly put you up for the night. He'll know all about the ships." She turned aside and started flipping over the octopus sticks and lathering the roasts with butter and garlic and a yellow spice that looked like curry. Talis found himself drooling at the smell.

"Can we buy some?" Mara pointed at the octopus. "They smell incredible."

The old woman chortled and her eyes flared in feverish delight. "These little devils? I'm just a makin' myself a little dinner. My grandson caught these in his diving nets. No need to pay me anything for 'em, feel free to enjoy one."

"How kind of you," Mara said, and accepted a golden-roasted octopus and let air blow around in her mouth as she chewed on the hot seafood. "Wow, this is delicious and different. I've never tried octopus before...so tasty and tender."

Talis accepted an octopus from the lady and thanked her, and inspected the small, roasted tentacles and took a tentative bite. The tender seafood tasted buttery and wonderful, and melted in his mouth as he chewed. When he'd read stories of the southern Jiserian cities, they always talked about the exotically spiced seafood and meats, spicy chilies, strange fruits and honey-glazed nuts. He found himself craving to discover the wonders of Carvina.

The lodging provided by Master Goleth's coin proved simple and clean, mere huts set along the palms with cotton hammocks for bed. Wide-mouthed Hestor had been elated at the Builder's generous payment for food and lodging, and promised to secure passage for them aboard the next smuggler's ship arriving within a few days time.

Talis and Mara spent four sun-filled days in the smuggler's cove, scouring for shells and driftwood along the black sand beach, swimming and diving for octopus and clams in the warm, colorful sea, and gazing at the vastness of the starry sky while the wind lulled them to sleep in their hammocks. After seeing the stars on the first night, they knew they had to take their hammocks outside, so they found several palms clustered close together and tied their two hammocks next to each other.

It was the first time in many months that Talis felt truly free and relaxed, and over the few wonderful days with Mara, he allowed the heat of the sun and sand to melt away all the built-up tension in his body. Mara swore she'd return here one day and take up the life of a smuggler: some weeks at sea, some in the mountains, and many more here in the picturesque cove. Talis told her he loved the idea.

Master Goleth had kept to himself the whole time, off on walks in the jungle, where Talis and Mara had spied him meditating next to a waterfall that spilled into a flower-rimmed pool. They had explored the jungle and discovered many streams that fed into the sea, and many beautiful pools filled with fresh-water fish and crystals. The terrain surrounding the cove was jagged and lush, and they found steep jutting spires of volcanic rock and several caves that wound deep down into the depths of the earth. One especially hot day they explored a cave for hours, utilizing the Surineda Map to keep them from getting lost. The experience reminded him of Ghaelstrom, and at each corner he expected to be greeted by a dragon's snout.

But all too soon the sails of a ship came into view around the palm-lined cove, and Hestor and the other villagers excitedly prepared several small boats to greet the large caravel as it swept into the cove. She flew a black flag emblazoned with the white face of a ghoul. *Pirates*, Talis thought, and narrowed his eyes at the approaching ship.

Master Goleth strode up alongside and stared out to sea, a grim expression on his face. "After they load the silver ore, Hestor told me we'd be allowed to board. She sails the Horn of Hardrin for Carvina, arriving at the smuggler's port inside the capitol. It's a vast city and will take us almost a day to walk from there to the Royal Court of Carvina."

Talis tried to imagine a city so massive that it would take a day to walk across it. The only other large city he'd visited had been Illumina and Darkov, and both were grand but also condensed, nothing as expansive as how Carvina sounded. If they were to try and visit the Emperor at the Royal Court, could they actually gain an entrance? Especially if Master Goleth introduced them as royals from Naru.

They strode over to the beach where the smugglers were busy loading crates of silver ore into the long boats. The caravel had released several boats of their own, and Talis spotted a bearded man standing erect at the bow. He wore a red silk shirt and black pants, and his mane of black hair was covered by the strangest hat Talis had ever seen. The black, three-cornered hat had a red-faced goblin on each edge, and three layers of red goblin heads adorned the crown. When he looked away, Talis swore the goblins' eyes followed him.

Hestor eagerly waved at the bearded man, and helped tug the longboat ashore so the man could jump off the boat's prow. The bearded man glanced around at the assembled villagers and gave the crowd a gold-toothed grin.

"A nice haul of silver this time, eh, Hestor? I'm surprised you have so much for me, I thought the Jiserians were busy trying to eliminate corruption?" The bearded man clasped arms with Hestor and studied him with curious eyes.

"Our bribes are taken easily now, Captain Cridd, a surprise to us all." Hestor allowed a broad smile to flourish on his tanned face. "The Jiserians seem scattered and disorganized, and the silver ore ripe for the taking. We plan on an even greater plunder next time, if you'll supply us with the jewels."

Captain Cridd released a pleasant belly laugh and slapped Hestor on the shoulder. "Jewels we can manage! As long as you can keep supplying all this fine silver ore. We'll do a righteous business together, Hestor. The gods love profit and wealth. May the sun shine soft and lazy, and the wind blow smoothly on our sails." He turned and glanced at Master Goleth, his eyes turning hard and mistrustful.

"This is Master Goleth," Hestor said, and spread a nervous hand towards the Builder. "He seeks passage with The Emperor's Revenge all the way to Carvina."

The pirate captain sneered at the Builder's robes. "A wizard? And you dare show your face here amongst a nest of smugglers and pirates? What is a master of the Order of Rezel doing here? And why aren't you aiming for Ishur?"

Master Goleth bristled under the pirate's words and raised a threatening finger at the captain. "Do I need to explain myself to a notorious brigand of the Melovian Sea?"

Captain Cridd looked pleased at the Builder's outburst. "You do, at least if you intend on boarding my ship. These are perilous times in the Empire. Talk of war has changed to talk of chaos and civil disruption." The pirate snorted at Hestor. "Exactly the environment that allows smugglers and pirates to thrive. So, Master Builder, might you have any information to help fatten our purses?"

"I've only just returned from a long journey and thought that you'd be able to supply me with more news." Master Goleth had softened his voice, and the effect on the pirate was immediate.

"As I suspected, a long journey." The Captain peered at the purse hanging from the Builder's waist. "A profitable one?"

"Winning favor from Lord Aurellia is always profitable," Goleth said, and chuckled at the look of horror on the pirate's face.

"L-l-lord Aurellia? But he's gone, vanished from the world, that's how all this chaos started. Seraka was burning the last time I visited...a mob had overthrown their rulers. Khael was tainted with a foul, somber mood. And my fellow captains returning from the west have told me grave stories of rioting and killing in Ishur, and a revolution in Ursula and Onair. The Jiserian Empire is crumbling from the inside, festering with maggots eating away at its organs. Only Carvina stands untarnished with the Emperor, the Stelan Knights, and the Order of the Dragons ruling strong."

"Now do you understand my desire to return to the capitol?" Master Goleth sighed. "I've no desire to join the fray in Ishur. After traveling so far with Lord Aurellia, I merely want to reunite with my family in Carvina."

Talis noticed the greed return to Captain Cridd's eyes. "And what will you offer me in exchange for safe passage to the capitol?"

"I'll allow your ship to stay afloat. I'm sure you'd hate to see all that silver ore plunge to the bottom of the sea. Is that payment enough for you?"

The Captain's face darkened and he studied Talis and Mara, and once again returned his gaze to Master Goleth. He snapped his fingers and three hooded figures from the longboat suddenly stood and strode over to join him. Talis tensed as they aimed gnarled and burned fingers at them.

"You don't go threatening Captain Cridd, I come prepared with my own wizards. Now unless you want to discover what manner of horrors these wizards can unleash, I suggest you reconsider your response to my question. What will you offer me? A ride on The Emperor's Revenge doesn't come for free."

"What would you consider as acceptable payment?" Talis said, earning him a glare from Master Goleth and a grin from Captain Cridd.

"The boy speaks! And a reasonable bargainer's voice, the voice of nobility. And whom might you be, young master?" The bearded man seemed perplexed staring back and forth between Talis and Mara.

"My name is Talis Storm, from Naru."

"Can this be true?" The captain slapped his leg and released a friendly laugh. "A son of the famous Storm family lineage alive after the destruction of Naru? A family known across the world for their once prosperous trading empire? I have dealt with his people many times in the past."

"You asked for news, Captain, and I am pleased to offer you some. Naru is rebuilt and her people restored from the plague of the undead. Saved from a spell cast from my own hand. I would be most grateful if you keep that news away from the Jiserian sorcerers and necromancers that have mauled my city. Perhaps we share a similar distaste?"

Captain Cridd nodded and huffed in response. "I'd sooner deal with the devil than parlay with those demons."

"I thank you." Talis gave the man a polite bow. "I have also asked Master Goleth to take young Mara and myself to the Royal Court of Carvina in the hopes of being granted an audience with the Emperor himself. We seek an alliance directly with Emperor Ghaalis."

"A wise move, young master. While the vermin rage and gnaw on each other in Ishur, you may find a receptive ear in the Emperor." The Captain cleared his throat a few times and tapped at his chest. "You asked me what I wanted in exchange for safe passage... And now I see the way open for our mutually beneficial partnership. I'll allow you and your friend to travel with me to Carvina in exchange for your vow of granting me exclusive sea trading rights for the Storm family business and all goods from Naru. Last word I heard from my fellow captains was your father was still alive and running his business from a small village along the Ursulan Coast. I'm sure you are pleased to discover that last bit of information."

Instead of retorting his knowledge of his family's safety, Talis nodded and thanked the man. "You have my vow, Captain Cridd. All sea trading rights for the Storm family and goods from Naru are yours for a span of say ten years?"

"Twenty." Avarice gleamed in the pirate's eyes at his quick retort.

"Fifteen years, Captain, and we'll agree at once. If you pass on the offer, so be it, I can arrange other means of transportation. But tell me, do you have enough ships to handle our trading requirements? My father does a brisk business."

The pirate spread his hands wide, his face displaying a wounded expression. "I have fifteen fine ships under my control, all spread across the known world. And after delivering this haul of silver ore to Carvina, I'll add another three ships to my fleet. Fifteen years and you'll shake on it and make a vow to the gods?"

"I swear to the Goddess Nacrea to grant Captain Cridd fifteen years worth of sea trading rights with the Storm family and all goods to and from Naru." Talis shook the pirate's hand and smiled as the man swelled in excitement over the deal. The Captain beckoned them towards the longboat and Talis and Mara collected their packs and he allowed Mara to board first. Master Goleth sent Talis a grateful expression as he followed.

Talis watched the Captain hand Hestor a heavy purse and the smuggler's surprised face nodded in appreciation. "More jewels for your bribes. Keep the ore flowing, and bring us gold and platinum next time!"

Mara leaned over and studied the sea as the sailors rowed the longboat out to the caravel. Colorful fish danced under the clear, emerald water, and she squealed as she spotted a sea turtle gliding along indignantly. Farther out the waves crested and fell hard, causing Mara to seize Talis's arm for support. She glanced excitedly at the three-masted ship with a buxom figurehead of a goddess mounted high on the prow. The crew of thuggish, bare-chested pirates lowered the ladder, and as Talis climbed up after Mara, he noticed the motley crew wore a wide collection of necklaces made of teeth and bone and gold nuggets. *Such a friendly bunch of pox-faced, toothy bastards*, he thought.

"Am I the only girl on this ship?" Mara whispered, and Talis glanced around at the lechery in the sailor's eyes as they stared at her.

"Get back to work, you lazy sacks of sow shit!" the Captain bellowed, and his wrathful expression sent the men scurrying across the deck and many climbed like spider monkeys up to the tops of the three masts. "Hoist the anchor and prepare to sail! I want you whore-loving whelps to move your bloody arses like I'm holding a sabre to it!"

The deck exploded in a fury of preparation for their voyage. Talis was amazed to see how quickly the crew worked in unison, and soon the caravel's three sails popped under the wind and the ship swung around and out into the open sea. They were finally leaving, and Talis was glad at the prospect of journeying along the southern coast, but as he caught Mara staring wistfully at the smuggler's cove, he knew their peaceful time along the beautiful beach was over.

Carvina and the Emperor awaited them. If they could survive the passage around the notoriously dangerous Horn of Hardrin...

8

The Sweet Sultry Sea

Callith rarely let Nikulo sleep at night, instead choosing to torment him for hours, even after the blissful haze of sleep had washed over him. The voyage across the Nalgoran Desert and on to the Ursulan Coast had been one long hot, hazy dream filled with ale and vice. Not that he minded it. He was thankfully free of the pain, and the voices had stayed in the background, allowing him a respite from the madness.

With the caravan parked on hill overlooking Ursula, he stared through the open canvas flap at the throng of whitewashed houses bathed in the soft glow of the rising sun. Fires dotted the central part of the city and he wondered what might have caused such blazes. Jolting him, the raging, maniacal voices of the Naemarians perked up in his mind like a guard dog that's scented fresh meat. *A ship, a ship, find a ship to Carvina!* cried the voices. If the voices were an actual person, Nikulo would have slapped them countless times and shoved a heap of shit down their mouth. *And set it on fire.* He was so sick of hearing them speak to him unannounced.

While frolicking with Callith and watching her sleep after she was spent, Nikulo had found himself with many quiet hours to think. He knew he'd acted badly by killing her husband, and he regretted it. And if he blindly chased off to Carvina, following the Naemarian's commands, he'd surely find himself with little benefits to himself. More likely risk his life. The Naemarians weren't interested in helping him; he knew they would consume his mind and body in pursuit of getting what they wanted: the Starwalker's fragment.

Even if there was a chance of finding the fragment again, Nikulo was determined to never again touch a fragment of such immense power. He simply wasn't able to channel such a staggering force. What would happen to his body after the Naemarians and the fragment's power possessed him so completely? Legends spoke of such creatures. Mist wraiths that roamed the land at night, searching for souls to devour.

His mind always reached the same conclusion after thinking for hours and hours about his predicament. He had to somehow sever the mental link to the Naemarians. And find a way fast before he reached the springs to the north of Carvina and disappeared forever. *Death and disintegration of your mind awaits you there*, Nikulo told himself, and he was certain it was true. He rather hated the idea of losing his mind. The last few torturous days in Naru were bad enough, but to endure a lifetime of suffering?

"Will you at least say goodbye before you leave?" Nikulo was surprised to hear Callith's sleepy voice. Her frisky figure rose from the bed and she stretched and yawned in a delighted sigh. She'd been rather energetic in the middle of the night. Her pretty blue eyes stared at him with a rueful longing. Did it really matter if he left so soon for Carvina? Perhaps if he pretended to visit the harbor each day and inquired rudely about ships he would be rejected and the Naemarians placated. Since they no longer inhabited his body, he believed they had no way of reading his mind. *But somehow they can sense where you are and what you're doing*, Nikulo had observed.

"Of course I will," he said, and gave her a lascivious grin that caused her lithe figure to tremble in a fit of giggles. She crossed slender arms over her small breasts in a sham display of modesty. *That wasn't how she acted last night*, Nikulo thought. He found himself counting dwindling reasons to leave for Carvina.

"Is it really necessary for us to wake?" She crawled over and stretched out her little hands to draw close the canvas flap, and she turned and displayed more of her fine figure to him. He inhaled the sweet scent of her skin and tried to rouse himself out of her entrancement, knowing they needed to make their way down to the docks. He was unsuccessful.

"You're going to kill me," complained Nikulo, and without coyness she straddled him and seized his chubby cheeks.

"If I'd wanted to kill you I would have done so days ago when I was still slightly angry at you." She prodded playfully at the mound of flesh protecting his belly. "You're so adorably soft."

Nikulo groaned and rolled his eyes, and tossed her aside. "Get dressed, there will be plenty of time for that later tonight."

Outside, the soothing sea breeze brought a wave of relief from the murderous heat that had plagued them all along their journey west. A low, wispy fog hung over the seaward side of the city, slowly melting away by the strengthening sun. With the light rising stronger now, he could see the dark stain of smoke and smoldering fires rimming various districts along the central part of Ursula. Was there civil unrest in the city?

He ordered the slaves to ready the caravan for departure, and found the driver's face obstinate.

"There's fighting in the city, lots of killing and anger." The bald man fixed his eyes west. "I spoke to a man and his wife while you were sleeping. They were fleeing the city and he warned us to stay away. There is not only fighting but also disease and plague."

"Did the man say where he was going?" Nikulo grimaced as an explosion near the docks shot a plume of fire and smoke into the air.

"North, to Ostreva. Though he doubted he could make it that far with a pregnant wife."

Another child born into a life of misery, Nikulo thought, and wondered what was the cause of the unrest. "Why are they fighting?"

The bald slave looked at Nikulo as if he were an idiot. "Freedom from the Jiserian Empire. The man said it was the same in Onair and all the other smaller towns and villages south along the coast. Their sorcerers and necromancers are brutal. They kill the people and raise them from the dead to fight against their own family and friends. The man said only a few Jiserians remain here in the city, but they are powerful and cruel and stubbornly resist leaving the city."

"We'll see about that," Nikulo told the slave, and grinned at him. "Ready the caravans, I'll deal with the Jiserians." He pictured pustules bubbling over on the faces of Jiserian sorcerers and necromancers, and smiled at the idea of spewing poison across their ranks.

Soon the caravan lumbered down the hillside and they passed motley groups of fleeing citizens, their clothes dirty and burned, and their faces stained with ash and soot. Several of the refugees tried to warn Nikulo about the dangers ahead, but he just waved them aside and said he was going to kill them all. This earned him more than a few mocking looks and contemptuous chortles. Callith, however, was proud of his bravery and seemed highly inclined to believe that he was capable of dealing with the danger.

"How will you kill them, my lord?" She raised fawning eyes to him in admiration and expectation.

"Not with a sword or dagger, though I've been trained in many weapons. I'll fight magic with magic, and from what I can see, those Jiserians are primarily using fire magic and their necromantic arts. They'll be unable to deal with my poisons."

The look of curious confusion came over her face. "Poison? Though you said you won't be using a dagger."

Nikulo grinned and flourished his fingers, and the girl nodded in understanding. "Dark arts for dark times. We can't have the city in turmoil, my little lark. Wouldn't want you in danger."

Callith blossomed and blushed under the pet name he'd given her after their first night together when her voice had reached a melodic fury that stirred the slaves awake. "My lord is most thoughtful for my plight. Will you be wearing armor or wielding a shield?"

She raised a good point. Depending on the number of enemy sorcerers to deal with, he might have to shield himself in some way against their fire attacks. Normally he had Rikar or Talis at his side, with flame bursting or wind gusting aside the enemy attacks. He was alone here and for a long moment he wondered where Talis and Rikar were and wished they were here to help him. *Even the traitor Rikar?* he asked himself, and nodded in response, believing his old friend and sparring companion tainted by the ring from the Underworld. *More than that, the twisting of hatred and bitterness and denial warps the mind of Rikar.* Nikulo missed him all the same.

A surge of familiar pain struck along his temples and his body seized up in response. "Leave me alone!" he screamed, surprised at his own outburst. Callith wilted away at his rage, hurt and uncertainty on her lovely face.

"What's wrong?" she said, and he silenced her with a raised palm. He squeezed his eyes shut and the pain burgeoned to terrific heights as the words flowed into his mind.

"Leave the city tonight for Carvina... There is a ship named the Fair Winds. Her captain will accept your bribe to board tonight after twilight falls. If you fail in this task, the pain will doubly return and madness will certainly follow." Nikulo seethed in fury at the words, spoken in a new, clear voice this time, stronger and closer than the voices he'd heard in Naru.

He exhaled in relief as the pain subsided and once again his mind was free of intrusive voices. The caravan wagon shook and swayed as it crossed a cobblestone bridge into Ursula. Scanning the fleeing citizens, he knew he had to do something to help them. Did it really matter if he died? Perhaps the pain of death was far less than the agony dealt to his mind by the Naemarians. And wouldn't Talis make a prayer for him, and perform the Rites of Zagros to ensure his safe passage to the Fair Seas? *If such a place even existed in the land of the Underworld.* Perhaps it was all just a lie.

"Was it the pain again?" Callith said, her soft hands landing on his shoulders.

"I will kill them all, the enemies of the Ursulan people and the ones that might harm you." He was amazed at the certainty and violence in his voice. "I will make you the savior of the city, and they will worship you as a goddess and protector of their citizens."

He paused and studied her bright eyes, wishing he didn't have to hurt her by leaving for Carvina.

"But tonight I must leave before twilight, and perhaps never again return."

9

Lair of the Nameless

Rikar loathed the empty darkness and the dread of waiting for the being Lord Aurellia called the Nameless Lord of All. The space between visitations with the enigmatic priests of this tomb had been long and tiresome, and Rikar found his sanity slowly slipping away. Not that he had much to begin with, ever since he'd first bowed down and prayed to Zagros in that dark temple in Naru. Had it been a year? Or perhaps more than a year since his rage at Garen Storm, and his cruel unwillingness to grant Rikar's father passage to the Fair Seas. It had all driven him mad and caused him to make his vows to the Lord of the Underworld. *Little good that did for father,* Rikar thought, remembering the devious dog-like face of Zagros.

Why had Aurellia commanded him here of all places? To the ruin of an ancient city that legend said once ruled the entire world? Aurellia confirmed this legend and claimed the great city older than Darkov and Urgar, even ten thousand years older than his visitation to the world four thousand years ago. The Dark Lord had explored the planet back then for powerful crystals and relics and magical weapons that might prove useful to his cause. He claimed a dark and hideous fate lured him into the lair of the Nameless, and cursed his life forever. And now Rikar's life was cursed.

The waiting and the endless chanting of mantras the priests had commanded Rikar to commit to memory chipped away at his saneness. The complex cacophony of chaotic sounds caused his consciousness to plummet into a black void so pure it flooded Rikar's mind with sadness. The span of each visitation to the void lasted only moments in his awareness, but he returned to wakefulness with an urgent need to relieve himself, knowing that hours must have passed.

He had fasted now for countless days and was far beyond the point of hunger pangs. Though the mental clarity that resulted from the fasting helped to keep his mind from crumbling apart. When Rikar had found himself in the middling world of Chandrix, he had fasted for several days at a time, but it was nothing compared to the intensity of this exhausting period of abstinence. He was weak and drained of physical strength. How long would the Nameless make him fast before granting him an audience? A cold, certain dread fell over Rikar and caused his hands to tremble in his lap. Why was he so insane as to desire ever interacting with such a cursed and hideous entity?

But the promise of power and dominion over this world had been clear from Lord Aurellia. His master would rule Vellia and Rikar could claim rulership over Yorek. And with his acceptance by the Nameless, Lord Aurellia had assured Rikar that his master could influence Zagros and assure a place along the Fair Seas for his father. At this point Rikar had given up hope of ever alleviating his father's torment, especially after witnessing the horrors of the Underworld. But he craved the idea of ruling this world and exacting revenge against Garen Storm...

An orb of sickly yellow light appeared far off in the distance and bobbed and danced in its journey over towards Rikar. The implacable eyes of a priest neared, and studied him with a cautious conviction.

"We believe you are ready to meet the master." The dancing yellow light reflected off the priest's shaved head and he turned and motioned for him to follow.

Rikar found his heart racing at the priest's words, and he practiced the prescribed breathing technique to calm himself. But as they snaked through the narrow tunnels and down stone stairs deeper than Rikar had ever been, his pulse pounded erratically and he was unable to eliminate from his mind rash thoughts of escape. He had come here willingly, and the priest claimed that he was free to leave whenever he wanted. Rikar doubted that was true. Leaving would likely mean a painful death.

One thing that had worried his mind over the long days of meditation: the wrathful eyes of the Starwalkers after he had brutally killed one of their quad. He realized he had only been able to succeed against them as their leader was without the fragment that gave him vast quantities of power. In the hands of Nikulo, that power had been fearsome against all in Illumina that day. Would the Starwalkers come and seek revenge against Rikar? He knew they would.

They had gone down eleven flights of stairs, and from his counting on prior days, he had descended a total of twenty-two levels. The priest cast several spells on an iron door with four indecipherable symbols etched in the metal. The magic seemed to remove many warding spells from the locks. From within his robe the priest withdrew a ring of ancient, iron keys and unlocked the four locks that secured the door.

"Enter the prison of the Nameless," said the priest. "And visit his sanctuary and refuge against the world." The priest touched the four symbols in a counter-clockwise order, and the door swung open of its own volition.

Rikar didn't want to go inside the shadowy room. His heart wrenched and his mind screamed for him to flee this place and fight his way to the desert surface. The ring on his finger seemed to pull him away from the room, like a magnet yanking the metal back to the stairs. His feet refused to move. There was something inside so absolutely hideous and malevolent and Rikar was certain that it craved the control over his mind and soul. If the Nameless were imprisoned inside and protected from the world, then his reach to the world was through his followers, spreading the stain of sin throughout the worlds.

No, I won't do it, Rikar thought, but he found himself being shoved by massive hands into the room and the iron door slammed shut behind him.

10

Death and Deliverance

After the tenth and twentieth citizen had scuttled screaming past Nikulo and the caravan, many with burned faces and bleeding wounds, he swore to mete a higher standard of brutality back onto the Jiserians. He encountered a squad of shambling, slobbering undead and wished that he'd asked Talis to teach him the spell of purifying the plague. Most of these undead were days or weeks old, displaying distended bellies and mottled, purple necks, and their shredded skin flapped behind them as they jogged after the shrieking people. A hand raised to his temple caused the squad of undead to stop silent in their tracks.

"I always wanted a flock of rabid pets," Nikulo said, and chuckled at the frothing, foamy mouths of the undead. Callith didn't share in his sentiment, and the girl cringed back in the wagon as if it actually offered her any protection. The slaves were less brave, and only Nikulo's shouts for them to stay and avoid being eaten alive caused them to cower close to the caravan.

Nikulo gained more pets along the way until he'd massed a company of undead soldiers to fight on his behalf.

The whitewashed walls of the houses they passed were blackened by fire and signs of combat. The streets themselves were filled with the broken debris of flipped-over carts and slain oxen buzzing with flies and gaping wounds that oozed maggots. They rode past a once thriving food market, a wreckage of wasted fruit, flanks of meat, and ripped and ravaged human bodies; a grim stew festering under the hot sun.

As they neared the charred central part of the city filled with collapsed buildings and stones strewn across the streets, he strengthened his hold over the undead soldiers' minds, knowing how easily another necromancer might be able to steal them. From his practice of mental domination at the Order of the Dawn, Nikulo had learned how to sense when another wizard was attempting to commandeer a creature he controlled. He compared the feeling to watching a serene pond for biting fish, and the faint tug they make on the line. No one was biting. For now...

Closer in they caught the confused eyes of bands of citizens in active revolt, armed with only crude cudgels and cleavers and farm axes. These ill-protected revolutionists made sweet bait for the hordes of undead lumbering after them. Lucky for them, Nikulo intercepted the hordes and saved the streets from a bloodbath.

"You fight for us, wizard?" asked a tall, grim-faced man who was one of the few to actually wield a sword. More of his comrades crowded in around the caravan, faces tensed and gaping in dismay at Nikulo's army of undead.

Nikulo snorted and studied the man, assuming him their leader. "I fight for myself. Little did I know Ursula would have war raging in her streets. I aim for the ports and out to sea. Who brings these undead, the Jiserian scourge?"

"Where are you from, young master? You wear the style of clothes from Naru, and though we know the city fallen to the Jiserians and filled with undead, we heard a rumor from a scout passing here a week ago that Naru is reborn and a savior come to renew and rebuild her back to her once grandeur."

"Tis all true, Naru is restored, though not fully. I've left Naru myself. There is a fear that the Jiserians will return." Nikulo leapt off the wagon and stood tall and faced the crowd. "Are you content to allow the undead to feast on your children and grandparents? They are going after the weak first, you know. You are ill prepared and poorly armed to deal with the Jiserians. Have you no magicians or wizards among you?"

The eyes of those in crowd were sullen and desperate, and no one offered a hopeful answer. Their red-haired leader spoke in a somber tone. "All our champions are either slain or turned to undead. Beware, as some of the undead are wizards who still possess the gift of casting. Will you help us defeat them?"

"I am called Nikulo, though who I am doesn't matter. What's the name of the leader that I fight with against our common enemies?"

The man brightened at Nikulo's words, seizing and shaking his hand in delight. "I am Yarin, a merchant and leader of our revolutionary group. We tired of the daily insults and torment of our imposed rulers, and managed to kill several sorcerers in their sleep before the streets erupted into bloodshed. From what we know, only a handful of sorcerers and necromancers remain. Emperor Ghaalis withdrew his fleet from our docks and ordered all Stelan Knights returned to Carvina. When we heard there was war in Ishur amongst the magical Orders, we struck out against the few Jiserians remaining in our city."

Nikulo frowned at the man's words and scanned the ragged crowd and the ruined city. A handful of sorcerers and necromancers did all this? The city was easily ten times the size of Naru, though far less dense. Still, the prospect of facing such powerful fanatics didn't thrill him. Did it really matter if he helped them? The Naemarians would certainly bring back the pain if they found him distracted from his goal of reaching the ship to Carvina.

"If we are to defeat our enemies I will need your help." Nikulo remembered back to history lessons of successful military maneuvers and strategies of legendary campaigns. *Distract, divert, divide, and destroy,* he thought, remembering the four D's of warfare. Likely these citizens were inexperienced in the ways of war and winning. "Do any of you have a map of Ursula?"

An old man ambled up to where he stood and at Yarin's nod, produced a thick parchment penned in an ornate and flowery hand. Nikulo studied the map and observed the position of the buildings in the center of the city, and asked a few clarifying questions as to the locations of their enemies. When he asked where the others of their resistance lurked, he gaped in bewilderment at their utter lack of organization or communication infrastructure. No wonder the Jiserians had had an easy time defeating them. They'd won already and were just entertaining themselves in the city's slow torment.

Nikulo sketched out a four-pronged plan of attack on the map, splitting the band of citizens into four groups to lure the sorcerers in four different directions. He knew the necromancers would avoid coming out in the heat of the day, shunning sunlight for the cool of the dark. His plan included dealing with them separately. As for the sorcerers, from experience he'd seen them keep their distance and fly high and away from bowshot and sword, only swooping down to strike when necessity demanded. That was where he would come in and shoot the sorcerers at a safe range. At least that was the plan...

The crowd divided into four squads as Nikulo had ordered, and Yarin joined the lead group that would strike from the west. Nikulo commanded double the number of undead to follow and protect each group, infusing their plagued minds with a fervent loyalty towards the living. He hoped there would be enough to keep the revolutionaries alive and provide a suitable allurement for the sorcerers.

Callith left the wagon and stood by his side, watching the ragtag squads marching off through the streets. She scoffed and shook her head. "Strangest army I've ever seen. Do they even have a chance of surviving against the Jiserians?"

"Not likely," Nikulo said, as the last of the citizens left the square. He had kept a group of around forty undead to protect them or to use as bait against the sorcerers. "Let's go. We'll move in after Yarin."

As they trekked through the littered streets, Nikulo thought about what could go wrong. The sorcerers might not take the bait and go after the squads, and the necromancers might not stay inside. If the Jiserians joined forces against a perceived larger threat, that could make things extremely difficult for him. He hoped that dispersed attacks over time would split the sorcerers and allow him to kill them one by one. But he hadn't anticipated that there might exist a rivalry amongst the Jiserians.

The first drone and boom of a fireball came sooner than he'd expected. Nikulo chased ahead and commanded the undead to follow, veering around overturned carts and piles of bodies decomposing in the street. Soon he spied a sorcerer hovering in the air above a crowd of cringing citizens, while the protective undead clambered up a building in the impossible hope of attacking the sorcerer.

Nikulo drew in power from the Ghaelstrom crystal and focused on the Jiserian sorcerer who had turned to face the revolutionaries running from an explosion of flames. The noxious cord of poison jettisoned from Nikulo's palm and tore through the air towards the flying sorcerer. Behind a burning, overturned wagon, Yarin released a triumphant shout as the shrieking sorcerer's skin erupted into blistering pustules and the Jiserian plummeted to the ground in a wet, bloody thud.

One enemy down, Nikulo told himself, and gave Yarin a victorious salute. The slaves and the caravan pulled hesitantly up to where Nikulo and Yarin's group were reforming. Nikulo noticed that several of Yarin's squad of bedraggled soldiers were missing, and one glance at the spot where they had tried to shield themselves from the sorcerer showed him the blackened bodies of the slain citizens. His plan had cost the lives of several innocent people. But he was surprised to find that more were not dead.

After the first attack, the other three squads were supposed to execute a series of assaults against known points of Jiserian control in the center of the city. But the experience with the flying sorcerer had taught him that the citizens were ineffective other than playing a role as bait. Nikulo decided it was far better for them to get roasted by Jiserian fireballs, and avoid getting burned himself.

"Young master Nikulo, I hope your plan works smoother next time. Several of my comrades were slain." Yarin bore a pained expression on his face as he looked at the burned bodies.

"Tell them to hide behind something stronger next time." Nikulo strained his eyes to study the sky above a far temple. Was that another sorcerer who'd spotted their soldiers in the far group? "We need to hurry, I think we've roused more Jiserians. Callith, keep the caravan and the slaves here until I return. I don't think you'll survive a fireball blast. Watch the skies for my signal, a single shot of flame soaring towards the clouds, and only come to the docks then. Otherwise I might be dead, in which case you'll be wise to turn and trek back to Naru, or flee up north."

They charged ahead through the terrorized streets, past government buildings and ruined palaces and destroyed temples, until they reached a grand plaza where unnatural storm clouds slowly blotted out the sun. *Necromancers fight under the protection of darkness*, he thought, remembering the words of Master Viridian. Nikulo wondered if he knew enough spells of elemental magic to aid him? He could summon light, but that would just mark him as a target. *It's quite possible*, thought Nikulo, *that the Jiserians are hoping for me to act as foolish as those feeble-minded citizens of Ursula.* He wasn't intending to meet their minuscule expectations.

From the four fringes of the plaza, the thick air released hundreds of small, shining shots that illuminated the broken landscape and caused Nikulo and the others to seek the darkness behind damaged trees and abandoned vendor stalls and cracked statues of the gods. There was silence as the shots ceased and the shimmering globs of burning pitch cast eerie, twisting shadows across the plaza. So much for dividing their enemy. If they moved, they'd likely be zapped by lightning strikes. Nikulo grinned to himself. But if he sent the undead out into the plaza...

He pressed fingers to his temple and commanded an undead man with a desiccated body to run out towards a mass of burning pitch, and readied a spell to strike out at a sorcerer. There was a pause as the undead man stumbled about in the ruined plaza, his foaming mouth confused and stupid, and his arms swayed around like branches under a rising gale. Nikulo waited for some secret verdict to unleash its wrath.

It did not come. And as the undead man stood stupidly in a shambling dance, the sky slowly cleared and the burning pitch waned to smoke and ash and coldness. Confused, Nikulo studied the air from the protection of a tree trunk and found that the sorcerers had vanished. What had caused them to leave?

"It seems the sorcerers have fled," Nikulo said. Then he thought of something and turned his gaze to Yarin. "Have you noticed anything strange about the Jiserian sorcerers and necromancers in the last few days?"

"Anything strange?" Yarin said, and scratched his scraggly beard, eyes locked away on some distant thought. "Well we rarely see the necromancers anymore, only the bands of undead roaming and feasting throughout the city. If it wasn't for the undead, you would think the necromancers had gone, for they are never seen with the sorcerers these days."

Then the realization hit Nikulo with the weight of a heavy block of stone. There was conflict between the necromancers and the sorcerers, and likely the act of Nikulo slaying the sorcerer and sending the undead out as bait confirmed the sorcerers' suspicion that the necromancers were in league against them. How could he incite and inflame the hostilities between them?

"Can you take me to one of the places where the necromancers are known to live?" Nikulo studied Yarin. "You had mentioned before that you thought they nested in the depths of various libraries across the city." Maybe if he could root out the necromancers from their hiding places, he could invoke open warfare between them.

Yarin nodded and glanced around, then facing the south, he led them down another street until they reached a towering marble building with twisting pillars and a full consort of deities and demigods mounted in a procession along the pristine pediment.

"No citizen dares venture inside anymore, not since the Jiserian occupation. The Library of Nestria has become the warren of the necromancers, and deep inside the basement archives they have founded a coven of the dead. If you choose to enter, we will not follow you."

Nikulo released a devious chuckle. "I wouldn't think of asking such a thing. I'm not even foolish enough to go inside myself. I'll let my pets do the dirty work for us. Let's see how these necromancers enjoy the wrath of the undead turned against them." *An unbreakable wrath filled with the power from the Ghaelstrom crystal,* he thought.

He sent a mental command to his horde of forty undead, a command most receptively received by their vengeful minds. *Go inside the library, go down and seek your former masters, and tear limbs from torsos, and heads from trunks. Feast and devour until there is nothing left of them.*

The undead chased off, teeth clattering together in delight, and they disappeared into the darkness of the library.

11

Music of the Maelstrom

With the aid of the sorcerer's spells, the Emperor's Revenge now sailed at a speedy pace under the strong gust blustering behind them. Talis had studied the sorcerers as they cast their spells, memorizing their chantings and hand movements, and he tried to practice the spells in the secret world of dreams, but was unable to succeed. Since his time studying with Master Viridian had been cut short, he'd only learned from him the art of casting Fire and Wind Magic. The knowledge of summoning storms and casting lightning bolts against enemies was unknown to him. So many spells to discover and perfect in what Talis saw as the vast sea of magical knowledge.

On the second night of their voyage, the ship surged and fell in a rhythmic rocking that reminded Talis of the frenzied beating of the drummers in the forest where the witch Ashtera had tried to slay them. The music of the ship's hull against the water was mesmerizingly beautiful, and Talis found himself spending countless minutes, eyes closed, listening to the sound.

Master Viridian had once told him that there were different types of meditation, one of the eyes and one of the ears and one of nothingness. Now, the sounds of the sea lured his mind into a trance of chaotic intoxication. It was the sound of the army of dead in the Grim March, and the sound of the nether hounds of Zagros charging across that vile plain, it was the sound of storm and ruin and destruction. It was the sound of war.

Talis found his mind drifting towards the sound of the voice deep inside the Ruins of Elmarr, and knew that voice as the singer of the same song. The smashing of skulls against stone, the splash of blood spraying at the slice of a sword through flesh, the rhythm of war and violence repeated by hardened fanatics of Nyx, the God of War. The fury of rage and lust for blood and power, repeated endlessly like the rhythm of song, like the rhythm of the ship's hull against the waves. That song was surging now throughout the world. Talis could feel it in the hammering of his heart.

What force was in opposition to the music of the maelstrom playing out in the world? Was it Emperor Ghaalis, had he turned against the strife and unrest in Ishur in the hopes of regaining peace and order in his Empire? Or was the void of power from Aurellia's departure the catalyst that struck the first chord in this chaotic song? Talis knew that unless he did something to stem the flood of chaos, the whole world would be engulfed in the madness of the mind of the Nameless.

"Mind if I join you?" Mara said, her voice soft and sleepy. Talis turned to see several locks of long hair fall over her amber eyes. She flicked the locks absently away from her face, revealing a troubled expression.

"I had a horrible nightmare." She stretched out her arms and allowed her small figure to be enveloped in his comforting embrace. He could feel the pounding of her heart against his chest slowly subside and smooth, as if the vile world of the dream were melting away. "You were being tortured inside a chamber devoid of light. I couldn't see you, I could only hear your screams and moans of agony. You cried my name over and over again, begging for me to stop the pain."

She paused for a long while, as if uncertain of what to reveal and what to keep to herself. Finally, she exhaled quickly and continued. "It was simply horrible. I can't understand why I would have such dreams. Can't we just go back to the smuggler's cove and hide away from this hideous world? I slept so peacefully there and my mind was free and calm."

"And something has changed since we boarded this ship?" Talis held her shoulders and studied Mara's eyes, hoping to find hints as to her unrest.

"Everything has changed. I don't sleep well on this endlessly swaying ship. The crew is always gawking at me, and several times I've caught Master Goleth mumbling to himself in a really mad way. And those sorcerers keep glaring at me with their scheming eyes. I just don't trust them."

"Soon enough we'll arrive in Carvina." He held her hands and gave them a reassuring squeeze. "Captain Cridd told me that we'll round the Horn of Hardrin sometime early this morning. He said that he ordered the sorcerers to smooth the weather around the Horn so we'll pass through without interruption." Though he doubted the Captain's confidence in the sorcerer's abilities in completely controlling the weather. According to Master Viridian, weather was the hardest thing to master and the most unpredictable in achieving results, often subject to mass movements of maliciousness by the gods of storm and chaos. And the sorcerers had looked tired in Talis's eyes, taking turns to rest and recover from their long exertion in commanding the wind.

Now the sails softened under a lull in the breeze, and Talis glanced up at the masts, expecting another pop in the sails as was usual during their voyage. But even after a long while the wind remained at rest, and Talis thought that perhaps the sorcerers were exhausted from holding the wind spell for so long.

"That's strange," Talis said, and jutted his chin towards the sails. "It's the first time this trip that the wind has stopped."

Mara's tired eyes followed his gaze and her forehead furrowed in fear. He strode across the deck towards the stern, where the sorcerers usually held their wind spells and gazed at the sky. The aft deck was empty. Talis glanced around, trying to spot the sorcerers, but there was no sign of them. He charged over to the cabin where they often rested and meditated and he found the door unlocked. Inside the room was vacant save for the hammocks and the empty trays of food.

"Where are they?" Talis said, and he found Mara worried and perplexed as the ship seemed to meander off course and her speed lagged her once consistent pace. They raced over to the helm, hoping to find an answer there, and found it in the burned and bloody body splayed on the deck. The wheel spun senselessly and Talis seized it at once, keeping her direction as straight as he knew.

"Can you hold the wheel?" Talis allowed her to take over, and he slung his backpack around and withdrew the Surineda Map. A faint falling mist was illuminated under the map's golden glow, and Talis commanded it to display the ship and her direction, and it zoomed out to show their proximity to the shore. They were headed directly towards danger, and the map flashed red at the rocks ahead.

Talis asked Mara to spin the wheel left and they adjusted their course towards safety, and from the map he realized that if he had waited a few more minutes they'd have ruptured the hull on the rocks and faced a watery grave. He told her he was going to rouse the Captain, and from her nod of confidence, left her to keep the ship guided away from shore.

Fist pounding on the Captain's Quarters, he shouted in alarm for the man to wake but found the man deep asleep. Talis was about to break open the door when he was greeted by the Captain's furious face and fuming breath that stank of whisky and onions.

"Why in the name of the gods are you banging on my door?" The Captain peered outside at the dark sky, his bed-strewn hair a tangled mess. "What do you want? It's the middle of the night. For the love of all that is holy let me sleep!"

"Was your first mate supposed to be sailing the ship?" Talis said, fixing his eyes on the Captain.

"What? Of course, he's on duty..."

"He's been killed by your sorcerers." Talis clucked his tongue in disapproval. "And they've vanished from the ship."

Captain Cridd's eyes went wide as he sniffed the air and pushed Talis aside, striding out onto the deck and he stared up at the sky, hands pressed to his hips. "Well then, who's steering the damned ship?"

"Mara is, sir." Talis followed the Captain to where Mara stood. She relinquished the helm to the Captain, and studied his face now filled with terror as he kept sniffing the air and staring up at the turbulent sky.

"A big storm is coming and I didn't even see it." Captain Cridd muttered curses and shook his head like he was disgusted with himself. "So damned used to those conniving sorcerers that I never envisioned being betrayed by them."

"They're from Ishur?" Talis said.

"Nay, from Ostreva. I only hire neutral forces. Don't want to be seen as choosing sides."

"Why do you think they would abandon ship and put us on a course for destruction?"

"Could be they didn't like having Master Goleth on board, could be they didn't like you." The Captain sneered at the storm and scoffed. "We'll never know, now will we? They're long gone and this blasted storm is about to crush my ship into a million splinters."

"I'll go wake Master Goleth, he might be able to help us." Talis jogged off and took the steps down below deck and found the Builder's cabin open and called out for him to wake. The wizard flicked his alert eyes open and raised himself up at once.

"Something is amiss?" Master Goleth said, and at Talis's insistent face, he followed him up above deck where they were greeted with a sudden splash from the sky. "Betrayed? Let me guess, those sorcerers left us to suffer under the storm?"

"And they killed the first mate at the helm. We almost crashed onto the rocks before Mara and I steered us to safety."

The Builder winced as the rain lashed his face and he seemed to crave the cover of his cabin. "Do you know how to tame the storm, young master Talis?"

"I never had the chance to learn." Talis felt his stomach twist at Master Goleth's disappointed face.

"You and I are in the same ship, forgive the pathetic pun." He gave Talis a defeated grimace. "Those of my Order were forbidden from studying the art of storm and fire. Ours was intended to purely master the construction and deconstruction of elemental matter. Which in this case proves a great disadvantage."

"Could you fortify the ship against the storm?" Talis remembered Mara's story about how the Builder had forged massive metal and crystal ships on Vellia, and the smooth ride she'd experienced across the vast oceans despite being waylaid by storms.

"Aye, indeed we could." Master Goleth's eyes brightened as they arrived at the helm and were greeted by the Captain's stoic expression studying the storm.

"Can she weather the waves?" Talis asked the Captain, and from his calculating eyes knew they could not.

"Not without a wizard to tame the winds and the sea. Few vessels chance a passing around the cape without magical aid." Captain Cridd looked to Master Goleth. "Can you do something to settle the storm?"

Master Goleth shook his head and Talis watched the Captain's face go pale in a look of defeat. "No, I cannot alter the storm, but my magic does allow for me to fashion you a stronger ship. If you have no objections to staying afloat."

"While we are at sea?" The Captain's confused face crinkled in disbelief. "How in the name of the sea gods is that possible?"

"Pray to your gods, while I build you a better boat." Master Goleth flicked his fingers and floated up through the air to the crow's nest, where his waving hands sent tendrils of silvery energy into the sea.

The Captain shouted down below decks. "All hands on deck! Batten down the hatches and prepare for the storm!"

In a few moments, the sleepy-eyed and fearful crew hauled themselves up to the deck, and the Captain ordered them to bring down the sails and tie them up. Everything of importance that could be swept away by the storm was brought below deck.

Mara nestled beside Talis, and sheltered her head from the rain by hiding underneath his arm. They watched as the Builder drew in the crystalline elements of sand and formed a protective covering around the hull that rose twenty feet above the deck. He started with the prow and drew in more and more elements until after an hour of forging a reinforced hull, he brought the crystalline shield together all the way around to complete at the stern.

The waves whipped high while the Builder fashioned the elements together, and some swells slammed against the unprotected bowsprit, shattering the wood under the force of the impact. Master Goleth flew down and returned to the deck, and studied the creaking and groaning masts. He cast more crystalline elements to wrap around and protect the integrity of the three great beams, and the ship held intact despite the terrific force of the waves. Because of the shaking and reeling of the ship, the crew was wide-eyed and they mumbled prayers to their gods.

Talis tired of staring at the raging waves, though in his observation the swells were rising minute by minute. The Captain ordered most of the crew below decks after the sails were secured, the decks cleared, and the hatches closed. He commanded several keen-eyed sailors to keep an eye out for rocks, though from what Talis could see, they had the most to worry about the waves.

Off a great distance ahead, where the sky had cleared a few hundred feet from the low, violent clouds, Talis spotted a massive wave rising high above the rest. He prodded the Captain and pointed off towards the swell, and the man's face fell to a grave look of hopelessness.

"Master Goleth!" shouted Talis, and motioned at the wave. "Can you build the hull barrier higher?"

The tired wizard stared with dumbfounded eyes at the wave, and shook his head in despair. "Not in time to save us."

12

Sowing Discord

The idea of slaying necromancers by using their own undead as weapons against them pleased Nikulo in the strangest way possible. He'd often wondered whether the undead might fight harder or act with more brutality against their once cruel masters. They most certainly did. He watched one undead ripping an arm from a casting necromancer, while their drooling comrades sank their teeth deep into the Jiserian's neck and feasted for a long while on their soft spine.

Nikulo could only imagine the horror and surprise of the necromancers as their undead chased after them in the library archives. He was certain that one necromancer must have looked at another, as if thinking, *Did you call them here?* And only to find themselves as fodder for the hungry undead. Nikulo had turned his head away in disgust, feeling bile creep up his throat at the sight of the undead ripping the necromancers into small mounds of bloody flesh. The remaining horde of undead burst out of the library and scrabbled around at the bloody bits, and slammed and punched each other in a wild feeding frenzy that Nikulo was unable to stop.

"I think we better get out of here and let them calm down." Nikulo turned and trotted off north to where they'd encountered the sorcerers in the plaza. When they'd reached a safe distance, he glanced back and saw that the undead had returned to feed inside the library. *Until there is nothing left of the Jiserian necromancers*, thought Nikulo. And he'd be happy to also feed them the poisoned remains of the sorcerers. If he could only find where they'd gone.

When they arrived at the plaza, they were greeted by the other three groups, who came to them with expectant eyes, and were flanked by their decaying host of undead protectors. When a few of the undead seemed to catch a whiff of some tantalizing smell in the wind—no doubt from the necromancers' blood—Nikulo commanded them to hide in the shadows of the northwestern part of the plaza.

"The City of Ursula is almost free," Nikulo said, and gave them a bolstering look that only yielded a tepid response. "How many remaining sorcerers do you think are still alive?"

"I'm guessing three or four remain after the one you slew. Still too many." Yarin tilted his head towards the west. "The sorcerers are known to enjoy the view of the sea. We can also trying stirring up a few other palaces that they've been known to occupy." When the man said *stirring up,* Nikulo pictured the undead ravaging the bodies of the necromancers. Not a pretty scene.

"Lead on. The day is getting long and I have a ship to catch. If we don't find the sorcerers before the long rays of afternoon, then you'll have to battle the sorcerers by yourselves." And a poor chance of success you'll have, especially without a wizard or even a decent archer to shoot the sorcerers at range. Nikulo supposed that all the wizards and archers in their army were slain by the Jiserians. *Or imprisoned*, he thought, and wondered if that was where at least a few of the Jiserians might be lurking.

"I changed my mind. Take me to your prison, I assume you have one of those here in Ursula?"

Yarin gave him a quizzical look, but nodded and led them up north past the plaza, to an administrative building graced with tall, sleek pillars and a wide frieze displaying symbols of justice and balance and punishment. Likely this was the famous Ursulan Hall of Justice.

"Another building that we've been forbidden to enter. Most of the Jiserian soldiers and knights lived here, though by now I believe all have left and returned to the capitol."

"We'll need to be quite a bit more cautious here, as the undead have trouble distinguishing between the living." Once they entered the building, Nikulo ordered the undead to protect the entrance, and signal a warning if any intruders came.

The vast, towering halls of marble and stone were empty, save for the sound of their shoes slapping against the floor. Giant statues of the gods stood watch, of Nyx and Nestria and Nacrea, and the hero Lord Heti of Calabastria,

100

with a slain dragon under his feet. Here the cry of justice could be heard from the walls itself, with no answer forthcoming.

They strode behind an impressive looking entryway into what Yarin claimed was once the office of the justices, and their armed enforcing branch that meted out the proclaimed verdicts of the court. The offices were empty save for a few severely decomposed bodies, with little left to even interest the flies. Downstairs Yarin led them, until they found a stairwell down three flights, finally reaching a locked door. Nikulo still remembered the few lessons he'd been taught of fire magic, and he released a slithering flame into the lock, melting the mechanism until the door swung open.

"Go and see if any of the prisoners are still alive," Nikulo said, and purposefully stayed behind to ensure that Yarin and the other men performed their duty as proper bait for any sorcerers like might be lurking inside the prison.

The prison was significantly larger than Nikulo would have expected, and he found row after row of mostly empty cells. *What are we doing in here?* he wondered, and was about to turn around and leave when he heard a shout come from the last row. He darted down the corridor and reached the cell where Yarin and a few other men pointed inside.

"Someone is still alive in here," Yarin said, and Nikulo peered in through the cell bars to where an old, shriveled man stared at him from the corner.

"Master Holoron?" Nikulo exclaimed, and felt his heart thump in excitement at seeing his old Legends and History Master from Naru. He cast a quick burst of flame and melted the lock, and yanked open the door with Yarin's help.

Master Holoron had once again closed his eyes in his sitting meditation, and only opened them when Nikulo handed the old man a water skin to sate his thirst. As one of the most senior of the Sej Elders, Master Holoron exuded a commanding presence that was felt by the men assembled around him.

"Young Master Nikulo, here to rescue me from my imprisonment?" Holoron allowed a faint smile to flicker across his mouth. "I'm afraid you'll have to help me out of here. Though I've managed to keep myself alive, the strength in my body has left me."

Yarin glanced at Nikulo with disbelief in his eyes. "How did the old man survive?" he whispered to Nikulo. "All the other prisoners have died, most of them several days ago. This prison has been abandoned by the Jiserians and the remaining prisoners left for dead."

"I may be old but I still have ears," Master Holoron said, his voice still filled with the humor and vibrancy that Nikulo remembered him possessing. "As foolish a wizard as I am, I allowed myself to be captured by the Jiserians and imprisoned in a magically warded cell with little hope of escape. Though the air still contains water, it was barely enough for me to draw from and keep myself alive. Just carry me outside and let me feed from the sun, and then I shall be renewed."

Yarin and another stout man helped carry Master Holoron up the stairs and outside to the front steps of the Hall of Justice, where the sunlight shone down from the western sky. The wizard let his mouth fall open and he breathed in the power of the sun through slow, deliberate breaths, and after each inhalation Nikulo could see the color and vitality return to the old man's face. Soon Master Holoron had enough strength to raise his palms towards the shimmering orb in the sky, and Nikulo could see his hands glow golden and the light of the sun poured into his withered figure, until the whole of his body shone with a brilliant orange hue.

The other men shrank away from the Master's shining shape, and only Nikulo stayed and marveled at the old man's power, a power that Nikulo had no idea that he possessed. The memories he had of Master Holoron were of his stories of ancient legend and lore told in a dancing prose and a witty way that kept all his pupils in rapt attention. Never had Nikulo known or even suspected that Master Holoron was a powerful wizard in his own right.

"Ah, the blessed rays of the afternoon sun." The old wizard's face had turned ruddy and was restored to his former vital self. "It is good to feel the power of the Goddess Nacrea shine on my old form once again. I bet you thought that only Master Viridian and Talis knew of Light Magic, is that not so?" His eyes twinkled in mischievousness. "Master Viridian was the leader of the Order of the Dawn in name alone. Though I doubt he would have been so stupid as to allow himself to be tricked and imprisoned by Jiserian sorcerers."

Master Holoron sighed and his eyes went wistful and sad. "How I miss old Viridian. Everything went to hell after he was slain." The old man fixed his gaze on Nikulo. "Why in the name of the gods are you in Ursula? Last I heard, you and Talis and Mara had vanished and the Temple of the Sun destroyed by the Jiserians. We thought that you were all killed in the attack."

"No, that old fox Palarian kidnapped Mara, and Talis cast a world portal spell and we followed her into Chandrix."

At the old man's befuddled face, Nikulo waved his hand with a reassuring gesture. "Tis a long story, Master, one that deserves time for the telling. The good news is Talis, Mara, and I returned safely to Naru around two weeks ago."

"But isn't Naru filled with undead? Last I heard before I left was that the necromancers had infected the citizens with their fiendish plague."

"All healed by Talis's spell. He has restored much of the city to its former glory—"

"Then what sends you here to Ursula so soon after you return?" Master Holoron's eyes turned suspicious as he studied Nikulo with a ferocious intensity.

Nikulo felt trickles of sweat dart down under his armpits as he withered under the wizard's gaze, until the old agony once again lanced his brain and the voices of the Naemarians filled his mind in feverish alarm. *The ship, the ship! Go to the docks and quickly board the ship!* The pain was suddenly fierce and the voices so irresistible that Nikulo found himself standing and stepping towards the docks.

"What in the name of the gods is compelling you to leave?" Master Viridian narrowed his eyes and Nikulo could feel a violent heat prickling under his scalp at the wizard's magical examination. "Something powerful and ancient attacks your mind, young master Nikulo. Though it does not possess your body any longer, it somehow still influences your mind...and it injures your sanity."

Leave, leave, you must leave at once! screamed the voices in unison, and they drove the pain so strong across Nikulo's brain that it caused him to collapse to the ground, a whorl of light and shadows twisting in his vision until the world went black and he lapsed into unconsciousness.

13

Night Fever

Mara never felt the massive wave slam against her body and catapult her far back into the swarming sea. She never felt the icy rush of water singe her skin and pour into her lungs and sink her splayed figure down to a watery grave deep in the bottom of the sea. Instead of unconsciousness and death, she witnessed Talis rush to the ship's prow and stand unyielding in the face of the magnificently destructive wave.

The wind was a wild, primordial beast, the very elemental disaster the poets had prophesied for the world many years ago. A deluge of water, a deluge of fire, a deluge of darkness demolishing all life across the land. And Mara gazed at the oft-named face of fury in the titanic wave and found the names insufficient for the insanity of its rage. It was beautiful and hideous and sweet in the song of its relentless pursuit of disintegration. Talis raised his palms in a kind of greeting, as if his hands were telling that terrible force, *I welcome and embrace you, and in that embrace I empower your eradication.*

The shock of the force of power from Talis's hands rippled in long arcs across the sea. The fifty-foot wave was vaporized into a fine, steamy mist that sizzled and boiled atop the churning sea. But the remaining swell still lifted the boat dangerously high, causing Talis and Mara to skid back along the deck, grasping for anything to stop their fall. Then as they crested the enormous wave, the deep valley below threatened to plummet the ship into obliteration.

Talis darted over to Mara and seized her wrist just as the ship dove down the swell, but they discovered that Master Goleth's crystalline shield was high enough to keep the prow from being pulled under by the mauling waves.

"We should go below deck." Mara had to shout for him to hear over the roar of the storm.

"Go ahead and be safe, I have to keep watch for more waves like the last one." Talis stared through the torrential showers, studying the cresting and crashing waves. "It's going to be a long night."

Mara shivered under the cold rain and shook her head, determined not to leave him. Although she could see his eyes were angry and fearful, because she refused to go, she thought he looked relieved at the same time to have her stay with him.

They leaned against the ship and watched the waves rise and fall, and cuddled close as the boat pounded against the ocean. She felt her stomach twist and flip from the ship's wild movement, and thought that at any second she might be sick. *Better to stay above deck and still breathe the crisp air,* she told herself. But instead of the thought steadying her she vomited off to the side and Talis held her hair back and she could feel the heat of his hand flow into her trembling body and warm her. His touch steadied her stomach and made the world clear again until she gasped in a huge inhalation and sensed that the ship had calmed somewhat.

She thanked him as he withdrew a handkerchief and wiped her face clean and offered her some water that soothed her parched throat. The waves did subside a bit, and in her now feverish mind she imagined them waning and the wild thrashing of the ship subsiding more and more.

"It's getting better." Talis's soft voice calmed her anxiety, and as she joined him in studying the sea, she could tell the truth in his words. They still waited for a long while more, and in their watchfulness Mara could feel the fever flourish and her face was so hot that she craved the diminishing rain, cool and calming on her forehead and cheeks. She opened her mouth to say something, and Talis interpreted this as a desire for water. He poured more of the wonderful liquid into her mouth and she drank and drank, but the coolness of it only seemed to fuel her rising fever.

"You're dripping with sweat!" Talis said, and wiped her brow. "Did I give you too much heat of the sun when I cast the spell?"

Mara shook her head and gave him a feeble smile of encouragement. "I think I'm ok to go down and rest. Can you help me? I feel all wobbly and weak."

As he helped her stand, the weight of her drenched backpack strained her shoulders. They hobbled together towards the stairwell leading below deck, and despite the still unsettling movement of the ship, they made it down and into Mara's small cabin, where at her insistence, he'd snuck in and stayed with her each night.

"Can you stay with me for a while?" She let her heavy backpack drop to the ground, but kept it close as she felt the twin daggers calling out to her in warning. When she and Talis had first enjoyed the freedom of the smuggler's cove, her mind had raged about leaving the daggers behind when Talis asked her to go swimming in the sea. In her silent entreaty, she begged the daggers to loosen their chain of torment, vowing to never leave them if they agreed to withhold the pain. This had allowed her to swim in the ocean unfettered, and roam around the cove blissfully unbothered.

But since their journey aboard the Emperor's Revenge, the daggers had proven jealous, guarded masters, and had insisted that Mara keep close to them, especially with all the danger lurking around. *I really should tell Talis*, she thought, *if he knew he might be able to help me. Or he might judge you*, a sinister voice told her. The voice of the Nameless, the voice that she'd heard in the Ruins of Elmarr. The voice she knew craved the death of all living beings. The utter disintegration of the individual into the consumption of the whole. And that voice had promised her—

"What was that?" Talis said, and peered into her eyes with a concerned expression on his face. He mopped her brow with tender strokes, and offered her more drink. "You were mumbling something about a promise…"

She shook her head and gave him a disarming smile. "The fever must be affecting my mind. I was thinking back to our trip across Lorello, and when you saved me in that horrible graveyard. I really owe you so much, Talis. And you saved me again, you saved this ship from destruction—"

He pressed a soft finger to her lips to quiet her. "You should rest and get some sleep."

But she didn't want to sleep. She felt her heart open in tenderness and love towards him and didn't want to close her eyes. A soft light was shining in through the porthole, and the sight of his beautiful face lured her to study all the contours of his forehead and nose and cheeks and ears. Above his lips, a soft fuzz was forming, and she knew it would one day grow into a beard like his father. She loved him for the man he'd become one day, strong and stern and proud, but still with the same kind eyes that fell softly on hers. She willed that he would one day love her as she loved him now.

When he moved to sleep in the top bunk, she opened her mouth and spoke in a hoarse voice, "Stay with me, there's room for you here. I don't want to sleep by myself."

He nodded and she slid further in and made room for him to crawl in beside her, and she could feel his body shivering a bit. Mara came out of her feverish state for a moment and realized they were still wearing wet clothes. "We should take off these clothes…we're going to get sick."

Talis's face went shy at her suggestion, so she squirmed out of bed and locked the door to their cabin, and as he stood, she turned him around while she pulled off her soaked pants and shirt, and dove under the blanket. She grinned at the expression of embarrassment on his face, but she refused to look away, finding herself curious and bold in her feverish state.

He gave her an annoyed expression as he unbuttoned his shirt, but she just grinned in a wild look of delirium and watched in wonder as he pulled down his pants and scrambled under the covers. She felt his soft skin and a strange sensation tingled across her body as he wiggled in next to her. An excited giggle escaped her lips, the kind of girlish giggle she hated hearing from the practiced mouths of pretty girls fawning over the attention of young men. But his sparkling eyes dilated in response and he fixed his gaze on her, and only looked away after a flush appeared on his face.

"You're shivering," she whispered, and stretched out her hands to wrap around his trembling arms. Likely embarrassed of their close proximity, he turned his back to her and she found her fingers feeling along the curve of his shoulder as it dove down along his arm. His body quivered in response. The fever flushed sweat again from her pores, and her mind felt muddled but wildly awake and alert. Her body acted with its own volition and she scooted up to press her chest against his back and she snaked her arm around him and felt his heart pounding against her palm.

"Are you sleepy?" Mara said, and found her throat dry and raspy. He shuffled in response and twisted himself around to face her once again.

"I don't know if it's such a good idea for us to be like this." His voice sounded unconvinced of his own words. Mara was unable to think as her mind was absorbed in the sensation of his quick exhalations wafting along her neck.

"I just want to hold you, that's all." She saw that her smile caused him to part his lips. "Is it wrong for us to just hold each other?"

He shook his head and awkwardly wrapped his arms around her, but still kept a distance between them as they held each other. A bead of sweat slid down and stung her eye with its saltiness. She blinked and wiped her brow and Talis ran a cotton cloth across her forehead.

"You're still feverish." His voice was softer and resigned now, as if he was no longer nervous to be lying next to her. But he still kept a safe distance, and soon turned to lie on his back.

But Mara was still feverish and found herself daring and careless about his sense of propriety. She snuggled in close to him and wrapped her arm over his now sweating chest and surprised herself by sliding her leg over his, and immersed herself in the new sensation of his skin against her thigh. Instead of responding to her movements, she was disappointed as he closed his eyes, and whispered groggily, "We should sleep."

After fidgeting around for a while, a wave of weariness washed over her mind and she found the images of exuberant faces luring her into the dream world. She followed the people down a long, shimmering corridor of white marble, and was greeted by a celebration complete with cheering and the raising of flutes of crystal glass filled with fizzing wine. Over and over she toasted and drank the sweet, fragrant liquid, and found the frenzy of the festivities lifting her spirits to a place of reckless abandonment. She danced with handsome young men dressed in radiant blue robes of the finest silk. Her raised hands snaked and slithered in poetic movements, causing her dancing partners to rave in exaltation at her sensuous swirling.

Laughter poured from her mouth and she danced and drank again, more each time, until the feeling of freedom and fury possessed her in a singular sensation. All the while a deep, immoral voice whispered in her ear, urging her to drink again, and dance more, and relinquish all thoughts and worries into the fire of her new freedom. Her body writhed and twisted and shook, until the world wheeled around in a whirlwind of sights and smells and sounds.

She collapsed on the ground, heart hammering in her chest, and she found her arms draped over Talis, her breath panting and quick, and they were kissing in a wild frenzy, his excited eyes adoring her in an animalistic rush.

14

The Historian's Truth

The way Master Holoron scanned the air surrounding
Nikulo's head, it was as if the wizard were probing for
invisible threads of energy still attached to his brain. The
pain had vanished. Nikulo blinked and yawned and
stretched his shoulders and found that the world was lighter
and imbued with a kind of protective bubble that stretched
around his body. Was he truly free of the agony and the
voices? Or would they return once again, stronger and
more violent than ever, bent on his total annihilation.

"You've finally come back from the void." The old
historian's serious face scowled at him as if displeased by
what he saw in Nikulo. "The foreign consciousness followed
you all the way to the very edge of the void, but then
retreated in horror from the nothingness of it all. I was able
to observe them as they followed you there and as they fled
back to the surface of shining consciousness, where all life
feeds and nurtures itself away from the thoughtless void."

"They call themselves Naemarians." Nikulo was
surprised at the gentleness of his voice, so unlike the timbre
of his voice over the last few weeks since the affliction had

seized him. And even his thoughts were different and through some new lens viewed the strangeness of his old thoughts and actions with a kind of perplexed feeling of disgust. Had he really done all those terrible things?

A frown creased Master Holoron's brow. "And they exist on that other world you visited?"

"There and here, and they claim they are in many worlds, in the water of the deepest springs, from the primordial water of the universe. The water that brought life to all worlds from the heavens." Nikulo found his fists clenched in fury. "Those entities are utterly mad and crave a powerful fragment I found when I was in the World of Vellia, a fragment that belongs to the Starwalkers."

"As a historian, your words fascinate me to no end. But as a historian who has only studied texts from the known archives, I'm completely baffled. Who are these Starwalkers and Naemarians? Tell me your tale, tell of your experiences, tell your old history teacher stories to fill his future volumes. We've all the time in the world. I've lured and slain the Jiserian sorcerers that were foolish enough to show their faces. The City of Ursula is once again in the hands of the people, thanks to you and those ill-prepared but persistent revolutionaries."

Still suspicious of his freedom, and mindful of the Naemarian's command to board the ship for Carvina, Nikulo addressed Master Holoron once more. "How long have I been unconscious?"

"For three days…three long days in the void. Those beings called the Naemarians were incredibly tenacious and quite unwilling to give you up. That fragment of yours must have been of utmost importance for them to acquire."

"And am I really free of them?"

A dark cloud crossed the old historian's face. "I fear that you will never be completely free of the Naemarians. And perhaps in the future you will wish their counsel from time to time. However, my power now blocks their influence on your mind, and I will teach you the spell to block them from hurting you and to prevent their thoughts from intruding on yours. You will learn to control them…in time."

A mixture of anxiety and relief fell over Nikulo at the wizard's words, and he could not fathom why he would ever want the Naemarian's counsel. At Master Holoron's prodding, he began telling him the story of their journey to Chandrix and to the World of Vellia and his discovery of the Naemarians in the ancient spring above Illumina.

Twilight fell outside when he had finished telling the main parts of the story, but he failed to tell his old master of his slaying of the caravan owner and of his time with Callith, other than to mention her in passing. The old historian raised an eyebrow and addressed him once more.

"She is waiting most devoutly for you, my young pupil. It seems you've made quite an impression on her."

Nikulo smiled at that, and feeling in need of moving his body, pushed himself out of bed and stretched and found life stirring through him in an electric rush. He followed Master Holoron out of the sumptuous chamber and strode down to great dining hall where he was greeted by Callith and Yarin and several of the men he recognized from their bumbling campaign against the Jiserians.

"At last you are recovered, Master Nikulo?" Yarin was now dressed in a fine white silk robe and his once ash-stained face was now pristine and proud. "We've done it at last! Our fair city by the sea is now back in the hands of the people. And the Jiserians are slain and our citizens are in the process of cleaning the streets and rebuilding the city. Won't you sit and enjoy a drink before dinner?"

What a different outcome than expected, Nikulo mused, and he walked around and sat next to Yarin, and opposite to him sat Callith. He had thought that by now he'd be deep in the heart of Carvina making his way north to find the Naemarian spring. But was he not pleased to find himself free of them, and to be able to enjoy the lovely sight of Callith once again? Strangely, a part of him missed the wildness and fury of the Naemarians, and the feelings they provoked within himself. And when he studied Callith's curious eyes, he wondered what part she saw in him: the murderous maniac or the tenderhearted fool?

"Master Holoron has informed us of your former affliction," Yarin said, and filled Nikulo's goblet with a fragrant ruby-red wine that roused Nikulo's spirit. "And how despite your illness you endured a great pain and helped us retake Ursula. Nobly done, sir, truly noble and commendable. I had no idea you were suffering whilst we waged war against the sorcerers and necromancers. How did you manage the pain and the affliction while in the heat of battle? Frankly, I'm astounded."

Nikulo waved away the man's compliments, and found himself surprised that Yarin and the others weren't already dead for their utter lack of competence in the art of warfare. *I suppose the gods love the comedy of the fool with lofty ambitions*, he thought. And did the Jiserians really put up all that great of a fight? He glanced at Master Holoron and wondered how such a powerful wizard could have allowed himself to be captured by such an ill-organized enemy.

"Master," Nikulo said to the old wizard, "you never mentioned the story of your departure from Naru and your capture by the Jiserians here in Ursula. I am curious to find out what happened after Talis, Mara, and I left through the portal. None of the Sej Elders were still in Naru upon our arrival."

Master Holoron seemed hesitant for a quick second, then he fixed a resigned expression on his face and spoke. "It was a foul time for the Order of the Dawn and the Sej Elders. Viceroy Lei had proved a traitor to his own people and to the King, who is now ruling in absence in Ostreva. When it was clear that the Jiserians would fully take over Naru, the remnants of the Order of the Dawn met in secret and we agreed to each go on separate missions in the hopes of once again restoring Naru."

He sighed in fatigue and rubbed his reddened eyes. "Mistress Cavares had the most complicated mission and required my participation. It was necessary for her to convince the Jiserians of her loyalty and support of the dark arts, for we of the Order of the Dawn required someone deep inside the heart of the Jiserian Empire, in Carvina specifically, to work towards our ultimate aims."

So that was why Talis had found Mistress Cavares inside Carvina, Nikulo thought, and waited for Master Holoron to continue his story.

"Our plan was to have Mistress Cavares betray me to the Jiserians in exchange for a position of power in Carvina. Under the guise of sneaking together to find a ship bound for Ostreva, I acted the shocked and surprised part when we were surrounded by a horde of Jiserian sorcerers, and Mistress Cavares bound me in her shadow tendrils. She crafted the runic wards inside the prison cell, but provided me with a failsafe in the event I required to escape. Though I was weak when you arrived, I had many days left before I would have needed to escape and replenish my power."

"Why did you stay inside the prison for so long?" Nikulo said, finding the story somewhat strange.

"It was quite simple, I had to maintain the guise of weakness under Mistress Cavares's runic wards for as long as I could, to ensure her safety in Carvina. If a Jiserian sorcerer were to discover that I'd escaped, they'd likely open a magical portal back to Carvina and have her arrested as a spy. After you released me, I needed to act swiftly and kill the remaining sorcerers with precise certainty, otherwise our entire mission would have been in jeopardy."

Yarin hesitantly opened his mouth to speak, and Master Holoron motioned for him to continue. "And do you believe Ursula still at risk of attack by the Jiserians?"

"Not likely. From what Mistress Cavares has gleaned, the Empire is fragmenting at the edges and Ishur is in chaos with complete civil war among the various magical Orders. Only Emperor Ghaalis maintains his firm grip of power within Carvina."

At Nikulo's quizzical expression, the old wizard said, "We can communicate in the world of dreams."

Several servants entered the room with steaming plates of fish covered in rock salt, a huge bowl of rosemary and garlic potatoes, and a dish of fava beans mixed with onions and chard. Nikulo found himself drooling at the dinner.

"Now you should eat, young master, and regain your strength." Yarin gestured at the food. "Will you stay in Ursula?"

"Master Nikulo will be going with me to Onair," Holoron said, his voice decisive as if there were no other alternative. "Soon Garen Storm will return to meet us here in Ursula, and he will travel east with his family to Naru. Do not worry, we will leave your city under the protection of a squad of knights from Master Storm's garrison, and a wizard, Master Jai, to aid your city. Though I doubt you will find any Jiserian sorcerers or necromancers visiting here anytime soon. The knights will train your people in the art of war and help you to raise an army. From what we have heard of Onair, there is a great need to root out the Jiserians occupying the remnants of that destroyed city. Though they may have left by now, we have to be absolutely certain they are gone."

"And what course will I pursue?" Callith said, her voice soft and beautiful, and the color of her voice reminded Nikulo of their tender nights together out in the desert.

Master Holoron studied Nikulo and glanced at Callith in return. "I suppose that is your decision to make, young lady, and perhaps involves young Nikulo as well?" His wrinkled mouth formed a warm hint of a smile.

"I would return to my family in Naru." Callith spoke with conviction, and her eyes darted over to Nikulo's. As he ate, he felt a twist of emotion flicker over her face at her inspection of him. "And I would talk in private with Master Nikulo after dinner, for there is much for us to discuss…"

"Then it is settled. When Garen Storm returns to Ursula in a few days, you will depart east under his protection." Master Holoron raised his glass to Nikulo. "Let us raise a toast to the hero of Ursula, Master Nikulo, whom the citizens of this city should forever give thanks for his selfless aid in the face of overwhelming opposition. To Nikulo!"

Everyone at the table cheered and called out his name, and Nikulo felt embarrassed for it, but bowed his head and played the role of humble acceptance, knowing himself a fraud and his actions done out of self-preservation. *But you did keep your promise to Callith to keep her safe*, he told himself, and he caught the look of appreciation in her eyes as she raised a glass to him and mouthed her thanks.

In the distant part of his mind he heard a faint, familiar voice. *But you failed us, young master, you failed us... A fatal mistake and one we will not so easily forget. We are as old as the stars, and we were formed from the original seed of life, and we remember everything. We could have given you everything, all our knowledge to guide you. But you choose to live as a mere mortal individual, one disconnected from the whole. It is never too late to listen, we are always here in your mind. Waiting for you to come, to come and drink from the water of life...*

15

The Vengeful Fate

Soberness had flared in Mara's eyes that feverish night when Talis had realized they were kissing in a wild fury. There was no guilt or shame, only caution and the cool calming of the fire that burned inside them. He had urged her off to the side and asked if she was ok, if they were ok, and she told him that nothing had happened. That it was all a fever dream and that they should sleep. He left her bed and found his clothes still wet, and crawled up to the top bunk and fell into a fitful sleep.

They didn't really talk about that night for the next few days while the ship sailed along the southern Galhedrin Coast. The storm had broken and clear skies guided them past the Horn of Hardrin and on to where the famous Port of Carvina awaited them with its five hundred foot statue of an unknown Goddess. She stared south, her palms spread in supplication, and her lips were parted in a snarl as if she were starting to sing a dirge. On the ship high above, a sailor was raising a white and red flag, replacing the pirate flag that had flown for most of their voyage.

"She's the drowned bride of Pagamon, the God of Thunder, and legend has it that she threw herself into the sea after her lover never returned. Later, the gods had pity on her and she became a Goddess herself, and rose from the sea to found Carvina, from whom the city gets its name." Captain Cridd had smiled upon telling the story, as if all who heard the legend would feel a warm fondness towards the capitol because of it. Talis felt nothing but dread as he stared at the lifeless statue with her menacing eyes and cruel, calculating face. Carvina was the home of his enemies, and a vast and powerful city it was, stretching as far across the horizon as he could see.

Other than the massive statue at the harbor, the most distinctive feature of Carvina was the silver palace complex that snaked its way around several jutting hills in the center of the city. Talis borrowed a spyglass from the Captain and surveyed the tops of the hills. Towering silver temples gleamed in the afternoon sunlight, and were adorned with gigantic statues of gods and goddesses and mythological creatures. Twisting silver pillars supported long, rectangular buildings and each corner of the roofs was shielded by the wings of angels (or demons). The city blazed in the sun and surprised Talis for its lightness and illumination. He'd expected a dark, dreary place of death and doom.

When he shared his surprise to the Captain, the man chuckled and nodded his head in understanding. "You are thinking of the City of Ishur, she's is an oppressive place and filled with dread and wariness. You have to watch your what you say and where you look in Ishur. They might blind you or cut off your tongue. Not like the fair City of Carvina. She is a beauty to experience and rich in history and art and music and food, and they run a massive arena with the world's most skilled gladiators. The Emperor Ghaalis merely uses the sorcerers and necromancers in Ishur to do his dirty work. The citizens of Carvina know very little of such things, or perhaps they care little of what goes on outside their blissful city."

Talis chuckled to himself at the idea, and wondered how the Emperor was faring with his people now that his Empire was experiencing a widespread turbulence. Did the Jiserians need to expand their empire to support such a vast and wealthy city? Perhaps to placate the luxurious lifestyles of the citizens of Carvina, the Emperor was forced conquer new cities and bring in the wealth and goods acquired. But it seemed hardly sustainable.

"And here I thought that Illumina was the most beautiful city I've seen." Mara snaked her arm inside his and leaned against his shoulder, a sweet sigh escaping her lips. "Carvina causes all cities to pale in comparison to her magnificence. Will we be safe inside her walls, Master Goleth?"

"As honored guests of mine, the city will welcome you. Though I imagine when the Emperor's Court hears you are from Naru, there will be much gossip and scandal. The official account of the siege is that the citizens of Naru acted in open rebellion to the Emperor and were utterly

126

decimated as a result. I imagine weaving in the tale of our travels with Lord Aurellia will incite an even greater furor."

"Do the people of Carvina even know of Aurellia?" Talis glanced at the Builder.

Master Goleth crinkled up his eyes at that, and thought about his words for a moment. "He is not a public figure, that is, Lord Aurellia has never shown his face to the crowd or openly visited the Emperor's Court from what I have heard. But he is known in whispers and murmurs in the dark. I believe they have even have contrived children's tales of his dark power and the legions of undead that he commands. He's quite the boogeyman in Carvina."

How strange, thought Talis, *that Aurellia is a shadow figure in the very Empire he supported for so many years. Perhaps he was even the same way in Darkov and the other kingdoms around the world? Likely Vellia was always his true home in his mind...*

"Do you think we'll get to meet Emperor Ghaalis?" Mara whispered, and Talis caught Master Goleth studying them.

"We'll be staying at the Regent's Inn, the place diplomats and foreign dignitaries always stay." The wizard glanced with fearful eyes at the shabby docks the ship was approaching as it glided through the gentle sea. "That is after we make our way out of this hideous area. Captain, is this where you always make port?"

Captain Cridd gave Master Goleth his best devious smile and shrugged, then turned to bark out orders for his crew. He was a smuggler after all, of course he would bring his goods into the dingiest port in the city. Though from what Talis could see, there were few poor areas of Carvina. Even the houses and the buildings near the modest docks were newly painted and well maintained, and the area seemed thriving with workers bustling around in activity.

As they gathered their gear and prepared to leave the Emperor's Revenge, the Captain came and shook hands with Talis and Master Goleth, and bowed in respect to Mara. "We all owe you our lives, young master Talis and Master Builder." He looked to Talis and nodded his head in admiration. "I saw what you did to obliterate that massive wave and keep watch over the storm that foul night. I will never forget the aid you provided us after the betrayal of those sorcerers. If you ever need help of me or any of my captains, just you let me know. And you won't forget our agreement? The gods be blessed, soon the sea with thrive with trade from the Storm family and may Naru once rise again in power and wealth!"

Talis said goodbye to the man, and helped Mara down the gangplank where Master Goleth wasted little time in leaving the docks. His long legs strode at a pace hard for them to keep up with, and Talis had to call out a few times, asking for him to slow down. At those times the Builder's face looked nervous and even afraid to find himself in such a poor part of the city. To Talis it seemed familiar and warm, like the lower part of Naru, and nothing hideous like Seraka or seedy like Khael.

"We must keep moving," the wizard said, and he glanced around and winced as he spotted something off in the distance. "It will look poorly if we arrive at the Regent's Inn too late in the day."

When the Builder charged off once again, Talis scoffed and rolled his eyes at him, and Mara joined in, giving Master Goleth her cute and conniving look of mockery behind his back. "The *Regent's Inn* awaits us, my dear. Let us not tarry here in this disreputable part of the city. The gods forbid such dissolute behavior." She made an expression like she wanted to vomit.

Talis chuckled with her and he expected a harsh retort from the wizard, but Goleth was so intent on studying the streets that he hadn't heard a word they'd said.

"Blasted damned circular streets!" Master Goleth swung his head back and forth, his eyes in a panic as the darkness fell over the city. "There's no order or logic at all in this part of the city."

"But of course not," Talis said, and cleared his throat. "Do you really expect the city planners to spend time in the poor, common quarters of the city? The money flows to where the money comes. I imagine this entire quarter provides little in the way of taxes. Likely when they come to collect, the people ask for work or for money to help feed hungry children. After a few years of that, even the most motivated tax collector will give up and go for easier targets." Exactly how the lower quarter of Naru worked. Only the official shops and artisans generated tax wealth for the King. The poor provided little, but made cash and kept it hidden from the government. Not that Talis cared, for the King had much and the people had little.

"Are you lost?" Mara said, and Talis could tell she was trying to keep the humor out of her voice.

"Of course I'm lost!" The wizard sighed in frustration and let his hands flap to his side. "I'm a master builder but I have a terrible sense of direction. And I hate this part of Carvina." He paused for a moment, his eyes vulnerable and disoriented, as if he were a boy remembering a painful experience.

"I suppose you might as well know," Master Goleth said, "you deserve an explanation for my strange behavior. You see, when I was young I traveled through these streets with my mother. We had arrived in Carvina at those same docks to try and find my father, who had failed to write to us for many months after coming here to work as a stonemason."

The Builder rubbed his weathered, wrinkled eyes and Talis could see a quick swell of sorrowful emotions flourish on his face. "Those men *hurt* my mother... I can still feel the anger and impotence I felt, so powerless and unable to do anything to stop them. I tried"—he raised his big fists and shook them at the stars—"oh, gods I tried to beat them, but I was so little and those men were so strong and they laughed at me while they hurt my mother in so many terrible ways. I never saw her again. They beat me and left me for dead on these streets, and I never knew what happened to her."

Mara gaped in horror at the Builder's story, and Talis could see that she felt embarrassed for having mocked him before. And Talis felt the same way. If he'd only known why Master Goleth acted the way he did, he would have never made fun of him. But Talis realized that perhaps many people were like that, acting in some strange way because something horrible had happened to them, something painful that scarred them for life.

"And did you ever find your father?" Mara said, her voice soft and penitent.

The wizard nodded and his eye twitched at the memory. "After those men dragged her away and left me bruised and beaten, I forced myself to crawl and eventually stumbled away to safety that very night. I left this evil area and vowed to find my father, and I did after a week of searching and begging and asking for help in finding him. An old priest took pity on me and fed me and gave me shelter until he located my father at a temple building site where they were erecting a new shrine. But my father had found a new wife and she refused to allow me to stay with them. That's when the priest arranged for my acceptance into the Order of Rezel."

Talis found his hand settling on the Builder's shoulder, and the wizard looked at him with eyes ready to burst with tears. "I'm sorry for your loss, Master Goleth, truly I am. And don't worry, I'll help us out of this place." With an appreciative nod from the wizard, Talis withdrew the Surineda Map case and unfurled the parchment. He commanded the map to show their position in the streets of Carvina, and asked for aid in finding the Regent's Inn. Soon a wispy thread of gold appeared on the map and gave them clear guidance.

But Mara asked him to wait, and Talis saw a dark malice appear in her eyes as she stared down the dark streets. "Such an evil deed against one so innocent deserves revenge. I refuse to allow those men to go unpunished. They deserve to die."

Talis found himself shocked at the look of fierce determination and fury on her face as she stared at the wizard. Even though Master Goleth's stunned silence provided no agreement to proceed, Mara fixed her eyes on Talis and motioned for him to use the map. He had no choice but to humor her request. But he couldn't help but feel it was a terrible idea. So he closed his eyes and asked the map to display the location of the men that hurt Master Goleth and his mother so many years ago. When he studied the parchment, the map jittered for a while and blinked in response as if thinking, then it moved over to the northeast and displayed twin grey lights.

Mara nodded her head and exhaled, catching Master Goleth's attention as she pointed at the Surineda Map. "There are the men that hurt you and your mother. And tonight they will die, by your hands or mine, I do not care, but I swear to the gods that tonight they will meet the cruel Guardians of the Underworld."

16

Twenty-Second Level

Rikar screamed in horror as a shadowy being engulfed him in the purest form of malevolence. All his meditation, all his training, fled him in an instant. A vast hand of darkness squeezed him as if there was something soft inside to savor and consume. The pressure was so immense he cried out in agony and begged for it to stop, but Rikar soon realized that his words were swallowed by the black void that surrounded him.

Then the pressure released and the darkness vanished and the feeling of the presence smothering the life out of him disappeared into a sea of silvery starlight. He found himself floating in the space between stars, and the breadth and awe of that place astounded him. There were thick patches of stars condensed together into a white ball that spread out into fuzzy edges, and deep, massive stains of inky blackness that refused to allow any light within their terrible boundaries. Concentrated light alongside utter darkness. Madness and sanity. Life and death. Chaos and order. The fundamental opposite forces presented before him in the auditorium of the universe. And all Rikar could think about was killing Garen Storm.

He was sure that many people would be absorbed with the beauty of the vision and find themselves caught up in rapturous euphoria, but Rikar only stared at the black stain and pictured it as a dagger striking the heart of his enemy. After all his meditation and fasting, the focus of his mind distilled into one pure malicious thought: bring death, bring pain and suffering, and cause cascading collateral damage to everyone.

The oppressive feeling of the Nameless returned to him in an instant fury. A thought penetrated through to his mind; a silent question of Rikar's worthiness. Soundless curiosity voicing the doubt that Rikar had often expressed to himself, *Why should I bother with you?* The being failed to even care about his memories, it didn't probe and it seemed to care little, and after its initial horrific force, touched Rikar's mind like the soft breeze of summer. And he heard another glancing thought (perhaps the last one), *What thing of interest do you have for me to see?*

Aurellia had done no coaching with him on what to expect with the Nameless. In fact the Dark Lord doubted that Rikar would even be able to gain an audience with the Lord of All. He had forced Rikar to leave and ordered him to try his best to slay the Starwalkers. *At least one must be killed,* Aurellia had said.

He found fear pierce his heart as he pictured the Starwalker woman being impaled by the crystal shards of

135

the temple, and Jared, the lead Starwalker, with his raging eyes locked on him in an eternal promise of vengeance. The Starwalkers would come for Rikar, now he knew it with an absolute certainty.

The voice again, stronger now, *Ah...now that is something of interest to me, the ancient beings of light who walk the stars. They possess the primordial fragments of power from the birth of the universe. I desire such power. Interesting. You have slain such a being?*

Rikar opened his mouth to answer, but found no purchase for his voice.

Speak in your mind, strange one. The voice had a pompous edge that irritated Rikar.

So he tried again, thinking the words this time. *I have killed a Starwalker, and they have vowed revenge against me. Can you protect me from their rage?*

The Nameless issued a contemptuous laugh that echoed across Rikar's mind and filled him with fury. *You come to me daring to speak of self-preservation? There is no self in the universe, only the whole... The life or death of your physical form does not interest me, and I doubt it interests anyone.* The being issued a great wheezing sound like the rattling rasp of refuse in the lungs of a smoker. *However, if you prove a suitable lure for us to catch our plump and shiny fish, then perhaps...*

A shock of light burst in his mind's eye and soon he returned to the darkness of the chamber, filling him with a mixture of dread and hope. *But without an actual promise to help*, Rikar thought. The door opened behind him and he could see a faint light outside, but not even the most

136

infinitesimal bit of light entered the chamber. *A prison, indeed,* Rikar mused, and allowed a smile to spread on his face.

As he was leaving the room, the voice returned, formidable and indignant this time, *Here is the not prison. The door seals the prison of the outside world of illusions. You have been permitted entry through one of the gates into the real world, where illusions vanish into the sea of the whole. You know nothing, illusion-blinded fool...*

17

Assuredness of Victory

The smooth sensuousness of Callith's skin tormented Nikulo as he sat with her in the palace library, feeling the fire burning at the great hearth. The flames flickered and danced around the logs, sending shadows flittering across her face as the fire burned low. She'd led him here seeking privacy after the long dinner.

"I probably should have you arrested for killing my husband," she said, and surprised Nikulo out of his stupid entrancement. "But considering that you were afflicted at the time, I guess I can't completely blame you for what you did." She winked at him with an irritably cute expression on her face. "But I can blame you for all the other things you did to me, in my moment of emotional weakness…"

"What?" Nikulo felt his face flush from the heat of the flames. "I thought—"

"Oh, shut up," she said, and leaned over to kiss him with the familiar passion he'd experienced on their nights together on the caravan. After she parted in a panting gaze, her eyes bright with longing, she raised a finger to keep him silenced. "One condition I have for you. You and the slaves will say my husband was slain by desert marauders, and that you saved us. And I will never speak a word of this again to you or anyone else. Do you understand me?"

Nikulo nodded, and felt like a puppy that's been scolded by his master for peeing inside the house.

"How old are you?" Callith studied him with unconvinced eyes. "You have such a baby face, I can't tell."

"I'm sixteen...soon to be seventeen." Nikulo frowned as she laughed riotously. "What's so funny?"

"I can't believe I'm actually older than you. You're practically like my baby brother."

Despite feelings of humiliation, he didn't resist her when she plopped her small figure onto his lap and kissed him again. "I guess I have no choice but to stop hating you, chubby little brother. You did save the entire City of Ursula from destruction, and you are quite famous in Naru as well. I imagine I'll have to keep you. Just don't do anything stupid like getting yourself killed in Onair. I'll never forgive you if you don't return alive and well for our wedding."

His eyes flared at the words and he almost stood and dropped her on the floor. "Wedding? Did I miss something? Like perhaps proposing to you?"

She rolled her eyes and gave him a pretty scoff. "Let me see, late at night in the desert, the four moon sisters shining outside, the ale flowing freely between our lips. I resisted, and you made so many sweet vows of love and promised to take me away and keep me safe. How that handsome mouth of yours babbled, *I love you, I love you,* so many times I worried the madness of the moons had overtaken your silly mind. You may not remember what you said, but I do and I believed you then, and I still believe that a part of you feels that way now. Or was that merely your member talking?"

At her gentle squeeze, he found a groan escaping his mouth and realized it was hopeless to resist her. "Ok, I give in…you win. Stop it, now, you little tart. We're supposed to be *talking* in here not doing this. What if Yarin or Master Holoron came in and found us?"

"Oh, I highly doubt they'd be surprised, any fool can see the way you gawk at me with those hungry eyes of yours." She placed a hand on her breast and assumed the noble face of one very serious. "He is such a beast, I tell you the truth, Master Holoron. What kind of a devil was he in school anyway?"

Nikulo pinched her and she squealed in delight. "I'll show you what kind of a devil I am. Just be patient and wait until I get back from Onair. We won't be long in dispatching those Jiserians."

At the end of the next day, Master Holoron and Nikulo found themselves docking at a small fishing village just north of Onair. They ate dinner and had a few drinks with a local fisherman and his family who were kind enough to put them up for the night. The man's beady eyes raged in fury as he told stories of the Jiserian invasion and the destructive waves that ravaged their city like it was a sandcastle. Their small village had escaped attention, but

140

the streams of refugees and injured poured out of the city for weeks after the sorcerers and necromancers had imposed martial law and ruled the remains of the city in absolute tyranny.

"They never liked the fact that the wizards of Ursula gave them such a good fight." The old fisherman wagged his head and guzzled some more frothy beer. "It was revenge, I tell you, revenge against the wizards for defeating so many Jiserian champions that had faced them in their sky duels. The young one here probably doesn't know that Onair possessed a legendary school of magic with some of the finest wizards in the land." He glanced at Master Holoron. "But I'm sure you remember the Order of Songs and their wild, frenzied dancing and contortions and singing, all to invite the divine through their magical castings. I witnessed it once and will never forget that powerful display of magic and music."

"I visited the Order many times and enjoyed learning from their old masters." The wizard stared off at the sea. "When I heard the news of the Order's obliteration and the slaying of their wizards—both the old masters and the young apprentices—I felt my world was being slowly ripped apart. And then it happened to us in Naru. All our knowledge and power and history fared poorly against the dark, distilled clarity of the Jiserian magic."

"And what have you heard recently of the Jiserians in Onair?" Talis studied the old fisherman's eyes as the man furrowed his brow in worry.

"Tis a very complicated and difficult situation since it has been confirmed that the necromancers have fled." The man scoffed and a flash of irritation crossed his face. "I suppose it is a good thing that the sorcerers cleared the city of the undead and purged the dungeons and the deep archives of those foul practitioners of the necromantic arts. But unfortunately the city is ruled by a strange order of magic from the City of Carvina, an order that mixes melee with the magical arts to augment their physical strength, speed, and their defensive capabilities."

He looked to Talis as if grasping for help in finding the right words to say. "How would you call it...a kind of second skin, sort of like an armadillo or maybe a turtle? They wrap themselves in a tough, scaly skin that makes them almost immune to sword and dagger. Brutal beasts, they are. They came in after the wizards of the Order of Songs destroyed the first group of sorcerers. They gleefully fought every gladiator and challenger for miles around, luring them with a vast fortune of gold and gems. None of the challengers lived to enjoy the bounty."

Talis glanced at the concerned face of Master Holoron, and waited for the old historian to respond, but he just finished his beer and stared in thoughtful contemplation at the sea. The fisherman excused himself for the night, and Talis was left alone with the wizard.

"Are you worried about what the fisherman said?" Talis kept his voice low and searched Holoron's face for any signs of doubt. "How will we fight those warrior magicians?"

Master Holoron exhaled and pounded his fist on the table, causing Nikulo to jump in surprise. "We can't fight them, they've been trained since birth to have a high resistance against most forms of magic. And even if you are a master swordsman, good luck in beating them in a fair fight. They are the champions of Emperor Ghaalis, the fanatical and ancient Order of the Dragons, the most feared fighters in the world.

"From my research into their history I've gleaned that the ancient founders of their Order made a blood oath to steal the beating hearts of every dragon in the world, and offered the hearts as a sacrifice to their cruel gods. Once they completed that horrific mission they perfected their magics with the aid and blessing of their gods. That is why there are no more dragons on this world, at least according to their lore, and I've heard no better explanation for the dragons disappearance."

Nikulo thought to Vellia, and the vast horde of dragons from Ghaelstrom, and couldn't imagine them all being killed. What nefarious minds were powerful and conniving enough to destroy all of dragon kind?

"You know there is a cult within the Order of the Dragons that claim that their members have gone weak over the years without dragon blood and hearts to sacrifice to their gods. They hold a great reverence for the dragons, and believe that their ancestors should have never killed all the dragons, but instead conquered them and bred them for repeated sacrifice over the years. They've sent scouts far across the seas and north into the mountains searching for any remaining dragons, but from what I've heard, none have been found."

"I hope Talis never transforms into a dragon in Carvina, they'll try and rip his heart out alive."

Master Holoron thought about his words for a while, and shook his head in disagreement. "No, I imagine they might worship him as a god and raise him up as the most powerful figure on this world."

"So what do we do about Onair?" Nikulo changed the subject, not wanting to picture Talis getting mixed up with such a strange magical order. "We're stuck here now that the ship has gone. Unless we wait for another one going north?"

"I never said we'd give up on our mission. I merely meant we wouldn't fight. There are other ways of winning than fighting. And here before us is a valuable lesson in the art of war. What is the goal we are seeking to accomplish?"

Nikulo thought about all the miserable refugees that had come to Naru after the destruction of Onair. If they couldn't win in a fight against the Jiserians, then what was their real goal? "To protect the people left in Onair?"

"Think more carefully. To protect them would put yourself in a position of requiring to fight those of the Order of the Dragons. What is our real goal here in this situation?"

"Well, we wanted to go down and get rid of the Jiserians and free the city." Nikulo felt himself getting frustrated at the wizard's cryptic questions.

"Precisely, the goal is to get rid of the Jiserians and free the city." Master Holoron bowed his head in respect to Nikulo. "And to achieve that goal, there is no reason for us to fight. We just need a way to assure victory for our goal without raising a finger to fight. And do you have any ideas on how to get them to leave Onair?" At Nikulo's no doubt exasperated look, the wizard continued, "We know what they want, do we not? I've just told you they crave dragons to breed and use as a sacrifice for their dark gods."

"So you are suggesting we offer them a way to find dragons? The dragons on Vellia? But they have no means to leave this world and journey to Vellia, Aurellia made sure of that by leaving. Unless there are others remaining in the Jiserian Empire that possess the knowledge? But without a powerful enough crystal, there's no hope of succeeding in the casting of the world portal spell."

"Ah, but there is someone in the Jiserian Empire who has such knowledge and holds a powerful crystal required to cast such a spell. You said it yourself." The wizard leaned forward and Nikulo shuddered at the devious look on his face. "Your friend, Talis Storm, would he not be able to provide what those Jiserians desire?"

18

Collateral Executions

As they snuck through the silent streets to the house of their destination, Mara imagined the feeling of the twin daggers in her hands, blazing and slicing as she cut the criminals down. Master Goleth's story had strangely affected her emotions and even now she found her arms shaking from the image of those horrible men hurting the Builder and his mother. She allowed Talis to lead the way so she could open her backpack and withdraw the daggers. The leather straps of the sheaths were perfectly sized to attach to each forearm, and the weight of the blades and the feeling of fury flowed into her mind at their close proximity.

I will kill those men myself with my own daggers, she told herself, and she pictured the blood erupting from the old men's necks. *Age demands no pity of me,* she thought, and as Talis pointed at a multi-storied house made of stone, she gripped the daggers and wielded them, a burst of bloodlust surging through her.

A quick glance from his wary eyes caused Mara to lower the daggers in caution, not wanting for him to recognize the design. "The door is steel and there are solid iron bars on all the windows. And I doubt at this late hour they'd open for someone knocking at their front door."

"Use the map to show us any dangerous people or traps," Mara said, and noticed the hesitation in Talis's response.

"Is this really necessary?" Master Goleth said, and his eyes looked tired and fearful as he stared up at the strong house. "I mean what is done is done, and will killing two old men who committed a crime many years ago really help anything?"

"Of course it will," Mara retorted, and frowned in response to his stupid words. Why was he being such a coward? They hurt and probably killed his mother, and he felt no rage against them? "What they did to your mother, they likely did to many other people, and from the look of this house, they probably continue to commit crimes every day. Let the Lord of the Underworld mete out his judgment for all their evil deeds."

She took a step towards Talis and jutted her chin at the Surineda Map. Her eyes fixed on Master Goleth. "Stay out here in the street and suffer under your memories, Builder, but I'm killing those men tonight."

Talis stopped opening the map and gaped at Mara in horror. "What's come over you? I want to see those men punished for their crimes as do you, but it's almost like you're enjoying the thought of killing them. And where did you get those daggers? They don't make blades like that in Naru."

"You know as well as I do that we're the only ones who can punish those men for what they did to Master Goleth's mother." She sighed in irritation and looked up at him with a pleading gaze, not wanting to answer his question. "His story really got to me, ok? We both have a mother and he had to grow up knowing that his mother had been hurt by those men. And his father refused to take him in... Can you imagine how you would feel if that ever happened to you? Those men are guilty. Period. End of argument. Now are you going to help me or not?"

The wariness in his eyes melted under the weight of Mara's stare, until he gave her a grim smile and nodded, his expression fierce and certain. "May the gods use our hands to execute justice in the protection of the weak and defenseless." He opened the map and closed his eyes, and soon a sea of danger appeared over the place where the house was drawn.

"Oh, Nyx, what have we gotten ourselves into?" Mara whispered, and studied the angry red dots milling around the map.

"Traps at the roof, looks magical." Talis pointed at arcane runic symbols pulsing on the map. "All the doors have magical wards, especially the back door. The front door looks strong enough to not to need any magic to hold it."

"It seems like those men who hurt your mother are now crime lords of some kind. No name above the door, quiet, unmarked streets... Or perhaps a cult of some kind?" Mara wondered how they could find a way inside. She studied the glass windows and realized those men were primarily thinking of protecting themselves from people entering the house to hurt them.

"They're arrogant enough to keep glass windows. Likely they're not worried about someone setting their house on fire." Mara gave Talis a devilish smile.

"But what about all the people inside?" Talis said, and studied the map. "You want to set an entire house filled with people on fire to exact revenge against two guilty men?"

"That sounds about right. If the gods find them innocent of crimes then I imagine they'll escape unharmed and unmolested by our attacks as they flee the building."

"So you want to kill them as they try and escape a burning building?" Talis gave her a look like she had gone completely insane.

"I can't help but believe that they will be quite violent towards us as they charge outside." Mara knew she was walking a razor-sharp line with Talis and he was close to giving up on pursuing their targets. So she tried another tact to convince him. "How about we set fire only to the area of the house where the two men are? Maybe if we are lucky they will die in the blaze. That way the others will have a chance of escape and we can hide over there in the shadows and wait for them to leave the house. We'll watch the map and track their movements. That way we shouldn't hurt too many people."

Talis looked placated and Mara gave his arm a reassuring squeeze and told him he was doing the right thing to help Master Goleth. The Builder cleared his throat and his face held a crafty expression.

"If you insist on going through with your plan of revenge against those two men, then let me suggest another plan of attack." The wizard cleared his throat in a raspy, purging fit. "Excuse my cough, it seems as if I've come down with something during our sea voyage. I feel quite fatigued and dizzy."

Mara tilted her head and studied the dark, deep circles under the man's eyes and his skin's pale complexion. Had he looked like this on the ship or was it only because they'd entered this part of Carvina?

"As I was saying, my skills as a wizard relate not only to building but also to deconstructing. Your plan to set fire to the building is fraught with impossibilities. For instance, if their security is sophisticated enough to cast magical wards over doors, I imagine that the glass windows will be magically protected as well. However, very few rune masters know how to protect against my kind of magic. One spell and I can eliminate the doors and bars and windows, and leave them completely exposed to outside forces."

"Really?" Talis said, and gave the wizard an amazed look of admiration. Mara knew Talis was still very interested in learning of the magic of the Order of Rezel, but like Mara, he only wanted to study directly with Master Goleth, from the only Jiserian they trusted.

"I suppose now is as good of a time as any," the Builder said. "Track those two vile men on your map and I'll create the most elaborate distraction you've ever seen in your life."

Talis and Mara followed Master Goleth over to hide in the shadows, and once there, Talis nodded at the Builder and studied the map. Soon he glanced up as the wizard stretched out his long fingers and aimed at the building, a look of intense concentration on his face, like when Mara had seen him for the first time on the island in Vellia.

Mara watched the Builder cast his spells and she thought the swirl of the elements looked like the building spells he had cast before, but done in reverse motion. The iron bars and steel doors literally melted into a sea of shimmering light and poured into a new object that he was fashioning from those stolen elements. At first Mara had a hard time telling what Master Goleth was fabricating, but soon the shape rose and refined and resolved into a tall statue of a beautiful woman with curly hair, her long arms stretched out accusingly at the now dissolved front door.

"That's your mother?" Mara said, and was surprised to find her voice choked with emotion. Tears spilled from her eyes as she glanced back and forth from Master Goleth to the haunting statue.

"They're coming!" Talis hissed, and he aimed a hand at the building entrance. They stood tensed and ready to strike, and Mara could feel her heart pounding inside her chest. She gripped her daggers tighter and pictures of rage and revenge swirled around in her mind like silent commands.

The first thug poked his head out of the entryway and gaped stupidly at the place where the steel door had been attached to the hinges. A larger, brutish thug shoved him aside and muttered curses at how his fat face was getting in the way. The man glanced around the street, a menacing, calculating look in his eyes, until he stared in confusion at the beautiful metallic statue of the woman pointing at the entrance.

"Get the sorcerers," the thug shouted, and he turned and charged back into the house, the other man following him as well.

Talis glanced at the map and Mara saw that the two old men were leaving from the rear entrance. "Let's go after them. Looks like they're trying to sneak out unnoticed."

As they headed out back down an alleyway, Mara noticed that the Builder had cast a quick spell and barred up the front door and windows with slashes of steel woven into a dangerous pattern. Now the thugs and sorcerers had no choice but to leave via the back entrance, and Mara was sure that Master Goleth was preventing them from flanking their rear and attacking them with the element of surprise.

"There they are," Talis said, and pointed at two burly looking old men surrounded by a gang of six toughs, and three sorcerers in green robes followed from the back of the group. Before Talis could cast a spell, the Builder flicked his wrist and formed a prison of those same steel spikes around the two old men, causing the thugs to shout in consternation and surprise. The sorcerers flared their hands around, eyes searching for the source of the attacks.

The thugs charged off after Talis and Master Goleth, who stepped forward to face their enemies in the alleyway, but Mara snuck along behind the shadows of several crates piled high. The passageway between the crates and the house was wide enough for Mara to sneak through. The dark street was illuminated by bursts of light magic and lightning bolts, and the sound of steel striking steel as the thugs hacked away at the barriers that the Builder had constructed to contain the men.

Talis was caught in a frenzied battle against the three powerful sorcerers who crafted runic symbols in the air between Talis and them, blocking or absorbing every spell that Talis cast at them. With each casting, the runes seemed to strengthen and grow brighter. But while the sorcerers were concentrated on Talis, Mara had stalked along the building and positioned herself behind the three shriveled sorcerers with pasty, wrinkled faces. *Two daggers for three sorcerers*, Mara thought, and remembered the technique that Master Relech had taught her for dealing with situations like this.

The blade in her left hand swung around in a wide arc and punched a hole into the unsuspecting, left-most sorcerer's heart. While the man crumpled to the ground, blood bubbling from his chest, Mara twisted and brought the dagger in her right hand around and sliced the other sorcerer in the neck, nearly severing his head. A spray of blood filled the air and Mara felt the warm droplets on her face and arms as the man gurgled and gasped for air as he collapsed into the expanding pool of his own blood. The third sorcerer pivoted and aimed his fingers at Mara, but before he could get off a spell, the man found an exotic blade buried deep into his eye socket.

The thugs, lured by the sounds of battle behind them, gave up on Talis and turned to inspect the bloody mess that Mara had created. What a sight she must have been for those men. She chuckled as their eyes narrowed in perplexed horror at the mess of blood over her face and white frilly blouse. With a quick pull she yanked the dagger from the last sorcerer's eye socket and beckoned for the thugs to come and dance with her. The feeling of pulsing power from the twin daggers raged inside her hands and heart and she stabbed the air in the direction of each thug in a children's game of choosing which pig she'd butcher first.

None of the hired thugs were brave enough to join in her dance of death, and the men bolted down a side street, filling the silent night with the sound of boots clapping against cobblestone as they escaped. The rage simmered slowly and Mara felt the blades' disappointment at not being fed their fill of blood. She wanted to chase after those men and stalk them down one by one, but she remembered

154

all the points of light on the Surineda Map. Weren't there more men inside who could threaten them?

Master Goleth melted away the sharp steel barriers and strode over to where the two old men cringed in terror, their baffled eyes studying the Builder as he approached. Mara glanced at Talis's concerned face as she joined the wizard to stare at the criminals who snarled at them like two old rats caught in a trap. She prodded the steel cages around the men, wishing her blades were longer.

"Leave them for me," Master Goleth said, and his unrelenting eyes offered no opportunity for argument. Mara moved aside and allowed the wizard to stand alone and face those two men. With a flourish of his hands the steel cage evaporated into elemental particles and swirled around and formed into a menacing-looking, serpentine short sword that fit nicely in the Builder's hand.

"You may not remember me." The wizard jabbed the sword underneath the wrinkled neck of the first old man. "But I remember you two, especially you, for my mother was the first to suffer under the punishment of your hands. She was so young and beautiful...why did you have to hurt her?"

A line of blood dribbled down the old man's neck as a flash of mockery crossed his face. "I don't remember you or your whore of a mother, and I don't really care. I've made it my business to hurt filthy women and poor innocent boys. Ah!" The wizard slashed the sword across the man's big belly and stared with some interest as his intestines spilled out.

"A declaration of guilt," Master Goleth said, his voice cold and flat. He turned the blood-soaked sword to the other man, whose eyes glowered at the wizard in defiance. "How about you? If I recall, you tried to stop your friend from hurting my mother at first, but then he called you a coward and to prove him wrong, you joined in and were even more brutal than he was against her."

"Was I twenty, or twenty-two years old? Or perhaps thirty, I don't remember." The old man sighed with a brazen expression on his face. "Just kill me already and be done with it. I did what I did to your mother and I can't take it back. And honestly, I'd probably do it all over if I had the chance. She was a beautiful—"

Master Goleth stabbed the man in the heart and twisted the sword around so as to cause the man more pain. He clenched his teeth and raged until his face went red and spittle spilled out of his mouth. His heavy head went slack and lolled to the side while the wizard yanked out the sword. Off to the side the first man groaned and tried to shove his intestines back inside his belly, but Master Goleth just wheeled the sword around in an arc and tried to hack the man's head off, but was gruesomely unsuccessful.

The wizard fell to his knees and Mara could see tears spilling down his weathered face. She was overtaken by a feeling of pity for the poor man, for losing his mother to such disgusting men. The daggers in Mara's hands screamed for her to inflict more punishment on the men, but her will was slack and deflated, and all she could think about was going to someplace safe and scrubbing the sick smell of blood from her skin. She glanced at Talis and wondered if she'd forever altered his view of her as some vile, incomprehensible creature. She wanted him to love her, not despise and distrust her.

"Let's get out of here," Talis said, and pulled Mara into the protection of his arms. His accepting face gave her a look of sorrow and compassion, and when he whispered, "Everything is going to be ok," a flood of tears poured from her eyes.

Everything is most certainly not going to be ok, she told herself, and closed her eyes as she allowed Talis to guide her through the dark streets.

19

Royal Colors

When Talis left Mara in the capable hands of the servants at the bathing hall of the Regent's Inn, he prayed to the Goddess Tolexia to heal the pain and confusion from Mara's mind. The frenzied look of fury in her eyes as she murdered those sorcerers with such gleeful precision frightened Talis to his core. That was not the Mara he knew and loved, more like the Mara from Vellia under the influence of Princess Minoweth's dagger and the dark taint of Elder Relech. But weren't they both gone now?

The memory of the hideous, crow-like Elder haunted Talis's mind, and the effects on her psyche were devastating. Talis was hoping that the Jiserian Empire would be in ruin by now and crumbling under the remnants left behind by Aurellia, but as he surveyed the clean and sumptuous City of Carvina, this was clearly not the case. Their magical might and military power made them just as big of a threat as before the invasion. At every suspicious glance from the guards roaming the city, Talis told himself not to be fooled by the beauty of this place.

This was the heart of the very enemy who had killed many of his people and turned Naru into an undead madhouse.

"Will she be ok?" Master Goleth frowned with such a harsh uncertainty that the crow's feet between his eyes pinched into two deep crevices. "She was quite brutal in her slaying of those sorcerers." *And she looked like she wanted to run off and hunt those other thugs down and kill them one by one,* thought Talis.

"She's never really had a rest since Palarian stole her away into Chandrix." Talis sighed and remembered the feeling of horror as Mara had disappeared into the world portal. "The shock and stress has shifted her sanity beyond the edge, I'm afraid. I never should have allowed her to come along this trip."

"The truth is she is important in our mission to the Royal Court. She is Viceroy Lei's daughter and rightful heir to his role as Ambassador to Carvina. It is possible that only she can mediate a peace treaty between Naru and the Jiserian Empire. At least that is how Emperor Ghaalis will likely see it."

So you are saying to make sure that Mara stays sane or we'll have come here for nothing? Talis thought. After his experience struggling against the three sorcerers guarding those two old men, he knew that there was little he could do against the skill and power of any unknown Jiserian magic he might encounter. His frustration in pouring the power of light magic against them—fueled by the crystal from Ghaelstrom—did nothing to break through their wards.

159

They easily outplayed and outsmarted him with a strange kind of magic that would have easily defeated him. *If not for Mara's aid, we'd be dead on those streets instead of those two old criminals.*

"I have contacted the royal messenger and sent word to the Emperor's secretary requesting an audience." Master Goleth passed through the door to the bathing room where a full range of servants waited to prepare them for the baths. "Depending on his mood, we should expect a response within a few days."

A few days? Talis thought, and reluctantly allowed a dour-faced manservant to collect his backpack and fire sword as they headed into separate changing rooms. The servants held the look of trained indifference on their faces as they helped Talis undress and gestured him to the steaming-hot water inside an elaborate marble bath.

"Though perhaps, since they've delivered me a return message," the wizard said, "we'll hear from the court sooner."

One of the servants handed Talis a sponge scrub-brush and soap and motioned him towards a wooden bucket and a flow of steaming water that jettisoned from the stone wall. Realizing he was filthy with the stench of sweat and sea, Talis drenched his head and body with the hot water and felt the troubles of the last few days wash away down the drain. He scrubbed and scrubbed his skin, trying to rid the stench of blood from his face and hands, but somehow the smell refused to go away. His mind kept picturing the spray of blood from Master Goleth's sword splashing him in the face, and how he'd tried to wipe the blood away with his hands. But the smell still remained.

He finished washing and dressed into new white linen pants and an ornately embroidered silk shirt with dragons etched along the arms. Had the wizard chosen this shirt for him? A grin from Master Goleth told him he had asked the servants for this specially designed shirt.

"Dragons for a dragon," the Builder said, "woven with my own magic. Wait till you see the jacket I've designed for you. You see, in the Royal Court of Carvina, it is just as important to shock and delight with an exotic image and a confident posture as it is in what you say. Promises and words mean little to the royals of the Jiserian Empire. Surprise them with your story and allure them with the creature that you've become, then perhaps you'll have a chance of winning the respect and admiration of the Royal Court."

In his mind, Talis imagined a vast and palatial court filled with silk-robed royals gossiping at his entrance, eyes gesturing in wonder as Talis strode down the purple silk carpet to bow in respect before the grand Emperor, the most-hated foe of Naru. Would Talis find the craving to kill the man rising inside himself upon first sight of the Emperor and all his stolen glory? Or would he like the man and find him honest and unaware of all the atrocities his Empire had committed? Would it even matter? Talis knew the only thing he wanted from Emperor Ghaalis was for his empire to leave Naru alone.

The same servant brought over a heavy silk jack of the finest white material embroidered with two slithering silver dragons along the front, claws outstretched on the each side of the jacket, and the dragons' heads spewed silver fire. Talis stretched out his arms and allowed the servant to place it on him, the cool feeling of the silk made him picture the beauty of the City of Illumina as the crystal spires caught the last rays of sunlight. He was a dragon mage cloaked in the image of a dragon, true to his kind. King Valeron would be proud.

Outside, at the explanation of Master Goleth, the hallway was lined with busts of former civilian leaders of Carvina, powerful men and women who ruled the economy, wrote the laws, and managed governmental bodies as representatives of each district of the city. The wizard had given him at exhaustive background of the political and economic structure of the capitol and Talis found it very interesting, a sharp contrast to the government of Naru. Here in Carvina, the Emperor technically was a figurehead of power who controlled the sorcerers and necromancers of Ishur, and they were not allowed to visit or occupy Carvina. The Stelan Knights were permitted in the capitol, but only inside the Emperor's palace and the vast majority of knights were stationed outside the city, on campaigns in the Empire's far outposts. Carvina was primarily ruled by elected civilians.

Talis turned his head at the sound of heels clicking against the marble floor, and he gaped at the sight of Mara. Her transformation into a regal princess was like a rose blossoming into fragrant beauty, and the view of her startled him down to the marrow of his bones. She wore a long silk gown of fiery red, the color of blood and power. Her uncovered arms and shoulders were toned and sleek, and the dress displayed a deep slit in the front, showing a revealing amount of her blossoming cleavage. Talis felt his face flush when his eyes settled there, and he remembered their feverish night alone on the ship. Once a girl only in proclamation by her parents, and more a boy out on the hunt with Talis, now Mara stood as the true Princess of the Lei family lineage, confident and strong and beautiful.

She beamed under his attention, her face completely changed from the vile expression of fury that she'd displayed towards the three sorcerers. Talis was taken in by her radiant smile and the quick tapping of her red-heeled shoes against the stone floor as she darted towards him in an exuberant rush. Her face blushed under the weight of his adoring eyes and she stopped just before committing the socially unacceptable act of throwing herself into his arms, something she regularly did when they were out on their own.

"So what do you think? Do I look terrible?" Her eyes looked playful and hesitant, as if she demanded words of praise to propel her all the way to the Royal Court.

But Talis was so stunned that he found himself unable to voice words on just how incredible she looked. Mara took the pause as a sign of disapproval and a pouting frown appeared on her pretty lips.

"Is it that bad?" She twisted around and showed the revealing open back that dipped down to the curve of her hips, causing Talis to gulp at the sight of her soft skin. Had she grown taller, or was it her high-heeled shoes?

"No, it's too good." He regretted the gushing, croaking sound his voice made as he spoke the words. "I-I mean it's really too good."

She smirked at him like he was an idiotic boy from a farm. "You said that twice, silly. Do you mean good as in like ice cream delicious good, or good as in regular good?"

"Definitely ice cream delicious good," he blurted out, and he felt like his face would explode from all the blood surging across his cheeks in embarrassment.

"I like ice cream good." She winked at his awkwardness and kissed him right there in the hallway with Master Goleth and the servants watching them. But he didn't mind at all. It felt good to forget propriety and just enjoy the moment. Besides, who knew what would happen to them after they visited Emperor Ghaalis… What if the Emperor reacted terribly and Mara was taken away from him again?

She seemed blissfully ignorant of his dark thoughts as she seized his hand in girlish delight and followed Master Goleth as the servants beckoned them down the wide, curved stairs that led into the crowded grand foyer. Couples in white and black silk meandering around the entrance stopped and whispered at Talis and Mara as they descended the stone steps. A flash of surprise on Mara's face was quickly contained as she must have realized that she was the only woman to wear red.

"Allow me to introduce you to Princess Mara Lei and Talis Storm of Naru." Master Goleth flourished a hand towards them as they approached a group of old, stodgy-looking men dressed in stiff, black suits. Most of the men raised spectacles to their curious eyes and inspected Talis and Mara, leaving a long glance for her red dress.

"Ah, but of course, from the wasted and wicked world of the Nalgoran Desert," said an elderly man who wore a four-pointed black hat. His hooked nose twitched as he studied Mara. "They let ladies of good reputation to wear red like that in Naru? It's no wonder the city was so easily cursed by the gods…"

Talis felt furious at the man's rude comment about Mara, but she just laughed confidently and smiled at the old man, keeping her voice smooth as she spoke. "In Naru our women are expected to be strong like the beautiful color of red. Are the women of Carvina expected to slink around in the shadows of their husbands?"

A few indignant gasps came from the covered mouths of the nearby women who were no doubt listening in on their conversation. The old man refused to back down and raised a finger to speak. "Our women support their husbands and don't spend time luring other bees to their flowers."

Mara chuckled with devious eyes. "The nectar of a white flower attracts the hunger of many bees. It is the sweet smell of its soft petals that lures the insects. I've found many weak men intimidated by the strength and intelligence of a woman, especially a woman who wields power and is unashamed to wear a strong shade of red." She winked at the old man and grinned when a surprised and flustered expression crossed his face.

"I must inform the Princess that in the Jiserian Empire, red is considered the symbol of the Emperor's power." The elderly man cleared his throat and looked apologetic as a result of his assertion.

Master Goleth raised a finger to interject. "That is most certainly true, Duke Vermouth, however it is also true that red is the color of the clergy of the Sorarkian Church, among whom they have priestesses who wear red during their rites of power. So you see, the claim to wear red does not solely lie with the Emperor. Although it is fashionable by those of the Royal Court to only wear white and black to pay respect to the Emperor. But there is no provision excluding foreign dignitaries from wearing the color."

Duke Vermouth sniffed as if something in the room were distasteful. "That doesn't mean the Royal Court might find the Princess embroiled in a controversy at her arrival looking like that…"

"Controversy would be perfect," Mara said, and gave the Duke a winsome smile.

20

Order of the Dragons

The lie, the lie of committing Talis to help the Order of the Dragons, the lie stretched out in Nikulo's mind and simmered there for a while as he pondered it. Would such a lie actually work? Would they believe them and leave Onair in the vain hope of actually finding dragons on another world? Nikulo doubted they would listen to them. He doubted he himself would ever believe such a fanciful tale, unless of course Aurellia had dealt with the wizards of the Order of the Dragons. Had he told them of his plan to leave and return to his home on Vellia? Likely he had, especially since Elder Raelles had returned to the Jiserian Empire and recruited so many sorcerers and necromancers to his cause.

But then again Nikulo didn't remember any sorcerers on Vellia with the abilities that Master Holoron had described. Perhaps they were more loyal to the Emperor since they were based in Carvina and all the other magical Orders were founded in Ishur? Where did their loyalties lie? Potentially Master Raelles never even visited Carvina on his return trip to recruit fighters for Aurellia's cause.

Maybe those of the Order of the Dragons were never loyal to Lord Aurellia, just loyal to themselves.

"We should leave under the cover of darkness," Master Holoron said. "Get some sleep and I will wake you in the early hours of morning." The old wizard hobbled away and left Nikulo to his thoughts.

He decided he should try and sleep, so he ambled over to the hammock that the fisherman had prepared for him and lay down and felt the gentle sway lull his eyes closed. He dreamed of dragons in flight above the skies of Illumina, the great horde of dragons from Ghaelstrom flying to help them in their fight against the Jiserians. The massive black dragon, King Valeron, sweeping his wings out as he landed on the ground near Nikulo, his great black eyes studying him with questioning look.

Nikulo heard the dragon speak to his mind. *Are you the one who will betray my people to the fiends of your world? How will you live with the blood of the dragons staining your hands and your heart? If you betray us, may your name be cursed by the gods forever...* The king dragon stretched out his long neck and Nikulo could feel those dagger-like teeth sinking deep into his arm.

Heart pounding, he woke with a start as Master Holoron shook his arm and told him it was time to go. Nikulo glanced at his arm, half-expecting to see teeth marks and blood gushing from the wound, but found nothing. He exhaled and slipped out of the hammock and stretched the discomfort out of his back. Would he really betray the dragons? Or could the lie be stretched further and somehow keep those sorcerers stranded on Chandrix, the middling world, where they could do no harm on either planet? Could he convince them?

Master Holoron and Nikulo trudged south through the darkness, following a faint faerie wisp illuminated in golden light as it danced ahead and found them a safe path to traverse. Another secret spell that the old, mysterious wizard possessed that Nikulo had never seen. He thought it strange that the wizard chose not to fly, as he was certain that the old man possessed such a spell.

"When we arrive in Onair, it will be particularly useful for us to pretend we've just come via the sea." Master Holoron huffed and breathed hard as they climbed a steep rise. Soon they stood overlooking the view of Onair and the sea, clearly illuminated by the brightness of the four moon sisters. The broken walls of the city looked eerie and desolate in the darkness, as if the city were a vast beast slumbering after a grave injury.

They hiked down the hill and stayed close to the rocky cliffs with a clear view of the hastily built docks where two ships were anchored in the low mist. Soon they stealthed along the hard, encrusted surface of the beach, and Nikulo drooled at the sight of the fat crabs sidling away from their approach.

"You are trained as a mentalist, am I correct?" The wizard glanced at him and continued without waiting for a response. "Can you use your skills on humans, perhaps to

170

convince the captain of that ship that we've just arrived with him from Carvina?"

"Likely, assuming they have actually come from Carvina. It is far easier to make such a mental suggestion when the truth is stronger than the lie." After a long while they reached the docks and sneaked down the wooden pier until they found themselves facing a large galley with the gangplank conveniently down. Master Holoron beckoned for Nikulo to go first up the plank. The wooden board creaked as Nikulo stepped along its length and finally he reached the empty deck with a guard dog that snarled at his arrival.

With a quick hand to his temple, the beast calmed and panted in a friendly, I-want-a-snack kind of way. Nikulo handed the black dog a piece of dried beef and the creature wagged his tail and smacked in satisfaction as he wolfed down the treat.

"Good boy," Nikulo whispered, and scratched the dog's ears. "Now can you show me where the captain is sleeping?" The animal bobbed its head and exhaled a smelly waft of air, and trotted over to a cabin on the aft side of the ship, its claws clicking against the wooden deck. The dog plopped itself in front of the door and whined softly.

Nikulo waited in the shadows while commanding the dog to continue whining until a stirring and creaking could be heard inside the cabin, and a groggy voice said, "Something wrong out there, pup?"

The door groaned opened and a scraggly-faced man with long, disheveled hair poked his head out and studied the tail-thumping dog. "Oh, I see, now. Yer just lonely and wanting a wee bit o' company, are ya?"

Nikulo pressed two fingers hard against his temple and fixed his mind on the captain's thoughts. Smoothly he inserted a suggestion that his two visitors from Carvina were needing to rise early today and visit the Jiserian rulers of Onair, and that he needed to escort them inside the city.

As a way of assuring verbal confirmation, Nikulo suggested to the man that it would be good for him to speak the words out loud, which he did in a dreamy, distant voice. The dog clobbered its tail against the deck at the captain's words.

"Oh, you're awake, Captain." Nikulo stepped carefully out from behind the shadows. "I hope I didn't startle you. We were to meet early and go into Carvina?" Nikulo gestured at Master Holoron, who slowly appeared to the inspecting eyes of the captain. "We're anxious to conduct our business with the masters of the Order of the Dragons. Especially since we've come all this way from Carvina." Nikulo was taking a gamble that the ship had docked in the capitol, and found success as the man nodded his head in groggy assent.

"Yes, yes, and you must be tired after making so many stops along the way." The captain arched his back as if invigorated by some noble purpose. "Let's make haste and get you inside, though I'm a bit confused." He rubbed his head and Nikulo prodded his mind forward. "Bit confused as to how I'd go about requesting an audience with them… They never see us. Only the soldiers deal with sailors and merchants."

Nikulo waved away the worrisome thought. "Never you mind, Captain. Just get us inside those gates and we'll handle everything past there. If anyone asks who we are, just mention we are two emissaries from the Royal Court of Carvina on a secret mission to meet the masters of the Order. They'll understand diplomatic privilege."

The feeble-minded captain bobbed his head stupidly and his eyes glazed over at hearing the words, *diplomatic privilege*, as if nothing more needed to be said after those words had been spoken. They followed the leather-clad captain down the gangplank and the dog loyally trotted ahead, sniffing up the scents along their path down the docks. The dog lifted its leg and marked a pile, its eyes staring ahead into the darkness where torches flickered at the city gates.

"Morning, soldier," the captain said, and inclined his head in a bow as the three of them passed a well-armed guard with suspicious eyes. The soldier settled on Nikulo and Master Holoron for an uncomfortable amount of time. Then the man continued on his patrol away from them and Nikulo sighed in relief as they neared the heavily fortified gate.

A tall, burly soldier wearing a strange, woven steel armor studied them with hawkish eyes as they strode closer.

He stood well over a foot taller than Nikulo, and his giant sword swung out to stop the captain's approach.

"What do you think you're doing?" The soldier lifted the captain's chin with the tip of his gleaming sword. The sailor gulped in response, his once sleepy eyes now fearful and alert.

"These men are emissaries from the Royal Court of Carvina." The captain froze as the soldier rested his blade against the sailor's neck. "They have business inside with your rulers."

"And my sword is hungry for blood." The soldier's words earned him a few appreciative grunts from the other men in their squad who sat lazily around a fire warming their hands.

"What Crestia means to say is…turn your sorry asses around and go back to that pathetic ship of yours," another older, menacing-eyed soldier said. "Or find your head lopped off your ugly body. Those men are no more royal emissaries than the wench I had last night was the legendary Princess Serine of House Ostreva."

The soldiers guffawed at that remark, and Nikulo found himself uncertain if he could affect the cynical, hardened minds of those men. Master Holoron seemed infinitely more confident as he spoke to them in a low, assuring voice.

"Let the poor man alone," the wizard said, and stepped in and moved the sword aside. "He's just doing as instructed and delivering us to Carvina. No need to frighten him. Can you see us more clearly now, in the light of your torches, that we are emissaries from the Royal Court? Would you dare turn us away and risks your lives as swordplay for those masters of the Order of the Dragons?" He studied Crestia with doubtful eyes. "You won't last long against them, I'm afraid."

"What do you know of the Dragons?" Crestia said, and lowered his sword as an uncertain expression clouded his face.

"As a royal emissary I know a great deal." Master Holoron sighed in irritation. "I know they're faster than you by far and stronger as well, and even if they weren't, there is no way that your pathetic sword could cut through their scaly armor. How many countless times have you seen them hack down challengers in the arena? Dare you wish to join those challengers in filling the trough of blood spilled by those masters of the Order? Now step aside and open the gates, and you can get back to the business of minding your wenches."

There was a long, tense pause during which Nikulo felt beads of sweat dribble down under his armpits. He glanced at the nervous, wary eyes of the soldiers who all seemed to be waiting for someone to issue a verdict. Finally, a soldier pushed himself up from a chair where he had been resting under a tarp. As he sauntered over to them, a long scar across his grizzled face gleamed in the firelight. His eyes stared off in different directions as he studied Master Holoron and Nikulo in a long, uncomfortable gaze.

"Since you seem to know the Dragons so well, old man, why don't you tell me which Master of the Order you seek?" The man Nikulo guessed was the commander stared at the wizard a long time as if he knew the trap he had set would catch its prey.

A wry smile crossed Master Holoron's face. "A name I can easily supply. Is it Commander?"

The soldier nodded and said, "Commander Drelan."

"Thank you, Commander. We are here to visit Master Varghul, the leader of Onair and likely the new bane of your existence?" The wizard gave Commander Drelan a knowing expression that caused the man's cold stare to deflate.

"Right this way, sir." The soldier completely changed his demeanor to that of a professional bound by duty to fulfill his task. Master Holoron bowed abruptly to the captain, and followed Commander Drelan fifty feet up to the gates now rising and clattering noisily.

Nikulo stared up in amazement at the repaired gaps in the walls where the waves had broken through, clearly visible by the incomplete construction that stopped around twenty feet up along the hundred foot walls. It was almost as if a titanic sea beast had come ashore and chomped several areas of the walls, leaving behind a horrific wreck.

The city inside was sparse and crudely constructed, and the lower part was filled with large tents and Nikulo could see the fearful eyes of women dressed in dour colors as they prepared breakfast for the sleeping men. Piles of resting dogs nestling together failed to bother at their approach. The entire area had a desolate, temporary feeling as if at any moment another massive wave from the sea might wash it all away and leave behind only sand and rubble.

After walking some fifteen minutes through more hastily constructed housing, they finally reached a second gate that rose at the Commander's signal. Compared to the chaos of Ursula, the City of Onair was run with the rude precision of a military camp at war, though Nikulo could see no evidence of conflict. The inner city seemed completely unaffected by the gigantic waves that had struck the outer walls and had inflicted horror on the houses and buildings there.

The core of the city was the picture of perfection, the exotic beauty that Nikulo had imagined from the etchings in his geography books he had studied of Onair. Tall palm trees dotted the landscape, with fig and date and olive trees scattered here and there across the multi-layered cityscape. The several storied houses were whitewashed with colorful paintings and patterns circling underneath the wooden roofs. On the towering buildings built with sharp, sleek granite pillars, the clean, geometric rooflines stood as sentinels to the vibrantly painted friezes below the beams. Nikulo gaped at the pristine condition of this part of the city, as if the invading sorcerers refused to touch the historic beauty of this place. For indeed it was a marvel to behold.

The only evidence of discord was a massive pile of sun-blanched human bones and skulls in front of one the most beautiful buildings—Nikulo guessed it was a temple from glancing at the golden dome. Across the white wall were characters written in an arcane, Jiserian script that Nikulo could read from his years of study with Master Holoron.

DRAGONS HAVE DEVOURED THE SONGS.

21

The Candle Flame

Mara nearly collapsed by early evening, after an exhausting day spent in silly social conversations, lavish feasts and long introductions to countless nobles with their odd sense of pride in wearing only black or white-colored clothes. Her favorite part of the day was when they sauntered over to a shaded veranda adorned with climbing roses for afternoon tea and cakes, including fresh strawberries and whipped cream. All the social torture was made palatable by the sweet deserts and fragrant tea.

The evening slowly stole hours away from the day, and the dark fingers of twilight stretched across the outdoor dinner party situated along a fantastic man-made lake with seven waterfalls spilling from the gaping mouths of seven gods and goddesses. In a peculiar change in the scene, all the women had disappeared from what the men coined, *The Resting Hour,* and returned renewed and radiant wearing sheer silk dinner gowns that revealed far more of the women's' figures than Mara's dress.

At the first cheerful note played from a lute, Mara could tell that the night's festivities were an anchor point for the nobility, as the amount of royals out milling around the lake at the dinner party tripled from many of the events earlier that day. With the orchestra playing full and furious now, the warm sultry air possessed only a faint hint of humidity, though enough to keep the night pleasant enough for Mara's exposed skin. As she stood arm-in-arm with Talis observing the migratory patterns of the royals, she felt a firm flow of steadying power from having him at her side. Something about his tousled hair and dazzling eyes filled her with a sense of belonging and confidence that she so desperately needed right now, especially after the incident with her slaying the three sorcerers.

Gasps and murmurs cascaded across the various groups as heads turned towards a stain of blood-red that showed far off in a slow-moving boat that appeared underneath a god's head. Mara craned her neck to see around stretching heads trying to get a better view of the arrival of someone very special. The blare of trumpets burst out. A luminous red falling curtain covered the sky from the zenith all the way down to the rolling surface of the lake. The boat and its riders had teasingly vanished in the shimmering show of power likely created by invisible magicians positioned mysteriously across the grounds.

And then an eruption of fireworks from hundreds of spouts in the lake jettisoned white and red pillars of fire high into the sky and ignited the curtain into a raging inferno that blinded Mara for a moment and sent her heart racing in ecstatic delight. With the smoke came a dark and dreadful mist that showered the celebration in obscuring phantoms and faeries that moved and swirled and danced around the heads of the partygoers. But soon absolute darkness rampaged across the screaming, wailing women and brought a roar of frenzied exclamations. The sounds seemed as if coming from the mouths of men sentenced to death, men pleading to indifferent executioners.

Mara felt the fury of fear surging in her chest, the same feeling as when Talis had led her into the Ruins of Elmarr, into the place of doom where the malevolent voice spoke words of terror to her mind. Was the same being haunting here in a visitation upon Carvina, summoned through the channeled spells of its most ardent sorcerers? The power surged and scintillated as a ripple of fire and electricity danced in sheets across the sky, so intoxicating that Mara felt her legs quiver and tremble under the force of magic, and she found her teeth clenched in a weird, uncontainable wrath. She longed to grip her daggers and destroy and destroy until the sky was a deluge of blood.

Silence and a wash of nothingness. A familiar hand holding hers. Talis staring over her with concerned eyes. The smell of smoke and cinder serenaded her nostrils and caused her to gasp in a sudden wakefulness.

"Where am I?" Her voice sounded surprisingly soft and sleepy, as if she'd just woken from a long, dreamless sleep. She glanced around and her eyes discovered a dimly lit room and Talis sitting at her bedside. His face held the concerned expression of a father studying a sick child.

"We're back in your room at the Regent's Inn." He looked as if he were uncertain of how much to reveal to her. "You fainted in the park. It was pretty intense when the Emperor arrived with his consorts and royal sorcerers and illusionists. You weren't the only one to faint. I saw countless women and even men gasping and convulsing with horrified expressions gripping their faces. It was a grim and devious scene. Master Goleth believes it had something to do with our arrival in Carvina and the letter that he wrote to the Emperor. He said that Emperor Ghaalis likes to awe first-time visitors to Carvina with a massive display of his power."

"Did I go into convulsions?" Mara studied Talis's face for hints of her unruly behavior, but he only shook his head and his clear eyes told that her she didn't act out of place.

"You just fainted after the darkness came. I felt your knees buckling and I scooped you up before you could fall." He grinned at her and cupped her cheeks with his hands and she pushed herself up and kissed him in appreciation for his chivalry.

"Gods, that's a relief. Here I was imagining myself spasming on the lawn like a deranged lunatic." She sat up and glanced around the dark room. "What time is it? I'm starving. Is there any place we can go and get something to eat?"

"We could ask the servants to bring us something."

She shook her head, wanting to go outside and feel invigorated by the cool night air. "I'll change into

182

something black and make sure I fit in with the crowd. I got way too much attention today wearing red. I don't know what I was thinking."

"You certainly did draw a lot of stares." He stood and helped her up and chuckled at her woozy face as she found her legs wobbly.

"Wow, I must have really been out of it," she said, and steadied herself against Talis's arm until they reached the changing room filled with clothes that had been made especially for her. "How late it is?"

"Like midnight?" A nervous expression flashed across Talis's face. "I hope it's ok for us to go outside."

She waved away the idea and rummaged through the collection of clothes and dresses hanging from brass hooks in the huge wardrobe. A short sleek black dress with frilly lace below the waist caught her eyes and she pressed it against her chest and stared at her reflection in the mirror. She wasn't what she'd call beautiful, not compared to all the other tall, gazelle-like girls that loped around in long, lavish dresses that accentuated their lean and lengthy arms and legs. Their slender figures had just the right amount of curves to inflict cruelty on the imagination of men gawking at them like puppies. But many men did stare at her tonight, and Talis beamed in pride at having her by his side.

"This one," she proclaimed, and decided for certain after Talis's bright eyes fixed the decision. She told him to turn aside while she undressed, but when he went to leave

183

she asked him to stay and keep her company. The black dress fit perfectly and she stretched out her arms and twirled in front of the long mirror, admiring her toned and slender legs that looked longer than the last time she had studied herself.

"Am I getting taller?" she said, and looked to Talis for confirmation.

"You are taller, actually. Your mother is quite tall, so no reason you won't grow more." Talis was being kind and Mara knew it; her mother wasn't tall, definitely not compared to how tall and thin the women were in Carvina. They looked like giraffes.

She seized his hand in an excited rush and slipped on a pair of shiny black slippers the servants had brought for her, and tugged Talis out into the hallway. They quickly escaped out a side door into the crisp, fragrant night air that possessed the faintest hint of a cool mist. The streets were still surprisingly bustling, with fewer couples and far more younger, livelier girls and boys threading through the streets with jubilant and conniving faces. Mara noticed the curious eyes of boys older than her, drugged and intoxicated eyes that roamed and laughed and raged ebullience and freedom.

Music poured out across the streets from performers singing and playing and dancing for coin, upended velvet hats collecting a bounty based on the skill and popularity of the artists. She caught sight of the most beautiful and exotic young woman she had ever seen, dancing at a wild street corner thronged with admiring men and jealous girls. The dancer wore diamonds slunk around her exposed, sensuous belly that gyrated and pulsed to the sound of drums hammering away in a frenzy of hypnotic rhythms. Her silk top teasingly revealed upright breasts that bounced in time with the music. Mara found a blush coming to her face at the woman's erotic movements.

She looked up at Talis's entranced eyes and elbowed him in the ribs to shake him out of his gawking. He glanced down and gave her an embarrassed but entertained smile that caused her to relax and enjoy the show. As Mara returned her gaze to the dancing, the woman's almond eyes caught hers and sparkled in a mischievous look. The dancer twirled and twirled in a pirouette of pleasure, and her delicate hands and long fingers flourished graceful gestures while her hips rocked and bounced in a seductive fury.

The music stopped abruptly and the dancer bowed, sending a wave of cheers and clapping across the crowd. Mara cheered along with them, waving her hands in an excited flourish that matched her free feeling.

"Such a wild and wonderful city," she said, and giggled as the crowd pushed them along towards a marketplace filled with steaming stalls where savory and sweet scents wafted into Mara's nostrils, driving her stomach to gurgle and complain in expectant delight. Soon Talis commandeered a place underneath a sprawling sycamore tree and offered her a white chair at a table already stocked with a selection of chocolates.

It seemed as if the youthful crowd was also hungry and thirsty from flirting and gossiping and enjoying the excitement of the street shows. Well-heeled girls plopped down on chairs while the young men stood and sipped on mugs filled with frothy beer, admiring the girls as they preened and exposed legs and flapped dresses as if pretending to cool themselves. It was quite a lavish scene.

A candle was brought to their table, and Talis, obviously showing off for her, aimed a palm at the flame and caused it to twirl and dance about a foot into the air. Several gasps went out as girls from nearby tables noticed the outburst of brilliant light. But Talis remained undisturbed, and instead focused even more on the flame.

"I've been practicing with fire and force," he said, keeping his voice soft and sultry like the night. He aimed both palms at the flame, facing each other in a kind of cupping gesture. "Flame feeds off wind, and wind drives fire crazy."

Mara chuckled and lifted herself a bit to see better. "Kind of like you and me."

"You do drive me crazy more times than I care to admit." He winked, but kept his eyes fixed on the flame. Soon the flame split into two, then three flames that illogically had twisted around in a fixed twirl where each flame did not touch the others. It was almost as if Talis had learned how to independently control each flame, and yet each flame still burned within the confines of its own spiral.

A smile burst across Talis's handsome face as he leaned back a bit and watched as the three flames continued to grow and spiral into the air, like three long-stem roses artificially twisted and splayed apart in the air. Shrieks of joy and exclamations of amazement echoed out across the nearby tables. So much for a night out unseen. Though Mara would've preferred anonymity, she was pleased to see Talis enjoying the entranced attention of the crowd that was gathering around their table.

"Flame and dragons married along the serpent's spine." Talis projected his voice in a high, mysterious tone as he snapped his fingers and caused three dragon heads to sprout and come alive atop each flame fingerling. Mara marveled at his sophisticated artistry, and the level of detail he could command, including causing the eye area inside the dragon heads to burn white-hot. How did he do it? She had never seen him practice such complicated creativity, other than flame-play at campfires and fires at the hearth.

"Three dragons consume each other in ecstasy," Talis proclaimed with a playful chuckle in his voice, and spiraled his index fingers and caused the dragons to face the sky and twist around like cobras under the bewitching tune of a snake-charmer. Indeed the dragon's mouths opened and devoured each other and dove down to the candlewick and burst back up as a single, larger dragon with churning, white-hot eyes that flared a bright heat. Mara jerked her head back in a giddy gasp of pleasure.

Then Talis clapped his hands and the flame was extinguished in a burst of white, fragrant smoke that smelled like temple incense. The silent crowd stood stunned and gaping at the rising, twisting smoke, as if expecting the smoke tendrils to come alive and form into some hideous beast.

"That was amazing," Mara whispered, but even the softness of her voice managed to startle the assembled crowd out of their reverie. She glanced around at the entranced faces of the youthful citizens of Carvina, the faces of people least likely to be amazed, considering all the spectacular displays of art and magic she'd already seen here in the capitol.

One bold and beautiful girl opened her mouth to speak. She was perhaps sixteen-years old with long, luscious yellow hair that danced as she shook her head in amazement at Talis. Her voice sounded enviously silky and smooth as she spoke. Mara instantly hated her.

"Dragons are forbidden from all displays of magic in Carvina." The girl's pleasant proclamation startled Mara, as she had expected the girl to praise Talis for his artistic expression. "From what city do you hail?"

Talis's surprised pause gave an opening for Mara to respond. "We're from Naru, a city to the north nestled in a vast oasis in the Nalgoran Desert. A city that has long been at war with the Jiserian Empire."

The yellow-haired girl pivoted her pretty face around and gawked at Mara as if shocked that she had the audacity to speak to her. "Naru?" She scoffed in a fetching, taunting exclamation that caused the girls around her to break out in a fit of pretentious giggles. "Didn't we completely obliterate that frightful little city? I heard father talking to his club friends that after our sorcerers and troops demolished any resistance, our necromancers turned the entirety of that vile population into frothing undead."

Mara seized the tablecloth and squeezed until her knuckles went white with rage, and yet through a cool force of will kept her face calm and indifferent. Talis rescued her from the embarrassment of an ill-mannered retort.

"I'm afraid that is all old news, Miss?" He paused expectantly and studied the girl's surprised face.

"*Princess* Devonia," the girl said curtly.

"Well met, Your Royal Highness." Talis swept his hand to Mara in a smooth motion. "Allow me to introduce you to Princess Mara Lei of Naru, daughter of Viceroy Lei and former Ambassador to the Jiserian Empire. And I am Talis Storm of House Storm."

She gaped at him in utter disbelief. "You lie! It is common knowledge that the Child of the Sun was slain early in the siege of Naru, when the Temple of the Sun was destroyed by our sorcerers."

Talis smiled with confident ease and raised an eyebrow at her. "And yet here I am sitting next to you. So interesting how the official accounts from ministries of information are quite often incorrect, as evidenced by my mere existence here before you. Do you require proof?"

Princess Devonia gave an incredulous huff and folded her long arms and cast him an intrigued glance. Mara found herself jealous at the charged exchange between Talis and the pretty girl.

"Let's see, how about light magic to illuminate the night?" Talis scanned around with an unsatisfied expression on his face. "But we'd need darkness first to make such a display meaningful." He raised his hands and waves of shadows tore across the square and extinguished all the candles and torches until gasps and shouts of concern filled the crowd.

"Now for the pure golden light of the sun." Talis projected his eerie voice like an actor on a stage. He allowed his palms to radiate with brilliant golden balls of light until Mara and the people around shielded their eyes from the intense light. Out of the corner of her eye, Mara could see that Talis was unflinching in his gaze as he focused on the golden orbs. A quick snap of his wrist sent the two fiery, miniature suns out to float over the heads of the shrieking, howling crowd.

A girl nearby shouted for Talis to stop the light, that it was blinding them, and Mara saw a wry, self-satisfied smile creep over his mouth as he clapped his hands together and made the golden orbs disappear. Darkness returned with all-encompassing dreariness. But soon spiraling tunnels of flame jetted and danced from Talis's fingers and fled out over the sparkling eyes of the fearful crowd until finding purchase on the candlewicks and torches, which ignited in a soft series of whooshes across the square.

But Princess Devonia was for some reason enraged at his display of power and pushed herself up to leave, her eyes flared in fiery fury as she glowered at Talis.

"So you come here to Carvina to invoke fear in the hearts of our serene citizens?" Her voice trembled as she aimed a finger at the crowd, but Mara felt her earlier hint of jealousy rise in strength as Mara realized with some feminine intuition that Princess Devonia held some feeling towards Talis. "You dare provoke the hysteria of soon-to-come revenge for the sins committed against your people?"

Talis waved a hand dismissively, and Mara noticed the Princess flinch at the gesture. "The people are often innocent and ignorant of the heinous details of war, of course unless the citizens are part of the collateral damage, then, like those citizens of Naru, the realization is strong and visceral."

He stood and proffered an arm for Mara. "We've come without revenge in our hearts. Our people our cured of the undead scourge by my own hand, and though many citizens were slain and scattered across the world, Naru is rising and rebuilding once again to her former glory." Though after he'd said the boastful words, Mara knew he regretted the declaration at the brief flash of self-loathing on his face.

Mara snaked her arm in his and they turned and left the Princess. But after a few steps Talis paused and aimed his gaze at Princess Devonia. "We've come bringing terms of peace for our two civilizations. One hopes that with the current state of unrest in the Jiserian Empire, the people desire peace and prosperity and the end of war and bloodshed."

Talis tugged on Mara's arm and strode off through the silent square.

22

The Servant's Wisdom

Talis lay awake in bed with a hungry belly, dreaming of Princess Devonia. He wished he had waited to eat before deciding to show off and perform his fire magic tricks to Mara and the people in the square. *Gods, why can't I go to sleep?* Talis thought, and turned over again for what was probably the fifth time. Sweat dribbled along his back from the heat of the magic still raging inside his body. He had held the power inside for far too long and he knew he'd regret doing such a long and complicated display of his recently created art. He'd learned to combine the forces of fire and wind magic in a contained display of artistic magic. All to impress Mara, or done to boost his ego?

In the darkness of the room, the image of Princess Devonia's haughty and beautiful face tormented him. Did Mara suspect something in his expression towards the Princess or in the way he had spoken to the girl? Princess Devonia was tall and slender like the sleek line of a flamingo. But the thing that kept driving him crazy was how her long, golden hair had spilled over and glanced his shoulder as she had inspected the three fire dragons he'd created. He could still feel it.

Her sense of authority and calm assurance in dealing with such unfamiliar magic had made him admire her power and nobleness. But when he had cast light magic, her thin crystalline shell of confidence had shattered under the realization that Talis was the powerful, hated foe of the Jiserian Empire. And the look of fear in her eyes when she had known for sure that he was alive and here in Carvina. That had excited him in a way that made him feel like a cruel brute.

Now he wished he could get Princess Devonia out of his mind. All her shocked expressions, her scared eyes, the sound of her gasping in horror, and the intoxicating smell of her dangerously sweet perfume. He felt terrible and guilty and wished he could expunge every bit of her memory from his mind. Didn't he love Mara? Not just after kissing her and being with her like that on the ship, but because of the light, playful dance of her eyes and her funny wit and charm.

Gods! Of course he loved her, she was Mara, his best friend since forever and then some. And he knew that she loved him too, he could see it in her eyes and in the warm familiarity of her touch. They were meant for each other. The gods had ordained it when they survived the journey into the Underworld. When they'd impossibly returned from two worlds away and together rebuilt Naru. After he'd brought her back to life with the sustaining power of the sun. The gods had fated them as a pair.

Though if he knew where Princess Devonia was right now he would fly to her room and do things to her that he never would dare do to Mara. He slapped his head for thinking such thoughts, and only heard the low, ominous voice of the Nameless hiss in his mind, *You can fight your feelings or give in and go with the flow down deep into the endless black ocean where all life comes from. You are an animal, and an animal is not unique, just one of the many million beasts that crave and crawl and crush the mind in favor of the feeling. Give in, you cannot resist her.*

A soft knock on his door woke him from his hysteria, and he pushed himself up and went over and cautiously opened the door just enough to see Mara's impish eyes. He chuckled and let her in, noticing that she wore a thick silk robe that seemed silly in this heat, though perhaps only he felt it was hot here in this room.

"You look wide awake," Mara said, and studied him as she came inside the room. "Dreaming of Princess Devonia?" At his no doubt stunned and guilty look, she gave him a second concerned glance and sat at his bedside. "Not that I can blame you, she's far more beautiful than I am, and...nubile. I mean she's like a year older than me and she'll probably soon be married off and be popping out kids." She frowned and stared at him with sad eyes. "I just hope they're not your kids... I always thought that we'd—"

"Don't talk like that." He placed a hand on her cheek and let his fingers slide down her neck until she closed her eyes and shuddered. "Did you hear how she talked about the invasion of Naru, as if it were some kind of joke? She just made me angry, that's all. I shouldn't had done all that and tried to prove who I was to her. I was so stupid. I should have just insisted that we leave and go someplace quiet and actually eat something. I'm starving, aren't you?"

She left her eyes closed and shook her head and collapsed to the side and sprawled out on his bed. "I'm so doomed. You're going to fall madly in love with her. I've seen it so many times before. Hatred leads to lust and love is the inevitable outcome of that vicious circle of hate and lust. I just can't compete with her beautiful body…she's just so primal and spewing the perfume of animalistic craving. Your eyes even dilated as you were staring at her."

But Talis could see a devious smile creep across her face as Mara's eyes glanced invitingly at him. "You're terrible," he said, and leaned in and kissed her soft lips. He tugged her robe and pulled her off his bed, shaking his head as if her being here was a very bad idea. "What time is it? Come on, let's go find a kitchen and some food, I am seriously hungry."

She huffed and gave him a pouting expression, but gave in and followed him outside the room where they found a side stairwell that wound down and around all the way to a servant's hallway beneath the main entrance level. The small window shafts revealed only the faintest amount of light, and Talis couldn't tell if it was the light of early morning or merely the gas lanterns that adorned the streets. He found the kitchen and looked inside, discovering an old, cheerful man humming a song and kneading dough over a massive wooden counter. The air smelled of onions and meat and flour. His eyes glanced at them in a warm, expecting look that reminded Talis of his grandfather.

"Come in young ones, you have the look of someone who is hungry. Craving some of my famous breakfast meat pies?" The man's watery blue eyes sparkled in the gaslit lanterns. "Won't be ready for another hour or so, but I do have some bread and cheese and sausage to offer you. Does that suit you?"

Talis nodded eagerly and the old man shuffled with a faint limp over to a cupboard, where he retrieved a plate and piled it with a substantial-sized sausage, a small round wheel of white cheese, and several pieces of crispy flatbread. At Talis's immediate enjoyment of the bread and cheese, the old man smiled in an expression of perfect contentment and he leaned against the counter and sighed.

"You know I've fed them all. The old and the young, the noble and the rich, I've even fed the Emperor several times here at banquets given in celebrations of marriage. He has the most beautiful daughter, Princess Devonia, do you know of her? She's not like her cruel brother, the boy is simply a terror to Emperor Ghaalis. I dread the day when that boy rules our Empire."

Talis had almost spewed out the food at the man's untimely mention of the Princess. He cast a wary glance at Mara, who shook her head in frustration as if she were unable to rid herself of the girl. If only he could have convincingly denied Mara's assertion about him and the girl, then maybe she would have believed him and stopped worrying about his feelings towards Devonia.

"You both bear the foreign look of someone who's come to Carvina from very far away." The old man returned to kneading the dough in strong, even strokes. "Let me guess, you're from up north, perhaps Ursula or Ostreva? No, definitely not Ostreva, maybe farther south, like Onair? But wasn't Onair destroyed by the sorcerers?"

"We're from Naru," Mara said, her voice flat and tense. "Talis's father is originally from Onair, so in a way you guessed correctly." She flashed him a quick smile that simmered with jealousy. "So tell me more of Princess Devonia. We only just met her last night." She shot Talis a harsh glance. "Talis here made quite an impression on the Princess, and it seemed like she was quite taken with him as well."

The old man stopped his work and glanced back and forth between Talis and Mara with inspecting eyes. "You're not brother and sister, are you? No it couldn't be, you're trying too hard to express your jealousy over the Princess. You're speaking in far too bright and interested tones." He chuckled softly and wagged his head in a friendly flourish of sympathy.

"I was once in love with a girl when I was young like you two. Silly of me, I never told the girl how I really felt. Day after day went by and I believed she'd always be there. I thought I had time to tell her, but it turned out I didn't. Soon I saw her hand-in-hand with another boy and I found out I was too late. Much too late to mend my broken heart."

At the old man's persistent and probing gaze, Talis felt guilty at his own actions and a sense of pity towards Mara as she looked away in embarrassment. Why was everything so confusing and complicated? Maybe in Naru things would have been simpler for Mara and him, but in a way he knew it wasn't true, remembering the old rivalry between the Lei family and the Storm family, and Lady Malvia's effort at trying to have her betrothed to other royals.

Was Lady Malvia worried that Mara would do something with Talis that might get her in trouble? Perhaps all the time Talis spent with her concerned Mara's mother. Talis nodded his head, remembering how Mara hadn't even said goodbye to her mother, and only left a note on her desk. He was certain that his parents would feel nervous at their lack of propriety.

Mara's soft voice broke the silence. "The thing is, Talis knows that I love him. He can feel it inside his heart. It's been there for a very long time." She glanced at him and tears welled in her eyes. "I can see it so clear and strong in the tenderness of his eyes when he looks at me. He adores

199

me and is always buying me such thoughtful presents. And—"

Her voice broke and she wiped her cheeks with the back of her hands, and the old man waddled over and gave her a handkerchief. He gave Talis a look of insistent urging and tilted his head at Mara as if he should go to her immediately. With a heavy feeling of self-loathing, he strode over to her, and though she resisted at first, he scooped her into his arms like a blanket enveloping a sleepy child. He felt terrible and wished she wouldn't cry over him. He didn't know if he was worth all her tears.

"Just stop it and eat your food, I'm really ok. I don't need your hug." She pushed him away but Talis just squeezed her and whispered in her ear that he loved her, and he meant it with all his heart. But as he closed his eyes and felt her body loosening itself of tension, and her small hands snaked around his waist, in the darkness of his mind's eye he pictured the ravishing face of Princess Devonia.

He knew he was doomed.

23

The Unknowable

Interrupting the endless infinity of timeless, thoughtless meditation, Rikar was summoned several times by the temple priests and asked to return to the locked chamber where the Nameless resided, though upon reflection, he doubted it was a chamber at all, more of another universe of some kind. After each visit, Rikar felt as if his mind had been torn apart and probed for any tiny detail regarding his interaction with the Starwalkers. What scared him the most was that the story was intermixed with Talis, Mara, and Nikulo, and the being asked him where his old friends could be found, and whether Rikar could entice them to visit.

The worst part of his last interaction was Rikar's feeling that the Nameless actually *knew* of Talis and Mara, though Nikulo seemed unfamiliar. Was Talis out there tracking him in the desert? Maybe he had used the Surineda Map and it had pointed him to the Ruins of Elmarr? A cold chill sank into Rikar and broke his meditation on the transience of life. What if Talis and Mara had visited here and somehow communicated with the Nameless? Or even worse, they were trapped inside the temple and maybe soon Rikar wouldn't be needed by the Nameless?

Then the cruel vision of the Starwalker woman being impaled on the crystalline shards filled his mind's eye and he knew that this would never be the case. He would always be of value to the Nameless, so long as he was still alive and the Starwalkers hated him—which was likely forever until they killed him or they were killed. The last part seemed doubtful, considering the vast power of the fragments in their possession. How many fragments did they control?

The door to his sanctuary opened and two temple priests entered, causing Rikar to panic at this strange occurrence. He'd never seen more than one priest together since he'd arrived at the Ruins. The first priest was the same one as always, but the second one was an old woman with a shaved head and a horrific patchwork face of the gruesomely disfigured. One eye was mounted higher than the other, as if a drunken surgeon had placed it there by mistake. The one functioning eye stared at him and projected a seething rage into Rikar's mind that caused him to froth at the mouth and clench his fist in fury.

The other lazy eye of the priestess lost interest and wandered around the room independently of the other, torturous eye. Mercifully, Rikar was released from the spell and he gasped and glowered at the woman, raising his hands against her, wanting nothing more than to obliterate her from existence.

"It is time for the bait to be placed in sight of our prey." The old woman sniffed and turned to go. She glanced at the other priest and said, "Make sure *Bait* behaves himself or he must be punished. I should think that ensuring that Bait is properly fragrant would be prudent before positioning him in the scent trail of our prey. Do everything with our Lord's complete satisfaction in mind."

The priest bowed to the old woman and kept his head down until she left the room. He turned his fanatical, gleaming eyes on Rikar and stretched out his hands. A wave of nausea overpowered Rikar as he allowed the ripples of blackness bursting from the priest's fingertips to enter his body. He knew better than to fight the priest; that would only lead to more torment and an even longer delay. And the otherwise infinite patience of the priest seemed to vanish under their now urgent mission to trap the Starwalkers and steal their fragments. Rikar guessed it had something to do with the prison that housed the Nameless, or possibly that the Nameless couldn't move at all beyond the chamber.

If that chamber were a universe, and this world were an illusion, then the Nameless was somehow trapped in between. Rikar was certain of it. The power of the fragments would help the Nameless break free and escape in either direction. Rikar hoped that the entity wasn't planning on coming to their world. But if Aurellia's master were truly the Nameless, then wouldn't it be part of their plan to join up and conquer the known worlds together?

Rikar still didn't believe that Lord Aurellia was interested in making peace with his brother and sharing in the domination of Vellia. He knew his master. He couldn't share power with anyone.

From the overpowering nausea came the spiking pain along the inside of his arms and legs, and on the soft part of his side, just below the ribcage. He screamed in agony at the feeling of needles piercing his flesh and he pictured blood blooming from the wounds and smelled the familiar coppery scent of his lifeblood slowly draining away. Soon he felt dry and withered as his vital fluid spilled into glass jars illuminated with an eerie, sickly yellow light that caused his blood to look like disgusting pus.

His spirit ejected from his body in a wrenching, tearing movement, and as he hovered around the sanctuary, he turned and noticed his shriveled up figure lying on the floor. His gaunt face held the look of shock and betrayal. His arms and legs were wasting quickly away, drying up and shrinking into themselves until only a gnarled, twisted, woody corpse remained. It somehow felt good to be dead and released from the pain and suffering of his body. Everything would be better now, more peaceful and his soul could fly to the Underworld and he could see his father again. He was free at last.

But for some reason he remained in that room and gazed at the priest dragging his body away and as Rikar followed him, another priest came and helped carry his insignificant corpse up the stairs, up and winding around the endless stairs, until finally they exited the temple and entered the harsh light of the Nalgoran Desert. When he noticed two wooden planks nailed together in a cross, and he glanced back and watched the two priests dragging his body towards the torture device, Rikar decided he'd seen enough. He tried to fly away, but to his horror found some kind of a strong silver chain yanking him back in the direction of his body.

He examined the chain and realized it wasn't a chain at all, but some kind of woven silver cord that looked and felt like the texture of a serpent's skin, and was cold and scaly to the touch. Looking up, he realized that for some strange reason, darkness had fallen in an instant, and the vast panorama of starlight swept across the sky. Had he drifted off and lost consciousness? The four moon sisters seemed to shine their light upon Rikar's now mounted and splayed body, as if his shriveled, wrinkled form were a pathetic sacrifice to the gods.

Off to the side came a cavalcade of candle-wielding priests walking in a solemn procession. A dark, purplish aura surrounded their hooded heads, and a solitary eye hovered high above the congregation carefully watching the ceremony. The priests positioned themselves across the sandy ground, and their formation created an odd pattern of lights flickering in the night. For a time they stood there and silently seemed to absorb the feeling of the stars shining down on their upraised faces. After a long while, a song escaped their lips, a melancholy song that reminded Rikar of the band of musicians from Onair that he had seen, of refugees singing a sad song mourning their loss, and of the beautiful city they'd left behind.

But this unfathomable song was unknowable to Rikar's ghostly ears, and was only made familiar through the sound of sadness in the tone of the singers. It was almost as if the priests were mourning the loss of their humanity, the loss of feeling itself, and the loss of family and friends and everything that had once been dear to them in their old lives. If he had a face, Rikar was sure that tears would be spilling down his cheeks. In a way that song reminded him of himself, and the old life he'd left behind.

For the first time in many months he thought of his mother. Was she still alive back in Naru? Had Talis saved her from the undead plague and restored her old life? If he had then he owed him, and Rikar didn't like owing anyone, especially not Talis. But what did all that even matter anymore? He was dead, and his body was stretched like a carcass across the wooden planks of a cross. His old life was over. But why wasn't he able to journey on and greet the Guardians of the Underworld?

He'd heard stories from Master Holoron of ghosts similar to this experience. A wraith bound to a sorcerer, like an undead body chained to a necromancer. Could the priest have bound his soul as a slave? Rikar reached around and tugged on the silver cord, and pulled and pulled until he floated over to where it was tied. Shocked, he found that it was attached to his own body, into the ganglion of nerves above his stomach. Why had the priest killed him and yet kept his spirit connected to his old, shriveled body?

The grotesque answer came swiftly. As Rikar was studying his emaciated body, eyelids flicked open around his body's dried and cracked skin, and to his horror, the eyeballs darted around in terror. Those eyes were not the unseeing, unknowing eyes of the undead, they were *his* eyes with his feelings of fear pouring out. Desperate, he tried to dive back inside his own body but found himself blocked and he bounced off and catapulted towards the starry sky until he was jerked back and knocked around by the cord. This nightmare was real. Rikar could feel the truth of it with his entire being.

His hearing came back to him in a burst of song, but soon the priests lowered their voices and raised their hands into the air. The flickering candles floated up a few feet above the priests and paused there for a while. As Rikar gazed at the luminous display, an explosion of light burst out and blinded him for a moment. *So strange,* Rikar thought, *that ghostly eyes can be blinded?* But then he remembered back to the light in his dreams and remembered the darkness of caves, and the bright, burning light of the sun. He still was able to perceive a wide range of sensations.

When he looked again, the candles had transformed into spidering lights that soared into the sky, weaving a great web of light, a fabric, a luminous mesh that stretched to the stars and covered the sky from the horizon all the way to the zenith. The mesh pulsed with a pattern, the rhythm of which reminded him of the priests' song. To Rikar's entranced vision, the song strummed in a series of lights and it seemed to him like a message in code, like smoke signals from a mountaintop created by primitive tribes, but this message was being sent out to the stars. Were the priests trying to reach out and summon the Starwalkers?

After the phosphorescent mesh was complete, the priests shuffled back in a single file to the temple, their hooded heads bowed low. Soon the massive, phantom eye faded away, as if the being's watchfulness were slowly waning away to nothingness. Rikar found himself alone beneath the stars and the pulsing fabric of light. But he heard the hideous voice of the Nameless surge inside his mind, towering over his thoughts in a mad rush.

You can survive all this if you listen and pay careful attention to my words. The loud raspy wheezing of the being returned and caused Rikar to raise phantom hands to his head. *Those humanoids that roam the stars will soon arrive on this pathetic planet, lured by the promise of vengeance. They want you dead, and upon seeing the sacrifice we've made of your body will find disappointment in their unsated craving for revenge. It will drive them mad with bloodlust. Then my most loyal priests will entice them into the temple with the sweet scent of your blood, and lead them down into the deepest level of this lair and into the chamber where I reside and keep your blood safe and secure.*

I will claim the power of their fragments for myself, and I will never again be contained...

The dark sky ripped and tore apart from within, a bright blossom of brilliant light that flowered open as if it were a white rose unfolding in the warm days of early summer. And inside was a long, spiraling tunnel, within the greater light, and there were found four figures veiled in shadowy cloaks. The quad jettisoned from the portal of light and hovered in suspicious fury as they stared at the wasted corpse on the cross.

The Starwalkers had come for him, come seeking the sweet savor of revenge.

24

The Royal Summons

In the serenade of lovesick dreams, Mara floated and slept and faded away into the fragrance of Talis's skin, the memory of his embrace still thick in her mind, and the scent of him woke her in a sweetness that possessed nothing of the jealousy that had kept her awake last night. She felt renewed, and as she stood and stretched and yanked open the curtains, the burst of bright light filled her with the amazing feeling that she knew was the purest form of love.

Talis had said it to her; his own voice whispered in her ear. He said he loved her, and that was enough to erase the jealously she'd felt towards Princess Devonia. A wave of Mara's hand washed away the memory of the girl's disgustingly beautiful face. Did she have a nasty wart in some hideously funny place? She probably nagged and was annoying all the time. There had to be a dark secret about the Princess that doomed her to a solitary life of misery. Mara certainly hoped so.

She flung off her nightclothes and strode over to the dressing room and flipped through her wardrobe, and finally selected a long, flowing dress that shimmered white and silky in the sunlight. It was perfect. Dressing quickly, she darted out of the room and went to Talis's room and knocked and waited, but he didn't come to the door. A servant girl glided over and bowed cautiously and whispered behind a covered mouth that the young master was downstairs having breakfast in the dining room.

Disappointed for a second, Mara nodded to the girl and realized that likely Talis had let her sleep in and recover from their late night. She followed the stairs down to the grand foyer and allowed her nose to guide her to the dining hall where only a few people remained at their tables, most drinking tea or sipping coffee and chatting. She must have slept in really late. Off to the corner of the room she spotted Talis talking with Master Goleth. She waved and weaved her way through the tables until she took her seat as Talis held the chair for her.

"We thought you'd sleep all day." Talis winked at her and flashed her an overly friendly smile that made her worried for some strange reason. It was like he was going out of his way to be nice to her. Wasn't he acting a little weird?

"So," Master Goleth pronounced, and raised a finger in an official-looking flourish. "We've heard from the Royal Secretary." At Talis's excited eyes, the Builder allowed a grin to cross his face. "Yes, yes, I knew you would be pleased. That's why I waited for the both of you. Couldn't spoil the news."

He took a sip of coffee and savored the taste as if wanting to torture them. Mara didn't really care, she wasn't all that excited to meet Emperor Ghaalis, and certainly didn't want to see Princess Devonia again, and from the old servant's words, she really didn't want to meet her brother either. He sounded like an arrogant, rude royal, like so many of them. Did she even want to go? Suddenly all her excitement at what Talis had told her last night, and from having a good night's sleep, vanished in the smoky haze of having to see Princess Devonia at the Royal Court. And to make things even worse, Mara hated the idea of Talis seeing the Princess again...

"That's wonderful," Mara said, her voice sarcastic. She cleared her throat and swallowed after her voice cracked. "The response was faster than you expected?"

Talis glanced with cautious eyes at Mara and she felt a bit embarrassed at the tone of her retort.

"Much faster, actually. I'm surprised that Emperor Ghaalis even paid attention. It's like someone pointed us out to him." *Likely Princess Devonia mentioned her encounter with us last night,* Mara thought. The timing was too perfect. "He certainly knew we were here otherwise he'd never had arranged that powerful display of magic. But going so far beyond protocol and granting us an audience right away...unheard of, at least in my experience."

"When are we expected to go?" Talis said, but all Mara heard was him asking when he could see Princess Devonia again. As if he were thinking the sooner, the better...

"This afternoon. Yes, don't look so surprised. We're expected right after lunch when the Order of the Dragons will perform a demonstration for the Emperor and the Royal Court. I doubt you've ever heard of them, but you're in for a real treat. They are simply amazing to behold." Master Goleth rubbed his hands together and stood as if ready to leave. "I'll leave you two to enjoy your breakfast. I've much to prepare before our visit. Make sure to dress in the complete formal attire I've had the servants set aside for you. I'll stop by your rooms well in advance of the time of departure."

The wizard walked out of the room as two servants brought covered silver salvers and set them on a wooden stand. One gleeful-faced waiter lifted the silver cover and flourished a hand at the steaming dish. He placed the plate of fish and rice and thinly sliced vegetables formed in an artistic twist in front of Mara. The servant ladled a white cream sauce over the fish, and bowed to them. The other servant poured tea for Mara and added a splash of milk to the spicy, aromatic tea. But she found that her hunger had vanished at the prospect of attending court.

Mara glanced at Talis and felt a lump of jealous guilt stick in her throat. This was so stupid, why was she feeling this way? Everything inside had been so confusing over the last week, ever since they'd left the smuggler's cove. The wild feeling that had washed over her that night on the ship after the storm… The rage and ecstasy she felt against those sorcerers as she destroyed their lives so gleefully. And the disappointment that had knocked her down so quickly when Master Goleth had insisted that he alone would kill those two horrible criminals. He had every right considering the hurt and terror they'd committed against the wizard and his mother, but Mara felt like it was her retribution to mete out against the two old men.

"Where did you go off to?" Talis's voice broke Mara's reverie and she realized with a flush of embarrassment that she was staring stupidly at the food, the fork and knife stuck in her hands, and the meal untouched. She sent him a quick, apologetic smile.

"Sorry, I was just lost in thought. All of this"—she flourished her fork and Talis winced as if she were brandishing a weapon—"is a bit too much for me to deal with, I guess. You know what I mean?"

"I suppose so." His voice sounded unconvinced and confused at her no doubt strange mood. She sighed and felt frustrated and for some reason just wanted to be alone.

"I'm being an idiot and I'm sorry for acting so stupid." She dropped the fork and knife on the table and stood, excusing herself to Talis in a hasty rush.

He seized her wrist and she felt her arm tense and prepare to strike him down, and the weirdest part was that she saw Princess Minoweth's dagger in her hand and the smooth arc as it cut across his beautiful neck and released an elegant spray of blood all over the white tablecloth. She gasped and blinked repeatedly, trying to eradicate the horrific image from her mind.

In a wild rush she shook free of his grasp and ran from the table, ignoring Talis's pleas for her to come back. Gods, what was wrong with her? If she'd had a dagger in her hand she would've killed him, she knew that nothing in her power could've stopped her from doing that instinctual movement. It was like catching a ball that someone throws at you. Snap. Just like that.

Back in her room, she locked the door and yanked the curtains closed to cover herself in the soothing darkness. For comfort she found the daggers and cradled them like they were two nursing babies that she alone could nurture and give them life to sustain and quench their hunger. They fed from her and caused a fury to rise in her heart. She didn't want to kill Talis. She only wanted to kill those two old terrible men, and the sorcerers that must have killed her father, and in a burst of hateful jealously, she wanted to kill Princess Devonia. Mara wanted to wipe that haughty smile from her pretty face with an angry slash across her pouty lips.

She threw the daggers into her pack and tried to clear her head. After thinking and sulking for a while, she got tired and disgusted of herself and decided to go and apologize to Talis for her ridiculous behavior. She glanced at her bag and decided to leave the daggers in the room, remembering the strong feeling of hatred and violence that had come over her from touching them. It was better to leave them.

At the door though, the pain surged in her stomach like the first time she had tried to separate herself from the weapons. She gasped, and in a burst of speed she turned and jogged back to where her bag rested by her bedside. What had changed? Since she'd made the agreement with the daggers she had often been away from them for long periods of time, like last night with Talis out and about the city. But something had changed and Mara could feel that the daggers were unrelenting in their insistence that she keep them close.

Could she put the daggers in one of the stylish purse bags that she had seen so many of the girls in the capitol wear? She headed to the dressing room and rummaged around through the dresses and shirts and bags and shoes that the servants had brought her. To her amusement, she even traced her fingers over the soft, silky and frilly underclothes that had been proffered her. Such strange and wonderful textures and designs, but for the life of her, she couldn't figure out how these would be useful in any way at all. But they certainly were pretty, though she couldn't picture herself actually wearing them. But would Talis like it if she wore them?

Finally she found a white leather purse with a stylish gold clasp of the sun at the top and she tried it on, inspecting herself in the mirror. It was small enough to look attractive, and large enough to hold both daggers. What else could she carry inside to conceal the weapons? She thought back to the square and all the pretty girls opening

216

their purses and withdrawing tubes of red coloring to paint their lips, and containers of rouge to dab at their cheeks. Other girls had pencils to paint their eyes in brilliant, glittery colors that seemed infused with light and caused their eyes to glow and dance with magic.

She sifted through the perfumes and cases and metal tubes on top of the dressing table, uncertain of how they were all used. Some of the older girls in Naru wore color for their lips and cheeks, but nothing compared to the exotic applications of color and sparkle that the women of Carvina wore. She sniffed and scooped up several of the cases and tubes and tossed them inside her purse, caring little for actually using them, she just wanted something to hide her daggers.

Talis's eyes were wary as he opened the door and he paused as he inspected her.

"I'm sorry," she said, and pushed the door farther open and kissed him on the lips before he could say anything. She kicked the door closed and flung herself pathetically into his arms and felt enraged that he didn't kiss her back with the same intensity as he had before on the ship. With a pouty separation she glanced up at him and batted her eyes in the way she'd seen Princess Devonia do to him several times.

"Are you feeling ok?" he said, and held her arms, a quizzical look marring his youthful face. "You're acting kind of strange."

The purse felt heavy on her shoulder, so she slung it around and slumped down on his bed, and stared out the windows at the clouds bunching together as if threatening a storm.

"Maybe I'm just jealous of the Princess." She thought that perhaps honesty would earn her a bit of sympathy. She flicked out her fingers in an elegant flourish. "She's just so refined and tall and *older* and more beautiful than me. Tell me the truth, tell me you're not attracted to her. I know you are."

The pause in his response…that just killed her and made her seethe inside.

"It's not like that, Mara. Now don't get all angry at me, what do you expect me to say? Yes, she's pretty, but she's also the daughter of the Emperor that wanted to destroy Naru and enslave or kill our people. Be reasonable. You know how I feel about you."

She wanted to scream and slap him for acting so calm and reasonable. If Princess Devonia had barged into his room and kissed him and kicked the door closed, Mara knew for a fact that Talis wouldn't be acting all *reasonable*. He'd be raging like an inferno, like the Fire Mage he was, all burning and flowing and bursting with power and lust. Why was he so contained and logical with her? Right now, what she wanted was the very opposite of logic…

"Get dressed," she said, and pushed herself up and glanced contemptuously at his disheveled clothes. "I'm going back to my room." *And you can just think logically all you want, but do it without me. Perhaps she would ask one of the servant girls to show her how to apply the colors on her eyes and lips and cheeks. Certainly Princess Devonia's brother would be more entertaining than Talis. An ill-logical brute might be a far more pleasant encounter than Talis and his stupid sensibilities...*

"And remember, Talis. The only reason we're here is to negotiate a peace treaty with Emperor Ghaalis. Master Goleth has arranged an audience with the Royal Court, but since my father is dead, I inherited his role as ambassador to Carvina. We'll leave either when we die or they die, or when we walk away with a signed treaty. I really don't care what we have to do to ensure peace for Naru. I won't have war returning to our people again."

Talis gaped at her, speechless, as she strode out of the room, her eyes refusing to look at him.

25

Cult of the Dragons

A shudder raged through Nikulo as he turned his eyes away from the horrible message etched on the temple walls. *The Dragons Devoured the Songs.* Indeed, how true, as there was no music remaining at all in the city. Only a shell of its former beauty, without the color and soul of songs pouring out in the streets. After the charm and beauty of the architecture, Nikulo could only see the coldness of an occupied city strangled by the cruel hand of a foreign oppressor.

Master Holoron caught Nikulo's eyes after he looked away from the Temple of Songs, and his old face held a tired sadness and an inner fury at seeing the script scratched on the wall. Nikulo wondered whether the old wizard would be able to keep himself from expressing violence against those of the fanatical Order. But because the hardened warriors were likely as powerful as Master Holoron had described, Nikulo guessed he would hold his tongue.

Commander Drelan led them to a plain-looking building attached to a tall tower that rose high above the inner walls. Nikulo saw a squad of unarmed soldiers without armor marching out of the building, and he guessed that the place was a barracks or the command center of Onair. He was surprised to see the soldiers occupying such a sparse and unassuming base, expecting they'd setup their headquarters in one of the more lavish, expansive buildings farther up the hill. He'd learn later that the Dragons always sought to blend into society in order to prevent their Order from standing out.

They were greeted inside the barracks by an old, wiry man standing behind a desk who wore large, square glasses that magnified his eyes to twice their size as he studied their approach. Even though the man was old, the muscles of his bared arms were hard and sleek.

"How can I help you, Commander?" The man's voice was high and nasally, like he had a head cold. He glanced at Master Holoron and Nikulo, and a suspicious look crossed his face.

"Secretary Mazgen, I have visitors from Carvina that have come seeking Master Varghul." Commander Drelan looked nervous at the old man's hard-eyed response. "They've just arrived by ship…"

"Commander Drelan, you will report immediately for reassignment." The secretary's cold expression reminded Nikulo of a snake studying its prey. The Commander looked like he'd been struck in the face. But the Commander saluted and marched into the barracks, like he was marching to his death.

The old man narrowed his eyes at them and rapped his ring on the desk. "Do I look like a blind fool to you? That a wizard and his apprentice could so easily walk in here and see Master Varghul? You may be able to bully or trick the soldiers outside to let you in, but you won't get past me so easily."

"I can see you are a reasonable man, Secretary Mazgen." Master Holoron bowed and a wry expression formed on his face. "You are quite famous across the academic world. I enjoyed your treatise of the history of the dragons. One of my favorites, actually."

The secretary scowled and shook his head in disbelief. "How did you acquire of copy of my work? I was under the assumption that only the Royal Library and our Order's archives held copies…"

"You should be pleased to discover your work has been distributed far and wide to Ursula, Ostreva, Trinic, Danberk, and of course, Naru, my home city. We historians have a strong desire to share our research and works across the world. Tell me, what are you doing so far away from the capitol?"

"I go where Master Varghul goes. But if you are from Naru, then that would make you—"

"Master Holoron. A pleasure to meet you finally, Historian Mazgen."

A confused expression came over the old secretary's face. "But I was under the assumption that you were in the prison of Onair?"

"Yes, I was, until my loyal apprentice, young Nikulo here, released me from the confines of my cell. I'm most grateful to him for saving my life." Master Holoron issued a bland look of appreciation to Nikulo.

"You expect me to believe that this *boy* was able to break you out of a cell protected by magical runes?"

"I do, actually. The runes were to prevent me from breaking out, and only the lock was there to keep people on the outside from opening the door. Nothing really to stop a young wizard from casting a fire magic spell and melting the lock. Quite simple, really."

Secretary Mazgen frowned in suspicion, but his face softened and he nodded in half-belief. "So you've escaped from prison to come to Onair and allow yourself to be recaptured and placed in prison again? I don't understand why you're here."

A devious smiled played on the wizard's mouth. "We both share a love of dragons and dragon lore, do we not? And we are all familiar with Lord Aurellia and his journey through the stars to return to his home world?"

A stunned expression paralyzed the secretary's body for a moment, then he shook himself and stared hard at Master Holoron. "Where in the name of the gods did you hear about that?"

"Why of course, from my young apprentice Nikulo here. He travelled with young Talis Storm and Mara Lei through the worlds portal to Chandrix, chasing after Aurellia until they finally reached Vellia. Do you want me to continue the story now, or would you prefer me continuing to the part about the dragons of Ghaelstrom, on Aurellia's home planet, with Master Varghul present?"

Master Holoron displayed a row of brilliant teeth to the secretary in a satisfied smile. The old man rummaged through the papers on his desk in a nervous, habitual movement. He glanced at Nikulo in a surprised, frightened expression and swept out of the room, leaving the wizard to chuckle at his quick departure.

Soon another soldier came and waved them inside, and like the other men, he wore no armor and likely if Nikulo encountered him on the street, he would have never suspected him as anyone special or particularly threatening. What was common with all the soldiers of the barracks was their thin, wiry build, average height, and dull, dead eyes like the dragons of Ghaelstrom that Nikulo had seen on Vellia. Utter lack of eye contact and emotion, these Dragons moved as if nothing mattered and there was nothing of any care or weight burdening their bodies as they glided along.

Inside a clean, well-organized office in the back of the barracks, they were greeted by the cold, inhuman stares of three soldiers all wearing similarly loose, priest-like clothing. Secretary Mazgen stood in attention at the corner of the room, an anxious expression on his weathered face. The man in the middle spoke first, and he sat at a chair in front of a broad desk with a map of the city, and colored markers and small silver figurines were placed in strategic positions across the map.

"Master Holoron, I presume?" The soldier scratched at an itch on his shoulder in a deft, oft-repeated movement. "I heard you wanted to see me."

The wizard shifted his stance slightly and studied the man with cautious eyes, unaffected by the stiff tension in the room. "Why have you stayed so long in Onair after the invasion was successful? Certainly you and your men would prefer returning home to their friends and family."

The soldier gave an irritated click of his tongue. "Dragons have no friends and we leave family behind when we join the Order." He spread his arms wide in a gesture of inclusion. "This is our home now. This *is* the Order of the Dragons. All members of the Order live here now."

"What of the other Dragons in Carvina?"

"You know a great deal about our Order, wizard." The man scowled in a rare display of emotion. "Perhaps this has something to do with the rune master that betrayed you in Ursula? What was her name…Mistress Cavares, am I correct? Yes, I thought so. Well, I have news for you, those are not true Dragons in Carvina but apostates, traitors to our Order and our legacy, bought off by the Emperor's gold."

So these Dragons were the sub-cult that Master Holoron had talked about, thought Nikulo, trying his best not to make eye contact with the soldier.

"So you are Master Varghul, the leader of the Order?" Master Holoron glanced at the map on the desk and Nikulo thought he saw a glimmer of worry on the wizard's face.

"What interests you on our map, old man?"

"Nothing, really," said the wizard. "It just strikes me as odd that you would have chosen Onair to call as your home unless there was something of value here. And I see you've marked the ancient archives with a figurine of a dragon. You've discovered something?"

Nikulo could tell from a twitch in the soldier's eye that the man was doing his best to contain himself. "You were invited here to tell us your story, not to interrogate me over the map."

"But you see, I'm not finished with my questions for you." Master Holoron's face hardened as he stared down the solder. "If you want to hear my story, you will answer. What have you discovered in the ancient archives?"

When the soldier was silent and seething, Nikulo thought that a fight might ensure between the wizard and the man. But they remained unmoving and quiet, and to Nikulo's surprise, the tapestry on the far wall was moved aside and a short, bald man entered the room. His face held the nonchalant but very confident expression of a king, or perhaps even of an emperor. Something about his eyes exuded power and inner strength. And unlike the other soldiers who averted their eyes every time Nikulo looked at them, this man locked eyes with him until it was Nikulo who turned away in a cold flush of fear.

"Even with your best mentalist tricks you were only able to infuriate the apprentice." The bald man waved a hand and dismissed the soldiers, and the three men left the room. Did Master Holoron possess mastery over controlling the minds of others? Then why did he ask Nikulo to control the captain's mind?

"I'd say my apprentice passed the test for someone of the second level, and I will allow him to hold his rank for now. Though I'd expect more from him if he hopes to advance."

Nikulo noted the frustration in the departing soldier's eyes for failing to keep his calm, though the bald man still kept a degree of humor on his face.

"Allow me to introduce you to Master Varghul," said Secretary Mazgen, and he flourished a hand in the direction of the bald man.

"It is a pleasure to meet you, Master Varghul." Holoron bowed in an elegant arc that Nikulo thought was a bit too much for the plainness of the room.

A tremor of wonder rippled across Varghul's face as he studied Holoron. And to Nikulo's surprise, the man returned the bow in exactly the same movement. "'Tis rare to see a practitioner of the old formalities. I welcome your gesture of respect. Why don't you have a seat and I will have some tea brought in?"

As the man nodded to Secretary Mazgen, Master Holoron and Nikulo sat at the two simple chairs in front of the desk and waited for Master Varghul to speak.

"In the archives we've found evidence of a surviving enclave of dragons in the far north, within the Islands of Tarasen." Varghul paused as Nikulo opened his mouth to speak.

"But that's where Master Palarian was from. Do you know of him?" Nikulo wondered if it was such a good idea to mention the fact.

"We know very well of Master Palarian, and his islands have long been the study of our Order. His existence and strong-handed rule of the Islands of Tarasen were the prime reasons why we focused our search there. He went there before the last of the dragons were slain, so we suspected that dragons might still exist there. So you see, although you've informed my secretary that dragons exist on Lord Aurellia's world, we have no desire to infringe on his proclaimed territory. We have a kind of a truce between us. And now that Master Palarian has relinquished his rulership of Tarasen, we plan to soon travel up north."

Master Holoron ran a hand across his mouth and knitted his brows in deep thought. "A very interesting revelation. And would you be interested in extending that same truce with the people of Naru? It seems that your group might be distancing themselves from the Emperor."

"The Jiserian Empire is in downfall and Emperor Ghaalis has surrounded himself with advisors and wizards who insulate him from the harsh realities of the Empire. If he bothered to send scouts to Ishur and to other smaller cities he would know the truth: his Empire is in shambles."

Master Varghul waved a hand in a light flourish. "But none of that matters to me. Coming to Onair was just a chance for my group to leave Carvina and prove our worth to the Emperor. He's rewarded us handsomely for solving a very difficult situation against the Order of Songs. A fine, beautiful Order that I regret with all my heart that I had to put down."

When the man spoke the words *put down*, Nikulo pictured the time his father had killed a rabid dog on the outskirts of the city. He shuddered at the painful memory of the dog's howls and whining as it died under his father's blade.

"Are those the wizards' bones and skulls in front of the temple?" Master Holoron accepted a cup of tea from Secretary Mazgen and nodded in thanks.

Varghul cleared his throat and shook his head. "Merely a display of power to dissuade further revolt. Those are the skeletal remains of many who were injured in the tidal wave. A foolish assault done by the first wave of sorcerers to invade Onair. After that the wizards of Onair obliterated the sorcerers in retaliation, and the Emperor called in my group to control the city. You need not worry, we plan to leave as soon as the ships arrive to take us up north to the Islands of Tarasen."

"You will leave the city to the Jiserian soldiers that remain here?"

"No, we have arranged for them to return to Carvina by ship." A rare smile crossed Master Varghul's face. "You see, the Order of the Dragons worships power and beauty, and the discipline of the artist. We could never bear to destroy the culture and high art displayed in Onair. And from our study of history knew that the City of Onair owed much of its art and refinement and civilization to the Order of Songs. How could we defile such an Order?"

"What are you saying?" Master Holoron leaned forward in his chair, his eyes wild and excited. "Is the Order—"

"Let me continue my story, wizard. Before we arrived at the docks of Onair we sent word to the Songs with a detailed plan of our temporary occupation in order to fool the Emperor and his advisors into thinking that Onair had been conquered and the wizards of the Order of Songs obliterated. We had no desire to fight with the wizards and knew it would have been extremely difficult to beat them. There would have been grave losses on both sides. However, we also clearly delimitated in our message that the Emperor would not stop sending forces against them until Onair was completely conquered. They agreed with our plan and we alleviated the people of Onair of suffering and bloodshed and prevented the destruction of this beautiful city."

"So the wizards of the Order are still alive?"

Master Varghul nodded, a pleased expression slowly appearing on his face. "They're living under temporary house arrest until the time of our departure when we will return the rule of the city to them. The Order of Songs will

once again sing and pour forth their music across this great
and sacred city."

26

The Emperor's Court

Talis could still picture the look of disgust and self-righteous rage in Mara's eyes as she stormed out of his room. Even though they now stood at the entrance to the Emperor's Palace, a grand marble building that looked as if it were the entire size of the upper part of Naru, he still thought about Mara and what was going on inside her mind. She still held the same cold, rigid determination on her face, and every time he tried to catch her attention, she ignored him with that provincial gaze of hers fixed forward as the royal attendants streamed down the expansive hallway.

The beautiful, billowy silk dress she wore was white and pristine, and wrapped her figure tightly, revealing sensuous lines that Talis realized he had often overlooked. What had shocked him the most was when she'd strolled down the stairs into the grand foyer, the area above her eyes painted in glittering royal red accents that shimmered in a magical light of their own. Her lips also held a trace amount of the red glitter, but her face was still natural and beautiful, with only the lightest hint of rouge on her cheeks. The overall effect stunned Talis and sent his heart racing at her aloof, indifferent expression and the chilly fixation of her eyes on some place far off in the distance. He recognized the expression as that of Lady Malvia, Mara's mother, when she arrived at court looking as if ice steeled her eyes.

Had he lost Mara? In his stupid staring at Princess Devonia and his inability to deny that he was attracted to her, had he lost the affection of the girl he cared for the most?

"Introducing Her Royal Highness Princess Mara of the Lei Family of Naru." The royal announcer swept his hand as Mara strode ahead, ignoring Talis's previous offer of escort into the Palace. He tried to overlook the intentional slight, but he could feel his face flush with embarrassment as he was left alone at the stairs, waiting for the announcer to introduce him.

The old man frowned at the card, and glanced up at Talis, giving him a puzzled look of disgust. "Introducing Talis Storm of Naru, Child of the Sun and Most Hated Enemy of our Empire." The royal announcer said the last words with venomous spite and Talis was worried that the man might spit at him as he treaded into the imposing palace.

Never did he feel more alone, but the feeling was similar to the last time he'd entered the Order of the Dawn, with Master Viridian's accusing eyes scowling at him. The lines of royalty gathered in the palace whispered at him with glowering and frightened eyes, lips spewing accusations and warnings of mistrust. No doubt his stupid display of magic in the square had fueled the rumors concerning his arrival, and put the royals on edge at his presence here. Master Goleth was taking the greatest risk by asking the Emperor's permission for Talis and Mara's entry, a risk not only for his own safety, but also for his family.

But the gaudily dressed members of the Royal Court only smiled and fawned in adoration of Mara, treating her as a new and attractive arrival, and the girls and young men gossiped and waved to her as she strode past. Mara invited their attention by casting pretty glances at the young men, and quick waves at the girls, both of whom flowered at her notice. Several of the brazen stares by boys his age enraged Talis and caused him to crave the release of flames into their wanton eyes.

The march down to the end of the long chamber seemed endless and filled Talis with tortured feelings of animosity against the Jiserians of the Royal Court. He wanted nothing more than to strike a treaty of peace with Emperor Ghaalis and leave this place and never return. But what was the point of leverage that he could use to ensure their safety? Even if the Empire was in a convoluted mess, the capitol was bustling and organized and oozed riches and stability. Talis guessed that there was enough wealth here to build several powerful empires. What was it that Emperor Ghaalis wanted?

At the end of the long line to greet the Royal Family, Talis could see the Emperor on the Ebony Throne, and Princess Devonia and her princeling brother sat at either side, without an Empress present. Talis felt embarrassed wearing his ostentatious clothing, though his indignation against the harsh stares and glowering eyes caused him to stubbornly stride past, allowing his anger to fuel his movement.

Once again a royal announcer called out his name and condescending title, and Talis was knocked sideways as a heavy, wet object struck him on the side of his face. From the stinking smell, he thought that someone had thrown a mound of shit at him, but looking down at the yellow, viscous liquid gelling down his face he realized someone had tossed a large piece of some strange fruit.

Laughter exploded across the chamber, and Talis could see that even the Emperor and Princess joined in the merriment, with the crowd waiting expectantly for his reaction. Mara searched the crowd where the fruit had been thrown, her eyes furious. Talis shook his head at her, not wanting to give their enemies any fuel for their hatred. They were here for one reason alone, to bargain for peace with Naru.

"This is the fabled Child of the Sun?" Emperor Ghaalis boomed out, his tone mocking. "Talis Storm, bane of the Jiserian forces, felled by a foul fruit?"

The crowd once again broke out into muffled laughter and derisive chortles, and the eyes of those around Talis fell heavily on him as if wanting a show, and perhaps some of the nobility gather here—like Princess Devonia—had witnessed his display of magic at the square. He wasn't about to invoke the wrath of the wizards and sorcerers no doubt assembled in anticipation of such a foolish outburst of power. And Talis reminded himself of the strange runic spell that had made his strikes useless against the three sorcerers.

"We've come this long way here to Carvina," Mara said, her voice loud and confident, "not to find ourselves mocked and disrespected by the Royal Jiserian Court, but to sue for peace and to put an end to this bloody stupid war. Your people enjoy peace and privilege, while your Empire is crumbling outside the capitol city. You've gone to great lengths to demolish Naru, my home city, and to infect my people with an undead plague."

She aimed an angry finger accusingly at the Emperor. "No more!" she shouted, and let her words echo across the chamber. "No more will we stand for your sorcerers and necromancers subjecting our people to violence and war and terror. Or we will bring violence ourselves against this beautiful city, and pour a torrent of fire and death across your pristine streets, unmarred by the war you yourself have commanded."

The Emperor stood, face red and eyes furious. "You dare come to my court and threaten me and my people? I heard from Master Goleth that you came with an offer of peace, and instead you dare say these words? Your father was a great diplomat, however I can see none of his finesse rubbed off on his daughter—"

"My father was a traitor to his people and a fool. How much gold did you pay him for his betrayal? What offers of power and rulership did you use to seduce him to turn against his own family and people?" As Mara's words hung thick in the silence that followed, Talis knew she was treading on dangerous ground and like her erratic actions towards him before, he could see some destabilizing force was acting on her mind. He moved up to stand beside her, and searched the crowd for danger.

The Emperor was about to speak again when Mara's cutting voice stopped him. "You weaklings of the Royal Court all bear the pathetic countenance of those who've never known death and war. How many of you have fought in the wars against Onair or Ursula or Naru? Did a single one of you send your sons to fight for the Empire? Or did this pathetic excuse for an Emperor send your slaves as chattel for the necromancers, to push their siege engines across the Nalgoran Desert until they died from exhaustion, only to be summoned back to a nefarious state of existence as an undead soldier?"

Mara studied the shocked crowd, an angry, taunting look on her face. "No one? Not one of you knows of the horrors inflicted by this Emperor of yours? You fail to realize the cost of your luxurious lifestyle and blissful, ignorant existence?" She laughed a mad, mocking laugh that caused the crowd to shrink back in fear. "You will know soon, I promise you, you will know of the coppery smell of blood painting your streets red, of the fetid smell of bodies festering under the hot sun, of the horrific sight of wild dogs tearing away at the flesh of your children. All this you will soon know."

Talis cringed at her words and froze as he glanced at her. She was glowing green like when Princess Minoweth's dagger had tainted her mind and filled her with a dark power. The crowd close to them had noticed this too. Knights protecting the Emperor tensed and brandished weapons as Mara slowly strode towards the throne, and to Talis's horror, she retrieved from her purse two daggers of identical appearance and gripped them in her hands.

"So what would you have, Emperor Ghaalis, a signed peace treaty with Naru, granting the freedom of Onair and Ursula, and a favorable trade agreement with House Storm, or would you prefer my dagger thrust deep into your heart?"

A look of sheer terror froze the Emperor's face. He tried to open his mouth in either laughter or a scream, but the blood seemed to drain from his cheeks and his skin turned bone white. To Talis's surprise, a frightened-looking guard thrust his sword at Mara as she climbed the steps towards the throne, but she just sidestepped and stabbed the dagger through his chain mail armor into the soft part of the back of his head. He fell face first and his sword clattered against the marble floor as his body thudded onto the ground.

The area around the throne exploded with screams and people shrieking as they fled. Guards and knights charged towards them and more knights went to shield the Emperor. But to Talis's dismay, no sorcerers appeared to challenge them, although his hands were stretched out and ready for any attack. And the Emperor, instead of standing brave and indignant, cowered behind his guards like a little boy scared from a bad dream. Mara laughed at him.

"Afraid of a girl and her little daggers?" Mara peered around a nervous, trembling guard. "And where is the Empress? Or does the Emperor prefer men?"

By now Talis could sense no magical resistance or interference in the area, and was more scared of a sword harming Mara. He aimed his hands at the knights in front of him, and released many tendrils of flame, causing their eyes to widen in horror and they turned away as the fire blackened their armor. As the soldiers broke rank from flames only hot enough to singe and scald, Talis was surprised to see that the Emperor was guarded by only a few of his loyal knights, and they were trying to get him to leave the throne. Clearly they had not expected any resistance.

"Please, don't kill me!" Emperor Ghaalis wailed. "I never ordered any of those assaults…it was all the doings of the magical Orders in Ishur, and that madmen Lord Aurellia. I wanted to stop them but I was warned against interfering."

"So you're just a puppet, then?" Talis said. "A figurehead Emperor that keeps the people of Carvina placated while the sorcerers and necromancers wreak havoc on the world outside?"

"They were desperate to find sources of power to aid them in their dark cause." The Emperor relaxed a bit as he could see that Talis and Mara had calmed their stance. "But you never should have come here, you'll only invoke the wrath of the Dragons."

"The Dragons?" Talis looked perplexed as he studied the Emperor's eyes.

Behind him, Talis could hear footsteps approach, and glancing back, Master Goleth strode up alongside them and frowned at the situation. "Why have you done this? You claimed to come seeking peace and you make such a move against our Emperor? He is the weak piece in the game, and the Empress awaits, and her children, and the Dragons. They want you to kill him and free his claim over the power of the throne. Do not give in to their wishes."

The wizard flourished his hand at the throne. "Notice that Princess Devonia and Prince Davos have left their father to your friend's daggers. Yet be sure they still lurk in the shadows, waiting to pounce once you slay the Emperor. This is all a trap and a setup...don't fall for their play."

Mara cleared her throat and shook her head as if struggling to resist some dark power. "I said I would accept a peace treaty. There is no need for any more bloodshed today."

"I can offer you the signed paper of the treaty you seek." The Emperor's eyes fell to the floor, as if unwilling to say more. But Talis imagined that the paper would be worth little to enforce anything outside of Carvina. Had they come all this way and failed to prevent more violence from reaching Naru?

"Any treaty he signs would be worthless," said a girl's familiar voice. "Unless of course you are a fool and believe in its value." Talis spotted a girl's figure appear from behind a stone pillar. Was that Princess Devonia? And as the girl strode closer into the light, he could see it was her, but a carapace of armor was slowly forming over her lithe body, covering even her neck and head in a shiny skin that reminded Talis of the scales that covered the dragons of Ghaelstrom. Her scaly armor was red and dangerous and her eyes glittered with power.

More figures appeared, all menacing and covered in dragon scale, and Talis could feel the air crackle with their magical power. His mind warned him to flee and change forms and fly back to Naru with Mara and escape this trap, to escape death and certain destruction. The Emperor seemed calm and confident now, and he returned to the Ebony Throne and his knights repositioned themselves in a fan around him, their eyes stoic and unmoving.

And the Dragons moved silently towards them, their eyes glowing in the now darkening chamber.

27

Starwalkers Summoned

Rikar watched in terror as the Starwalkers strode up to the wooden cross and inspected the dry, windswept corpse, sniffing suspiciously at the skin. The smallest of the four Starwalkers, a bald, stocky man who wore a black silk robe with a gold, strange rune on the chest, aimed a stone at the temple. Rikar could tell by the shape and how the starlight glittered off the stone that it was a fragment, like the one that Nikulo had possessed. The man was certainly their leader, as the other Starwalkers held nothing in their hands.

As the four stalked towards the gaping mouth of the temple, Rikar enjoyed the idea of them being trapped in the confines of the chamber. If this went all as planned by the Nameless, would he find himself free, whatever freedom was in this half-state between life and death? Free to return to the land of the dead and join his father in the suffering of the Grim March? Or did the Nameless have a way to grant him life again, a form of physical renewal through his blood they'd collected in the jars? Though glancing at his shriveled body, he doubted whether that was even possible.

He tried to follow them into the Ruins of Elmarr, but the silver cord that connected him to his body held him firm and close, and he was left to stare at the sand swirling under a gusting wind and the stars twinkling knowingly at him overhead, like they were the ancient witnesses to all his foolishness. Time swept on and jumped and popped like the thrashing of a curtain under a stiff breeze. The desert churned and rolled and the stars twisted and turned in the sky as if a picture wheel played with by a child.

Soon morning's first light colored the horizon in a delicate wash of pinks and purples and reds, illuminating the scattering stain of storm clouds off in the distance. While Rikar was watching the brilliant sunlight break over the beautiful dunes, he caught a flicker of movement off to the side and turned to witness the priests marching outside in a ceremonial line. Of particular interest, he spotted four priests each holding ornate iron urns that billowed out black and grey puffs of smoke. Did they contain the remains of the Starwalkers? Had the Nameless succeeded in luring them inside and slaughtering them like pigs in the chamber?

He felt a kind of euphoria overtake him as he spied the glass jars that contained his blood, which were being carried by several temple priests over to where his corpse still hung on the cross. The same priest that had cast his hideous spell over Rikar followed the glass-carrying priests to his body. They placed the four jars at each cardinal location around Rikar's remains, and to his surprise, opened the lids.

The priest began chanting strange words that sounded like the words he'd said over Rikar that had slain him, but this time the order of the words seemed spoken in reverse. Black spirals spewed from the sorcerer's hands and flowed into a black, dense mass of smoke in front of Rikar's splayed corpse. Four tendrils from the black mass dove into the jars of blood and formed a kind of tube that sucked the thick liquid into the smoky mass. Soon the glass jars were empty and the dense mass seemed to come alive with a kind of strange, surging power that possessed Rikar with a feeling of familiarity and endearment.

Empty now, the glass jars were removed by the priests and in their place were positioned the four smoking urns. Why were they putting the urns near his corpse? The smoke was wafting up into the black cloud and mixing with the remains of his blood. For a painfully long time Rikar was fixated on the image of the smoke being pulled into the now growing, electrified mass. After what seemed like an hour or more, the urns stopped smoking and the priests came over and dumped the ashes into the living, churning black cloud and a burst of brilliant light exploded in a fiery blast.

When the dust and smoke cleared, Rikar moved in close to see what had happened to his corpse, and to his horror, found that the black mass had disappeared. What had happened to it? Had the spell or the experiment somehow failed and he'd be forced to live life as a wraith, stuck in between the world of the living and the dead?

Then a faint flicker appeared on the sand. Was that a jewel or a crystal of some kind? But the thing—or whatever it was—moved in a kind of wriggling, worm-like movement. As Rikar went even closer to inspect, he could see that it wasn't a worm at all, since it moved in a serpentine motion as it darted across the sand towards the wooden cross. The shiny, shimmering surface of the snake possessed a kind of starlight luminescence on the scales, but the overall color was definitely red like the rich rouge of blood.

Somehow Rikar felt a chilling dread come over him as he watched the serpent slither up and snake around the wood and it soon glided up and penetrated the crusty remains of his corpse. At that tiny tear in his tissue, a ripping feeling wrenched the inside of his spirit and caused a great, wracking pain to jolt through him. But the pain and the agony only got worse. Much worse than anything Rikar had ever experienced. It was as if four demons were pulling several sides of his soul and tearing him apart.

Screaming did no good as he had no mouth and throat and lungs to express the pain. He fled as far away from his corpse as the silver chain would allow, but still the throbbing, shooting pain surged into his stomach and shook him in epic convulsions. The pain was flowing, he realized, from his body, through the silver cord, and into his soul. Instead of fleeing from the feeling, he forced himself to return to his body and inspect what was causing all the agony. And the evidence was clear in the color returning to his skin and the bulging under his cheeks and in the stirring of his legs.

He was beginning to connect the pain with the regrowth of his skin and muscles and tendons. Even his brain was sparking with little zaps of electricity. He gazed dumbfounded as his body came back to life. And the times when he could see the serpent slither underneath his skin, he found himself sick with disgust.

Overall, his features were similar to what he'd remembered of himself, though he never really fawned over himself in the mirror. He seemed taller somehow, and his face held the menacing expression of a zombie. The color of his skin was definitely lighter than before, and it glowed with a kind of faint phosphorescence. Gone were the black hair and brooding eyebrows.

The priest clapped his hands and surprised Rikar from his reverie. He turned and eyed the priest as he started casting another spell at Rikar's now groggy and trembling body. The priest strode ceremoniously up to the cross and placed his hand over the body's midsection—at the originating point of the silver cord. He closed his eyes and chanted shrill words as he felt along the air where the cord was, and as if he could actually feel the cord itself, stretched his hands along its actual surface, and tugged and tugged the cord, pulling Rikar's spirit closer to the stirring body.

"This will burn a little," whispered the priest.

A little? Rikar wanted to say, and found himself dreading what the priest had in mind.

Several other priests came and unbound Rikar's body from the cross and helped the groggy figure to its feet. As they held the body firm, the first priest positioned himself behind Rikar's spirit, and chanted a new spell that caused a red shimmering brilliance to form around the shell of his soul. In a burst of power striking him from behind, Rikar felt himself pushed and propelled forward, until he penetrated the heavy mass of his body in a wrenching, tearing movement.

For a long while he felt nauseous and unsettled, like when you wake from the nightmare of a fever dream drenched in sweat. But in the heavy, gloomy feeling that followed, he sensed a clean, distilled power pouring through him that was foreign and frightening at the same time. It focused his mind and raised his awareness, and as if with renewed senses, his mind surged with new information that had escaped him before: the lull of a locust's wings, the itch of a priest's dry skin, the interruption of the flow of sand over a skull, and the deep, dreadful drumming of a heartbeat somewhere far down inside the temple.

All the sounds flooding his mind caused him to go mad for a moment, until he forced himself to only listen to the shifting of the nearby priests as they observed him in rapt attention. Rikar was afraid to open his eyes to the blinding light of late morning, and instead he inhaled a deep breath of air and his nostrils were filled with a myriad of scents: the distant fragrance of a desert rose, the coppery smell of spilled blood on the sand, the acrid odor of the priests sweating under the hot sun, and the most distinct smell of all, coming from within the bowels of the temple, was the smell of death. The same festering smell as the Underworld.

"Rise, Lord Rikar," said the voice of the priest who had killed him. "And give thanks to our Master and Lord of All for bestowing such generous gifts of power to you."

Without thinking, Rikar opened his eyes to study the man and instantly regretted it. The light was painfully bright and caused his hands to shield his eyes and he cringed from the sun. Normally it would take longer for him to adjust to the brilliance, but for some reason he mind sharpened and the view dimmed in response and in seconds was bearable. He wasn't used to such resilience of vision and senses and wondered what change had wrought such a difference. *The smoke and the ashes of the Starwalkers...they're a part of you now*, he remembered.

The priest placed Rikar's ring on his renewed finger and handed him a white robe to wear. Only upon feeling the soft texture of the robe against his fingers did he realize that he was naked, and the sun felt soothing and serene as it warmed his bare back.

"Our Lord and Master has gained a fragment of the stars from the quad that sacrificed themselves for our cause. Perhaps you can feel the change inside of you? Their essence has helped to reform your physical body, and with it, the Master has granted you new powers that will take you some time to discover within yourself."

The priest spread his hands wide and closed his eyes to feel the sun warm his face. "You must go and help the Child of the Sun, the Master commands it, and help the girl who wields the twin daggers and dances with the dead. The three of you are commanded to obey our Master and recover more fragments for his freedom. You must go quickly, as the Order of the Dragons will soon destroy them in Carvina. I will show you the way to the Emperor's Palace in the capitol. Without their help, you will be unable to succeed against the Starwalkers, so we must leave now."

Why did he have to help Talis and Mara? What did they possess that was needed by the Nameless in his pursuit of the Starwalkers? But he knew better than to question the priest, and realized that life was far better than death, and it was the Nameless and the blood magic of the priests that had brought him back to life. *But then again they killed you in the first place,* thought Rikar.

He stared at his hands and felt the intermixing of power from the ring and the new, strange and foreign energy coursing through his body from the Starwalker's essence. As the priest cast a spell and flew off over the desert towards the southwestern hills, Rikar let the rage surge inside himself and he shot like a shooting star after the man. He laughed freely as the wind whipped over his face, relishing in the feeling of power and finally being free from that constricting tomb. And no more was he a ghost; he was alive and filled with the magnificence of life and liberation.

Once he gained favor with the Nameless, Rikar was sure that he would secure claim to the rulership of this world. And then, without hesitation, he would kill Garen Storm and ensure that no blood rites were made for the man in the Temple of Zagros, and doom Talis's father to the endless torture of the Grim March.

After he helped Mara and the pathetic fool in his fight against those so-called Dragons of Carvina.

28

Chaos and Obliteration

With a wild and wonderful feeling of violence pulsing through her heart, Mara found a grim smile forming on her face as the dragon-scaled figures stalked towards them. She tensed and waited, eying Princess Devonia and her cat-like movements as she strode across the marble floor. The daggers poured power into Mara's body and she could see herself fade into a green, ethereal glow.

"Mara?" Talis shouted, and he whipped around to try and find her. She giggled and whispered that she was ok, and he relaxed a bit as he realized that she was invisible.

Master Goleth put out his hands as if trying to stem the flow of blood. "There is no need to fight, we came here to talk—"

"Move aside, Builder," shouted the deep, booming voice of the Emperor. "If you ever want to see your wife and children again, you will stay out of this fight. The time for talking with these young, arrogant ones is over. The girl made the first move of violence against us, and now blood must be paid for in blood."

There were at least twenty of the Dragons threading through the tall pillars and stalking towards Talis, their armored joints smooth as they strode silkily in a pack dog formation. Master Goleth shuffled away, his eyes hesitant and sorrowful as he stared at Talis. And the Emperor still sat bemused upon his throne, with several of his knights studying the Dragons approach.

"Father," said Princess Devonia, "you might want to leave the chamber and find protection elsewhere. The morbid-looking fire mage is likely to set the palace on fire. I suspect that Master Goleth and his allies will have quite a time rebuilding. Tis a shame, really, to have to destroy something so lovely."

But the Emperor made no movement to leave, and instead stupidly chuckled as Talis bent down and pressed his palms out. Mara took advantage of their distraction, and stalked around the throne dais. If the Dragons demanded blood for blood, them she needed to start spilling some. Old blood, noble blood, Emperor's blood. Regardless of what Master Goleth had said about the Emperor, Mara hated his haughty expression as he watched Talis, like a boy expecting a circus show for his birthday. *More like a horror show*, she thought.

At the throne there were three Stelan Knights guarding Emperor Ghaalis. And they were scared. Ever since she'd vanished the knights wore tense and worried faces, and their leader kept whispering warnings to the weak Emperor. *Pop the blood bags*, was what Elder Relech had said when he'd commanded Mara to kill innocents on their dark outings together. But in the case of the Emperor, it was more like slice the pig's throat and let the beast drain dry until it's dead.

"Your Imperial Majesty," the lead knight was whispering, "I must insist that we leave. The girl is invisible, and she could attack you at any moment."

Out of the corner of her eye, Mara could see Talis send a burst of testing wind against several Dragons who'd ventured too close, and the strike had sent them skittering over the marble floor and slamming against the hard pillars. But in response to the attack their skin hardened to a shiny sheen that seemed to make them invincible from the hammering impact of hitting the stone.

"Wind magic will do nothing to harm a Dragon," Princess Devonia said, her voice self-assured and calm. "And burn the whole palace down if you like, I really don't care, but flames won't harm us either. Our skin protects us from magic."

How about my blades, Mara thought, and stretched out her hand and sliced the soft neck of the Emperor. A spray of blood shot from his throat and painted the face of the shocked knight in a pretty red fan. The twin daggers raged in her hands as she stabbed the kidney of the closest knight on her right, and ducked down behind the throne as another knight twisted his sword around and sheered the upper part of the Ebony Throne in a vain attempt at lopping off her head.

As Mara stabbed the soft spot behind the knight's knee joint, she heard a gruesome, wet *whoomp* as something soft exploded and sent a shower of blood and bits of bone into the shouting, collapsing knight, knocking him back onto his ass. Mara found a vile laugh escaping from her mouth as she spotted a splinter of bone protruding from his eye socket. Was Talis spoiling all her fun?

A pain surged through her scalp and she screamed in agony as someone yanked her up by her hair and left her dangling to gape in horror as a knight brought around his massive blade to slice her in half. She shrieked and slashed her daggers at the knight's steel plate armor, but it did little to stop him. As Mara felt certain that her death was near, a green light blossomed around the raged-filled eyes of the knight, and the world went weak and distant, as if she were a drunk viewing the slurred scene, with time racing randomly and slowing suddenly, and even going silent and still in a timeless eternity.

The daggers twisted and turned, and in a torrential rage burst alive as if awakening from an ancient slumber. Eerie green fire poured out from the blades and rushed into the knight's mouth and filled his body with wave after wave of demonic-headed fire. Excruciating screams sped from his shivering mouth as Mara could see the demons eating away the man from the inside. A quick flood of blood streamed down his eyes as the demons consumed his brain and the soft tissues of his skull. Mara wrinkled up her face in disgust as she found herself falling from the knight's now limp grip.

She scrambled up to her feet and spun around the throne expecting another blow from the knights, but only found bodies bleeding on the red rug. Talis cast several wind magic spells to knock a group of Dragons away from him, and Mara realized that many more adherents of the Order had appeared, numbering at least a hundred Dragons protected in their weird, scaly armor and brutal claw-like fists and feet. But the way Mara felt, fear melted away in a wash of crazed laughter, and she charged after a Dragon sneaking up behind Talis.

Green shadows enveloped her as she vanished and raced after the man clad head to foot with dragon scales gleaming in the fiery remains of the burning Dragons. She tried to pierce the weak point under the Dragon's arm as the man went to smash Talis in the head. The Dragon growled in fury and spun around from the glancing blow and smashed her in the face. The instant the blow was about to land, the daggers fired in fury and a kind of green shield soared up and subdued the blow, causing Mara to only feel a slap sting her face.

She ran forward and climbed up the scales of the man's chest until she stood on his shoulders, and twisting around, she clenched her legs around the Dragon's neck, and caused them both to tumble backwards to the ground. As the man beat at her legs in an attempt to break free, she pulled both daggers in a quick stab underneath his scales, and the blades bit and broke though and punctured his heart.

Shoving his heavy body off of her, Mara stood and scanned around at the countless Dragons threading around bodies and blood, advancing on them with their cool, deliberate eyes studying Talis and Mara. They raised no hand to cast a spell, and moved in a madly precise formation, fanning out in clear attempt to surround them.

A quiet command to her daggers brought invisibility to her once again. In the cool calm of their advance, Mara studied the Dragons and spotted Princess Devonia stalking around with another Dragon that had a similar face as the Emperor. Was this her brother? Why were the children Dragons but the father only a weak Emperor with no power? Then Mara remembered the mention of the Empress, and Talis knew that she was a Dragon. But where was she hiding?

Talis caught Princess Devonia's approach, and he furrowed his brow at her and said, "Can't we end this? I've found your weakness and have it in my power to obliterate your entire Order until every single one of you is burned up from inside. We've come here seeking peace…can we end the fighting once and for all?"

"Never," hissed the Princess, and aimed her clawed fist at Talis. "As much as I enjoyed your pretty fire magic show in the square, I know you'll never be able to sustain that amount of power against our entire host."

"Try me," Talis said, his tone challenging and curt. "Perhaps you'll be next, Princess. Would you like to feel the heat of my fire boil you up from the inside?"

Princess Devonia scoffed and flourished her hands in quick snapping movement, forming a crystalline shield around her figure. "Good luck trying. Not all Dragons are as susceptible to that spell. You'll need to try another approach. And the only answer for the violence you've wrought here will be for us to rip your flesh from arm to leg and paint the walls with your blood. We'll make a memorial out of the display, and add the blood of every single person in Naru to adorn the shrine. Our dragon gods will be pleased with the sacrifice."

Mara was glad to see that the Prince had failed to raise a similar shield, and instead he chose to hide himself behind his sister in a cowardly move. He was a handsome boy her age, but his eyes held the raw cruelty of the overly privileged and the seldom punished. She already knew how to slip her blade up under his scales and let her daggers kiss the soft skin underneath. Wasn't it the Prince's time to die? Surely she was hearing the voice of Zagros call out to her? *Slay the tender mortal and feed me his royal blood. I've more demons to spawn and release unto the world...*

Who was she to disobey the Lord of the Underworld? With several stealthy steps she darted over and in a raspy whisper said, "My prince, my love, come to me," and as he turned his horrified eyes to face her, she jumped into his arms and snaked a hand around his head, and kissed his mouth with her dagger. Blood gushed from the wound and his sister screamed in a wild wail that echoed across the chamber walls as they fell to the ground in a rush. Such pretty eyes he had, blue as the summer sea.

A clawed fist smashed into her shoulder but the daggers once again flared out and shielded the blow, but the force was strong enough to send Mara tumbling across the ground. Now the furious Princess seethed with rage and ran after her, but a quick shot of wind magic from Talis sent the girl flying a hundred feet across the chamber, knocking over several Dragons in the process.

She looked up in time to see Talis facing three Dragons, and to her horror found his body radiating with the red light of overheating fire. How had she not noticed this before? As he tensed his palms together, the middle Dragon exploded in a brutal burst of blood that catapulted his allies off to the side in a somersaulting spin across the marble floor. After the last attack, the color of Talis's skin had risen up another feverish shade of red and he panted from the exertion.

"Talis!" she screamed, and darted over to him, picturing the girl wizard who'd exploded at the top of the Order of the Dawn. "Change form, Talis. Do it now!"

His head lolled about and he looked over at her in a feverish, glassy-eyed stare. As she shouted another insistent command for him to change into dragon form, a flicker of realization flipped on in his eyes. He flourished his hands weakly in what seemed like the last movement he could make, and Mara found herself stepping back as his figure bubbled and expanded and transformed into beautiful, gold dragon.

Their attackers stopped their advance, faces frozen in fear, eyes wide in terror and awe. Some Dragons even prostrated themselves and chanted weird, wild words in jubilant tones, as if Talis were their savior and god come to save them. In the serenity and shock of the distraction, Mara ran over and jumped onto Talis's back, and his long, sinewy wings beat in a furious rush as he lifted high above the stunned Dragons.

Fire poured from his dragon's mouth and he bathed the cathedral-like chamber in a hot flash of orange and golden light. The flames were so intense that Mara winced and hid herself against his warm, scaly body, imagining that the fire released now would have killed them both if he'd stayed in human form only seconds longer.

Shouts could be heard from below, not screams or moans of pain as Mara had hoped, but commands issued and orders given, and through the dancing flames she spotted the Dragons of the Order jogging in formation out of the burning palace. Talis swooped and flapped his wings and with his fiery breath bore a broad hole in the stone ceiling, and flew outside and up into the stormy skies threatening the City of Carvina with rain and lightning.

Far below, Mara could see the Dragons streaming across the square and several groups dragged long, pole-like devices. When Talis dove to have a closer look, Mara shouted at him to stop but the wind was too strong and swallowed up her words of warning. The Dragons quickly raised the devices and aimed them at Talis as he realized too late that the things were preparing to shoot. Like the sound of a ballista shooting massive shafts, Mara heard four *thwumps* from below and she screamed as a tangle of sticky cords covered them and constricted his wings, stopping his wings from flying, and soon they fell into a deathly spiral towards the square.

As consciousness slipped away and the world faded, the only thing that went through her mind was, *I'm going to die young like the legends of old.*

29

Tears and the Goddess

Talis did his best to break free of the bonds that constricted his wings, but the more he struggled the tighter they strangled him. Mara was riding atop his back and he knew that in maybe ten seconds they'd smash into the ground and she'd be slain. In a quick burst he transformed back to his human shape and twisted about and searched for Mara. Where was she? There! She was just above him and he shot out a burst of wind magic and stretched out his arms and seized her unconscious body, and shot out another stronger gust of wind magic in a vain attempt at slowing their fall.

They were traveling too fast and the pressure of wind magic sent a terrible strain along his arms and back as he tried to balance and not flip over on their descent. Just to the left was a lake dotted with boats, and in a last second burst, Talis shot them over to the water and they crashed down deep into the murky depths of the cool lake.

In the slow-motion, emerald-green blur of algae and fish and turtles, Talis searched with a frantic slashing of his hands through the murk and he kicked and swam around root tendrils trying to find her. He had forgotten to inhale a deep breath before he'd penetrated the lake's surface, and his lungs burned and his mind raged in desperation as he hunted for her small figure. He knew she was likely drifting motionless in the water and would drown if he didn't save her.

But he couldn't find her no matter where he looked and he knew that unless he went to the surface he was going to die. He shot out a burst of wind magic and propelled himself the surface and inhaled a huge gulp of air, scanning around for signs of Mara. Despite the Dragons that darted across the square towards him, he ignored his enemies and plummeted into the water and shot wind magic again, realizing with his now cleared mind that it was much faster than swimming. He sped through the water, and dove down deep to the place where the light had been similar to the depths of his previous fall.

A shiny bauble caught his attention, and he shot off in the direction of the light, thinking that maybe it was a piece of Mara's ruby necklace or diamond earrings. But instead of jewelry he spied a school of shimmering fish and discovered that it was the fish scales catching the light filtering in from above. But what was that inside the school? He spotted a delicate hand drifting and his heart leapt with joy as he realized that it was Mara the fish were swimming around and nibbling on her toes and fingers. He swam forward and scooped her into his arms and with a burst of wind magic, spiraled up to the surface.

262

With a surge of light magic, he filled her small figure with the warm power of the sun and she coughed and coughed and gasped for air, opening her eyes in a strange fury. Off to the lake's edge he could see the relentless Dragons diving into the water in a slow, plodding attempt to catch them. Talis laughed to himself, delighted that Mara was alive, and he gripped Mara tightly in his arms and shot out wind magic, propelling them across the water and away from the approaching Dragons.

As they reached the shore, Talis turned back to help Mara out of the water, but strong hands seized their arms and yanked them to their feet. A mob of Dragons surrounded them and stared with cold, serpentine eyes. Talis had the feeling that they were waiting before issuing another wave of violence. Princess Devonia ambled through the crowd and glowered at Talis with tearful eyes and trembling lips, as if she were barely able to contain her rage.

"You little bitch!" she screamed at Mara. "You killed my brother!"

Pond water was dripping out of Mara's nose as she stared blandly at Princess Devonia, her expression unconcerned at the girl's tirade. She ran a soggy arm across her nostrils and twisted up her face at the Princess as if wondering how she should respond.

"Think of it as payback for killing my father in the war. Though we are hardly even, considering the countless citizens slain in the multiple assaults on Naru. Just a small taste of the violence to come."

Princess Devonia scoffed and spread her hands wide. "You are in no position to make threats, little assassin. The best you can hope for is to beg for the mercy of a swift death. More likely we'll opt for the slow torture of Master Vaern in the Iron Dungeon." She stared longingly at Talis. "But this intriguing creature is an altogether different matter."

The way the girl looked at him, Talis would have guessed that she wanted to eat him, as if she hungered to consume his flesh in a cannibalistic kind of way. He shivered in response and his mind raced, trying to think of a way of escape.

"Take them away and bind their hands in leaden sacks to prevent any trickier of magic from interfering with their imprisonment." Princess Devonia frowned as Talis narrowed his eyes at her. "The Council of the Order will convene and decide their fate. Though we may well feast on dragon heart tonight!"

"What?" Talis said, his voice mocking and disbelieving. "Does your bizarre Order worship dragons and desire the consumption of dragon hearts?"

A wry smile crossed Princess Devonia's face. "Why do you think there are no dragons roaming the skies? The legacy of our Order tells us grand tales of the dragon hunts and the mystical rites performed with dragon hearts. Yours will be the first dragon heart we've consumed in thousands of years."

"But I'm hardly a dragon. I've just been taught the art of changing into beast form, which for me happens to be a dragon. If you want to see dragons soaring high in the sky, you'll need to visit the world of Vellia, where you can find massive dragons flying freely. I know, I met the Dragon King himself."

Princess Devonia scoffed and glanced around at the others standing around, their eyes laughing in ridicule. "You've quite the imagination! Do you actually expect us to believe such a tale?"

"You might want to listen to him," said Master Goleth, pushing his way through the crowd of Dragons. "I've seen the dragons of Vellia and the Dragon King with my own eyes. And so has Lord Aurellia." A ripple of whispers spread across the crowd at the mention of the dark lord's name. "Unfortunately, it is unlikely that you'll ever see the world of Vellia, not unless you possess the knowledge and power necessary to cast world portal spells. And Talis is correct, he is no dragon. Kill him and you'll find only a human heart."

"Then he is of no use to us at all," shouted Princess Devonia, her voice sharp and bitter. "And we should just kill them both now and be done with it."

This is it, Talis thought, *we're going to die.* He glanced at Mara and saw the fondness of love and the fierce determination to live beaming from her eyes. Her wet, glistening arms held the twin daggers inside their protective sheaths, and her hands twitched as if craving to feel them again. She faded away from his view and all he could do in response was to close his eyes and fix the memory of her beautiful face in his mind, hoping he'd never forget.

They'd kill him and she'd live, that was the way he wanted it. Mara was a survivor and she deserved to live. There was no way he could win in a fight against all these Dragons. When a clawed fist went to his neck, Talis remembered Master Palarian's words, from the Netherworld so long ago, *"If you treasure her, like I see in your eyes that you do, you should find a way home, and protect her."* But how could he escape and stay alive and ensure he could help protect Mara? A wave of remembrance of the Netherworld washed over him and he felt like such an idiot. The shadow spell…of course, that was the answer.

As the Dragons chanted the arcane words of some strange incantation, rain gushed down in a flood, and Talis felt the spindly shadow lines of energy swishing out from his stomach and he guided them to catch hold of a shadow cord. Just as the Dragons raised their voices in a frenzied pitch, he found his body whipped forward in a mad rush of blurred lines of shadow energy.

When he opened his eyes he could see that he was standing in a small silent square in front of an old white shrine with a statue of a beautiful goddess, her gentle hands on the head of a child. Behind the shrine stood a decrepit temple, the wooden door ajar, and the wind blew it slowly open and closed in a soothing motion. Feeling compelled by a strong shiver down his spine, he ambled over to the temple and climbed the steps and entered the cavernous candle-lit chamber. He released a sigh, relieved he had escaped with his life.

He strode down past similar statues of the same goddess but in different poses: helping a sick girl, giving food to a hungry child, bringing a quarreling brother and sister together, and the most beautiful statue of all stood at the dais, of the radiant goddess, her hands outstretched to the sky, receiving a divine blessing. Mounted beneath was a long stretch of candles, some flickering and alive and others snuffed out by the rising wind from the storm outside.

The face of the goddess was lit by some mysterious rays of sunlight, but Talis could find no source and was convinced it was because of magic of some kind or a holy relic truly blessed by the gods. He bowed down before the statue and clasped his hands together and prayed to the Goddess Nacrea for Mara's safety and sanity, refusing to believe that the daggers could overtake her mind. Her will was too strong and he believed that eventually she would overcome and find a way to preserve the integrity of herself, despite the dark power trying to overtake her. He prayed and prayed until tears streamed down his cheeks as the warm, beautiful feeling of the Goddess poured over him and caused his eyes to stare at the ceiling where the dark rafters unfolded like rose petals peeling apart and exposed a kernel of brilliant, expanding sunlight.

He could see the same beautiful face of the statue shimmering inside the piercing light, her golden eyes staring at him with an intense look of pity and concern. She stretched out hands through the ether and her delicate fingers touched his tears, and in a flash of brilliance, she was gone.

30

Shelter and Storm

When Talis had vanished in a flash of silver and black light, Mara thought for sure that the strange ceremony by the Dragons had obliterated him so completely that he was forever gone. But their shocked faces and glances around caused her to realize, in the purest wave of relief, that he must have escaped by casting some shadow spell. Instead of trying to systematically slay every Dragon one at a time, Mara relaxed and slipped away from the mob, aiming her wet path in the direction where Talis had been facing.

If she could find him then things would be better, she knew it was true. They could escape back to Naru through one of Talis's shadow portal spells or simply fly north and return home. If there were any threat of Jiserian invasion then they would deal with as it came. For now, as long as they could stay together and protect each other, she believed they would survive. He had saved her once again, and somehow sinking into the depths of the lake had caused a renewed hope to surge inside her heart. If the taint of darkness in her mind could only be washed away...

She gripped her daggers and felt the furious power working its way through the caverns of her mind, as if serpents slithered and searched for an ankle to poison. But she forced herself to remember Talis's hurt eyes as she ignored him in the palace, and pushed the power of daggers down below the surface of her thoughts until the dagger's dark suggestions were just a hushed murmur beneath the main avenue of her thoughts. She knew she had to control the power to preserve her sanity.

Her feet wandered as she shuffled through the snaking streets, and the rain soaking her white dress appeared ghostly to her eyes. She hoped that through some divine intervention she might stumble upon Talis and they'd escape together. But this part of the city seemed strangely silent and empty, as the citizens were avoiding going outside because of the violence in the palace. In the quiet, the city had a delicate quality to it, and Mara could see the beauty of the whitewashed architecture without the wildness of the crowd surging through it.

Above, the stormy sky seethed with a rising fury, and a gale's blast buffeted her face and caused her to shield herself from the wind. A faint whisper sounded in her ears, like when the wind rushes by and talks to you, so softly sometimes you can barely make out the wind's words. But this voice was stronger now, urging and insistent, and it told her to keep walking straight ahead, and oddly enough, guided her left and right, and around buildings and shops and trees as she strode in a clear, peaceful trance, as if she were treading freely across clouds.

A ray of sunlight pierced through the strangling clouds and shone upon a shining statue of a pretty goddess protecting a child, and Mara saw herself in that child and felt the warm embrace of light filling her soul with sorrow and gladness. The wind gusted up and pushed open a door to a temple and for a moment Mara was afraid of being seen, but she laughed as she remembered that she was still invisible, though she wondered if it was ok to remove the spell since she was so far away from the palace.

She released her invisibility and relished in the return of her body to her eyes. Why had she waited so long? Even if she encountered the Dragons, she could always hide herself from them. When the sound of feet came from within the temple her heart raced and she hurried on, not wanting to interact with anyone, certainly not a temple priest. She rounded a corner and felt relieved at escaping unnoticed, then a shout caused her to quicken her steps and run down the street.

Footsteps chased her and her chest pounded from the exertion of running as fast as she could from her pursuer. Rain streamed down her face and she felt cold from the wind and the storm pressing chilly air down from the sky. Feeling stupid for not going invisible again, she was about to cast the spell when she paused and listened, wondering if she recognized the voice of the person chasing her. She turned around and found a silly smile stretching across her face as she spotted Talis breathless and jogging towards her.

He paused and caught his breath, his kind eyes savoring her in a warm look of love and amazement.

"I prayed to the Goddess Nacrea," he said, still panting hard from the run. "I prayed for your safety, and for the fortitude for you to fight against the dark power of the daggers. I know those are identical to Princess Minoweth's daggers, I just don't know where you found them." He looked up and raised his hands to the sky. "All praises and blessings to the Goddess Nacrea, for hearing my prayer and bringing Mara safely to me."

Mara looked at his beautiful face as he stared up at the sky and a soft golden light swirled around his figure and filled him with an angelic quality that caused tears to flood down her cheeks and she gasped in sorrow and regret at hardening her heart to him. She loved him, it was so simple and pure, she loved him and no other boy. As she immersed herself in the vision of Talis praying to the Goddess, a silver streak shot across the stormy sky, and for a moment Mara thought that the Goddess might pay them a visit like before in the Temple of the Sun. But no Goddess appeared, only the sound of cascading explosions rocking the air above them, and Mara swiveled her head around to study a blinding array of lightning and spiraling storm tunnels shooting down at the city.

Was Carvina under invasion? Talis caught Mara's concerned eyes and he sidled over to hold her hand and inspect the tumultuous violence arcing across the sky. Thunder boomed in hundreds of massive, rumbling explosions that shook the ground and quaked the buildings from side-to-side until a flash of white smoke blanketed the sky. A wailing, whining, whirring sound echoed out as an enormous detonation shot a titanic plume of smoke and rubble so high into the air it seemed to cover the city in a seething, demonic face of destruction.

Talis and Mara dove to the ground as whizzing iron and stone fragments bounced off the eerie-green shield that activated from Mara's daggers, protecting them from the storm of particles that shot across the city in the explosion. Buildings crumbled and collapsed, and the sides of structures and houses were shredded from the blast. A giant tower off in the distance cracked and tumbled over, sending the massive stone blocks crashing into a nearby temple. The quick succession of damage to the city was so expansive and violent that it shocked Mara speechless. Her ears ringed in a tinny sound and although Talis was speaking to her, she couldn't hear a thing.

31

The Baleful Hand

They stayed on the ground for a while until the explosions died down to a dull series of thuds and concussive blasts, and Talis cleared his ears. What had made that massive explosion? He knew he had to see what was going on from the vantage point of the sky, even at the risk of getting caught by the Dragons again. He spoke to Mara and told her to stay here, but go invisible, and he pointed at the sky.

Still his ears were ringing and he could barely hear what she said to him, but he just nodded and motioned for her to go and she mouthed the words, *I love you, be careful, please!* He kissed her lips and watched her disappear, and moved over into the center of the square and transformed into a dragon.

The area was so small he had to scramble and claw his way up to the top of the buildings and he flapped his wings and took flight high above the smoking, burning, shattered city. Far below around the palace burst a clustering series of explosions, the colorful beauty of which was frightening to behold. He spied a silvery figure spinning around in circles, shooting quick blasts of power that seemed to be causing all the damage to the city. Who was that sorcerer and why was he attacking Carvina?

Something in the strength and intensity of the blasts seemed familiar to Talis. He dove down after the shimmering figure, uncaring now of the strangling nets from the Dragon's ballistas. As he neared the sorcerer, the figure paused its attacks and turned to face Talis.

"Thank the gods they didn't kill you already," shouted Rikar, a broad, mirthful smile filling his face. "Where is Mara?"

Surprised, Talis studied the sorcerer again to be sure it was really Rikar. Although the voice was definitely Rikar's cocky, aristocratic accent, his hair was now golden like the sun and his skin pale as the four moon sisters. A star-like luminescence seemed to surround him as he hovered in the sky, one foot on earth, and the other foot in the vast expansiveness of the many worlds. He was completely renewed, and from the devastating impact of his attacks, utterly transformed in his magical prowess. Talis felt a twinge of jealousy strike his heart at seeing Rikar in all his regalia, his face proud and strong.

With a flick of his snout he motioned for Rikar to follow him down to where Mara was hiding in the small square. He sped off over the inferno that raged over the once beautiful city, and Rikar flew alongside until they reached the cracked and shattered buildings that surrounded the square. Dust billowed all around and caused Talis to sneeze and smoke shot out from his nostrils. He scrambled down the inside of the square slowly, hoping that Mara would stay safely away from his approach. When he reached the bottom he changed into human form and called out for her.

Rikar landed with a hard thud that pulverized the cobblestones, shooting a dust cloud around his radiant figure. His relaxed eyes held a strange calmness that seemed foreign to the friend and traitor that Talis once knew. Mara appeared from behind a broken marble statue of a lion and strode over, staring with suspicious eyes at Rikar.

"What the hell are you doing here? What did you do, decide to dye your hair blonde?" Mara scoffed and tilted her head querulously. "No, there is something strange about you, a kind of pale magnificence that likely means you've either stolen something of fantastic strength or allied yourself with a very powerful entity."

"Good to see you too, Mara. And I see that you're well-utilizing Princess Minoweth's dagger?" His head did a double take as Mara held up her other hand. "Wait, twin daggers? How did that happen?"

Mara sniffed and glanced guiltily at Talis. "It's a long story, actually. And you have a lot of explaining to do. Like why you are here in the first place and why the massive change in appearance?"

"And change in power and ability," Talis said, and pointed at the destroyed wall of a building. "It seems our old *friend* has come to Carvina seeking to demolish the place. Good thing we weren't in the epicenter of the explosion."

"I knew you weren't, actually." Rikar tapped his head and grinned thievishly. "A long story of my own to tell, but now is hardly the time. I sense those Dragons stalking over the city, looking for you. Even though I created a nice distraction, I doubt the damage killed many of them. We need to leave...like right now."

"Where exactly do you propose we go?" Mara gave Rikar an exasperated shake of her head. "You come here out of nowhere and expect us to follow you? One moment you're our enemy and the next you flew to Carvina to try and rescue us?"

Rikar cast a quick spell and started rising into the air. "May I?" At Talis's nod he cast the flying spell over Mara and Talis and they flew over to where Rikar was preparing to catapult into the sky. "Back to the lair, the Ruins of Elmarr, to the prison of the Nameless."

The Ruins of Elmarr? Talis remembered the overwhelming feeling of malicious that had come over him as he was compelled towards the ruin in the desert. Why would Rikar want to take them there? Now wasn't the time to argue, so Talis decided to go along with Rikar and at least distance themselves from the city.

"But we have to go retrieve our backpacks from the Regent's Inn," Talis said. *And the Surineda Map*, he thought. Why had he been so stupid as to leave it in the room? He flew high and scanned over the city, trying to find the right direction in the smoky landscape. There! Off to the south, past the gardens where Talis and Mara had traveled through last night, and past the square where Princess Devonia had watched his foolish display of fire magic. Soon he landed on the stone street, surprising the servants that scurried away from them in horror at their approach.

The Regent's Inn had survived most of the blast, but broken windows and stray rocks had still sprayed the once beautiful inn with devastating shots of rubble. Talis shouted at the bell clerk to take them quickly to their room, and the man obeyed and they charged off after him up the stairs to where they collected their packs and changed into their cleaned travel clothes and leathers. Hoping he'd gathered everything he needed for their trip, they jogged back outside and scanned around before stepping into the street.

And with a nod from Talis and a grim look from Mara, Rikar shot off into the air and they followed fast, feeling the wind and smoke and dust rush past him as Talis chased after the last person in the world he wanted to follow.

32

Temporary Obedience

The speed and exhilaration from flying with Rikar's spell caused Mara to flush in excitement and strength, a feeling heightened by the dagger's dark power that surged through her body. She believed that anything was possible after witnessing the tremendous destructive force obliterating the once pompous and debauched city. It was a shame that Princess Devonia had likely survived the attacks. Mara hoped she could send the pretty bitch to the Underworld and speed her reunion with her brother. A sweet snack best saved for another time...

Compared to flying as a dragon, this ridiculous speed was like galloping instead of crawling. Several times her daggers brought to life the shimmering green shield and protectively smashed seabirds that strayed too far inland. Mara glanced at Talis as he squinted and stared ahead, his expression intent on not losing Rikar. The stupid traitor flew like a madman. What was he doing in the Ruins of Elmarr? Was he allied with the Nameless, that hideous voice that still haunted Mara's mind? She shivered in horror at the thought of returning to that place.

To Mara's surprise, they were approaching an expansive city with steep mountains off to the south, a red-tinged city built along the beautiful, emerald sea. The closer they came to the city, the more Mara spotted spirals of smoke scattered everywhere. Was this the great City of Ishur, the city that Master Goleth had said was deep in civil war and violence between the magical Orders? But wasn't Rikar supposed to take them to the Ruins of Elmarr?

Talis must have been thinking the same thing, for they both sped up alongside Rikar and shot him questioning looks that caused him to slow down and hover on the outskirts of Ishur.

"What the hell is going on?" Mara said, and was determined to hear Rikar's story before they proceeded any farther. "I thought we were going to Ruins of Elmarr?"

"Before we go on, I think we're owed an explanation." Talis pointed to a mountaintop off on the southern side of the city. "Let's fly over there and rest while you tell us your story."

Rikar's face looked strangely impatient and nervous, but after he glanced around as if scanning for danger, he nodded in agreement and sped off towards the mountain. Soon they arrived and landed in the shade of a stand of soldier pines and stared out over the rock-strewn landscape to the west as the sun floated just above the horizon, an orange ball slicing through a stream of feathery clouds.

Talis and Mara dropped their backpacks onto the pine needle bed and she sat with a sigh. She glanced up expectantly at Rikar, and with a shrug of his shoulders, he began telling them the story of why he'd followed them through the portal, and what he'd done inside the Ruins of Elmarr. Mara found the hairs of her arms standing in sheer terror as he described his interaction with the Nameless in that dark prison chamber. And when Rikar told of how his body had been brutalized by the priest and brought back to life with the essence of the slain Starwalkers, Mara shivered in horror as she imagined the hideous ceremony.

She wondered if even Elder Relech could be so cruel.

"You're crazy if you think we'd return to the Ruins of Elmarr with you," Mara said, and shook her head in disgust at Rikar. "No, listen, I mean it. Before you argue back, realize that we came to Carvina in the hope of striking a peace treaty with Emperor Ghaalis. Don't scoff like that, I'm serious. He did grant us an audience but it was a complete setup."

"And you expected something different from the Jiserian Emperor?" Rikar laughed and stared at her with mocking eyes, making Mara furious at his flippant attitude. "The Jiserians hate Talis for killing so many sorcerers and necromancers and standing up to them. You should have heard Lord Aurellia talking about you. He was actually amused as he seems to enjoy creating chaos and conflict."

"Well, he's worlds away now," Talis said, and frowned at Rikar as if wondering what he was doing here with his old enemy.

"Not for long. Do you think he'd really be satisfied to give up any portion of his power and dominion over this world?" Rikar looked with deliberate, haughty provocation at Talis and Mara, as if daring them to challenge him. "He only went to Vellia because he wanted something of power to aid his cause. I think he'll be coming back, especially if we succeed in stealing fragments from the Starwalkers."

"We? Are you absolutely insane?" Mara whispered, feeling disgusted at herself and disbelieving that she'd even thought of getting involved with Rikar's ridiculous plans. "Have fun with that! There's no way we're going anywhere near another Starwalker. You're the one they want revenge against. What do we have to do with it?"

"Do I know the mind of the Lord of All?" Rikar flipped his long, golden hair away from his eyes, and it infuriated Mara how serene and self-assured he looked. "There is obviously something you're not telling me, since it seems like the Nameless knows both of you. It's like he's watching you and tracking you, and he has to be whispering in your head, just like I hear his voice inside mine." He tapped the side of his skull and it made a soft rapping sound.

Talis looked wary as he paused for a moment. "We stopped at the Ruins of Elmarr. Some *feeling* possessed me and compelled me to land and go inside the temple ruins you talked about. Still, I resisted and we left, but it is true, several times I've heard the voice of the Nameless in my mind…"

"So have I," Mara admitted, and wished she'd stayed quiet, for Talis scowled and looked at her with doubt and fear in his eyes. "After we visited the Ruins I had a nightmare. I saw a dark chamber, and Princess Minoweth's dagger appeared…and the next thing I knew I woke and the twin daggers were in my hands. It was like the Nameless had fed off my memories and somehow recreated the daggers. I don't know, it's all seriously strange and honestly, I don't want anything to do with that power chained there in the desert. It's a hideous feeling…"

"You may not have a choice." Rikar's eyelid twitched as if remembering some painful memory. "We've all been touched by the Nameless. You can resist all you want, but if you make yourself an enemy, it will only hurt those close to you and likely bring destruction once again to Naru."

"But can the Nameless ensure that Naru is unharmed by the Jiserians?" Talis said, and Rikar smirked at his suggestion. "I mean he probably only cares about his own desires. What is the destruction of city to the Nameless? Look how easily you were dispatched to wreck Carvina."

Rikar released an evil laugh. "The Nameless didn't tell me to do that. I was merely commanded to go and help you and retrieve you both. That was a bit of my own flair at work. Besides, Lord Aurellia hates those of the Order of the Dragons, and likely will reward me if I actually managed to kill a few of them."

"Not to mention that Zagros will reward you for sending him more innocent citizens that you killed." At Mara's mention of the god, the rumble of thunder sounded in the southern mountains, and she closed her eyes and saw the dog-faced Lord of the Underworld.

"Enough of this," Rikar said, and pushed himself to his feet. "The Nameless has commanded us to tilt the balance of power in favor of his loyal sorcerers in Ishur. You can deny him and both you and Naru will suffer as a result, or you can obey for the time being and see where a temporary obedience leads you. But right now, I don't see you having any other choice."

"Can you give us a moment to talk?" Talis said, and Rikar nodded and shuffled away to stare at the City of Ishur.

Mara met Talis's concerned eyes and wished they'd never followed Rikar in the first place. She stretched out her fingers and scooted over close to him and scooped up his hands, melting a little at the soft feeling of his skin. Wasn't there another way? They could fly back to Naru and prepare for a Jiserian invasion. But as Mara pictured the ferocious intensity of the Dragons, she knew that Princess Devonia wouldn't stop until she'd killed every single citizen of Naru in revenge for Mara's slaying of her father and brother.

"What should we do, Talis? The last time we listened to Rikar we ended up in the Underworld."

"But in all fairness, it didn't turn out all that bad, and if we'd listened to him in the first place we would have avoided almost getting killed in that hideous graveyard."

Mara shivered at the memory of that place. "So you're suggesting that we follow him to the Ruins of Elmarr, and what, swear allegiance to the Nameless?"

"You forget, I've already sworn a blood oath to Aurellia. And if the Nameless is really Aurellia's master, then I might not have any other choice, ultimately. Don't look all distraught, we'll get through this somehow, I know we will. The important thing is for us to stay together. I mean it, I don't ever want to lose you again. When you went into that palace all furious at me, I was really scared that I'd lost you." He sighed and in the stillness stared into her eyes. "Do you still care about me?"

A rush of emotion flooded her heart at she gazed into his beautiful eyes, and she nodded her head and squeezed his hands. Of course she cared about him, she loved him and hoped that he felt the same way. "I only have feelings for you, Talis. I have always felt this way, even though you didn't see it. I guess boys are stupid that way." She laughed wistfully and glanced up at Talis. When he smiled at her, a sympathetic expression formed on his face, and she relaxed and gestured at Rikar. "Let's go before he gets all the fun of wrecking Ishur."

"Let him do the attacking," Talis said, a worried look crossing his face. "I'd rather know who I am killing first. Rikar might be commanded by the Nameless to kill people who aren't our enemies. Who knows, maybe the magical orders that are allied to the Nameless are the very ones that attacked Naru."

"Well, let's find out, shall we?" She allowed him to pull her up and they walked over to Rikar and joined him in staring at the vast City of Ishur.

"So who are you attacking down there?" Talis said. Mara thought she spotted a twinge of jealousy in his expression towards Rikar, and who could blame him? Talis had always been competitive with Rikar, ever since their competitions in the sparring arena.

"Not just me," Rikar glanced at Talis with questioning eyes. "You'll need to help if you are indeed joining me in pursuing the Starwalkers. And don't worry, we're attacking the two Orders that led the assaults against Naru, the sorcerers who work for money and the necromancers who work for blood. In both cases they were commanded by the Emperor himself to strike out against our city. Considering you've beaten them before, this should be easy, right?"

Talis shook his head. "Be careful with the sorcerers and runemasters. In Carvina I fought three sorcerers who cast runes in the air that absorbed all the power of my spells and it even made them stronger. If it wasn't for Mara, they'd likely have won."

Rikar frowned in puzzlement at his words. "Sorcerers and runes? Hah, I wish we had Mistress Cavares to help us out on that one, she would have proven very useful."

"Just watch out, shoot testing shots of weak power to see if any of the sorcerers cast that kind of spell. With the amount of power you're commanding, it will only make them stronger and more difficult for us to deal with."

"And don't forget about me," Mara said. "I remember what those spells look like. I can always help go after them, assuming you can keep the flying spell on me during the battle?"

"We'll be quite a team," Rikar said, and grinned with a strange fondness that made Mara suspicious. She preferred him as an enemy. It was weird to have him on their side.

With a flourish of Rikar's hands, Mara found herself floating alongside Talis, and the three of them flew down the mountain and shot towards the tall, red buildings in the heart of Ishur, where thick, black smoke poured from a raging fire.

33

The Skies over Ishur

Of course, as luck would have it, the sorcerers that Rikar first encountered in the heart of Ishur flung brilliant blue runes into the air that sucked all the power out of his attacks. As much as he hated to admit it, having Talis and Mara there to back him up really helped. Talis would position himself to the side of the sorcerer they were attacking—creating a distraction—while Mara came in from behind for the savage, bloody kill. With Mara's daggers providing her with complete invisibility, they were almost an unstoppable force.

That was, until to Rikar's horror, at the zenith there blossomed a brilliant blaze of white light that unfolded in flaps around the blue sky, and four figures flew out and hovered over the City of Ishur. Rikar felt his heart make a weird tremor and he had to force himself to breath as he gaped at the sight, watching and wondering what they would do next. *They're going to kill you*, thought Rikar. Though likely they were going to do something far worse.

Then the strangest thing happened. Instead of attacking or swooping down on Rikar, the Starwalkers began singing a sad song, a chorus, of love and loss and despair. He recognized the clear and beautiful voices as from the song the Starwalkers had sung on Vellia, and Rikar wondered if there was a connection somehow. But this song was different than the one before, more of a mother bird singing because she has lost her little ones. A searching, probing song meant to evoke a response from the lost Starwalkers. None came, for as Rikar knew all too well, they were utterly destroyed.

He waited, despite being caught in the middle of a battle with three sorcerers who now stared dumbfounded at the strange star portal still open in the sky. Now everything seemed meaningless next to the power and grandeur of the god-like figures surveying the cityscape. When they discovered that their comrades had been slain like that, in a way so cruel and inhuman, they'd certainly rain fire and obliterate the Ruins of Elmarr and bury that foul presence underneath the sands of the Nalgoran Desert forever.

Talis had sidled close to Rikar and now pointed at the figure of a Starwalker descending from the sky.

"I recognize him," he whispered. "He was in Illumina that day. Can it really be Jared?"

"Why would they send him?"

Rikar felt a faint whisper of wind behind him, and he turned to see Mara appear. "Jared knows us. Of course the Starwalkers would send him after the Nameless killed the first quad in the desert. But I'm guessing that Jared doesn't know that they're dead, otherwise they'd likely send more quads to fight. Look at them, they're not even thinking of fighting, they're just singing a song to find their friends."

Mara was right. The more Rikar studied the sky where the Starwalkers searched, he realized that they were confused somehow, likely perplexed because they could sense their friends. They waited as if wondering why they didn't respond to their song.

"We should go to them," Talis said, "before their confusion turns to frustration and indiscriminate anger."

As Talis turned to fly, Rikar seized him by the arm and shook his head. "No, it should be me that goes, it's me that they want."

"We'll go together. I know Jared and he'll listen to me." Talis raised a palm to placate Rikar. "They don't want you, they've only come to find out what's happened to their friends. We need to talk to them, or they'll certainly start blasting this city to bits."

With the renewed intensity of the Starwalkers flying across the city, and their song changing to a frantic rhythm and shrill tones, Rikar knew that Talis was right. So he flew up high above the red buildings and black, billowing smoke and hovered there waiting as Talis and Mara joined him.

Soon the nearest Starwalker sighted them and slowly flew over while two others of his quad joined him, women with long, billowing golden hair and the same silver and black shimmering robes that Rikar had remembered from

Vellia. Another man flew over to Jared, a youthful, fierce-looking man with silver hair and dark skin the color of chocolate, and his alien eyes surveyed them with curiosity.

"How is it that find myself once again in the presence of these three young humans?" Jared spoke to the other Starwalkers as if explaining an unknown story to them. "Two of them loyal and true and pure of heart, and one a murderer, but is it really him?" The Starwalker flew close and Rikar found his hands twitching nervously at the man's quick advance. "You look very different from the last time I saw you in Illumina. Your hair and skin has changed. Some mystical force has completely renewed your body? A familiar energy now courses through you and radiates like the stars..."

Jared gasped in shock as his eyes went wide and he wailed a mournful exhalation and shook his head in disbelief. "Can it really be true? That the essence of my fellow Starwalkers resides within your cruel body?" He came so close that Rikar flinched as if worried the man would strike him down in an instant, but the Starwalker only sniffed. "Your skin even possesses the smell of the Starwalkers? How is this possible?"

Rikar tried to retreat from the uncomfortable distance between himself and the Starwalker, but Jared narrowed his eyes and Rikar felt woozy and delirious in an instant. Jared came very close to Rikar again and small, spindly snake-like cords shot out from his fingertips and attached themselves around Rikar's wrists like an octopus latching

291

onto its prey. To Rikar's horror, the green strands clenched tight and he could feel something sink into his skin and caused his arms and fingers to spasm uncontrollably.

"How, how, how?" Jared shouted, and his bull eyes glowered at Rikar, a wrathful agony twisting up the once beautiful features of his face into a horrific scowl. "You have all four inside you? As if you ingested their blood and ate of their flesh? But, no, not in your stomach…in your blood and in the cells of your body, in your mind, in your energy. Somehow you have been remade with their very essence? What kind of foul blood magic is this? Jeremiah tampered with the dark arts, but nothing so cruel and nefarious as this…"

"A cruel deed has been done to Rikar by the one called the Nameless," Mara said, her voice soft and sad, and Rikar was surprised that she spoke up for him. "It is the same being that has slain your Starwalker friends, deep in the black heart of the ancient Ruins of Elmarr. But by what dark method, none of us know."

The Starwalkers stared at each other with sorrowful expressions and the women whimpered weakly and darted their tear-filled glances at Rikar, their eyes like long needles of hatred stabbing into him.

"Must we accept the words of these mortals as truth?" The dark-skinned Starwalker aimed a finger at Mara. "How do we know they are not simply leading us away from finding our brothers and sisters?"

"Janesh, I understand your concern, but it is undeniable that bits of the essence of all four members of the quad now reside within this young murderer." Jared studied Rikar with doubtful eyes. "Though I am quite certain he doesn't possesses the power to kill them. This causes me to believe that likely the girl's story is true. And if it is true, then we are in grave danger remaining on this world. We must consult with the high council. Especially since a fragment is now in the hands of an enemy."

"But what does this mean for us?" Mara's forehead creased in worry as she glanced at Talis and back to the Starwalker. Rikar felt like something terrible was going to happen, and the voice of the Nameless was shrieking frantically in his mind, warning him to leave and fly away. He knew that if any more prodding pressure pushed his mind he would fall off into the black emptiness and go insane.

Almost in unison, the sky around them filled with sorcerers and necromancers rising up from the streets of Ishur. Jared wheeled around slowly and surveyed the threat, his amused face forming a grin.

"Why look, have we guests come and worship us?" A look of humor passed between the Starwalkers, but their bull-like eyes retained the alien coldness that sent chills prickling along Rikar's arms.

"I imagine these robe-wearing magicians are loyal to the one you call the Nameless?" Janesh fixed a fierce scowl on Mara.

Rikar cleared his throat and forced himself to concentrate. "I sense the Nameless is furious and he now commands his loyal servants to protect us."

Janesh spread his arms wide. "These insects dare challenge gods?"

The image of Rikar slaying the Starwalker woman played out in his mind, but he forced himself to remain quiet and expressionless for fear of invoking their wrath. Though they were certainly powerful, they were not gods, nothing like the power and fury of Zagros.

"Be wary of these insects, brother," Jared said, the corners of his eyes crinkling as he studied the threat. "You may find some of them scorpions."

The Starwalker clapped his hands and a white, shimmering star portal flowered in the sky and caused the crowd of sorcerers and necromancers around them to cringe in fear at the power and glory of the portal. Jared snapped his fingers at Talis, Mara, and Rikar, and they went woozy and the world went bleary from the spell. Rikar tried to fight against the power of the Starwalker's mind, but he found the effort like swimming upstream against a raging river, and he gave in and allowed himself to be flung along the swift current until blackness overtook his mind.

34

Between the Stars

When Talis woke he found himself alone in a glittering, glassy world like the view of a sun-filled day staring through a faceted, clear crystal. Glancing around, he discovered he was lying on a low bed in a room made completely of glass or crystal or perhaps even gigantic diamonds. Some light outside the room or within the crystals illuminated the facets and sent light beams across the whitewashed floor. One entire side of the room opened to a tropical garden with a low waterfall spilling into a lily pad covered pool. The foliage reminded Talis of the jungles of Lorello.

In a fright he looked around and soon discovered his backpack beside the bed and the Surineda Map case still safe inside. Wanting to find Mara, he withdrew the map and felt the familiar force of fire magic slither up his hands as he closed his eyes and sent the map his command to locate her. The map immediately came alive and drew a shimmering point of light in a room next to his. He sighed and strode over towards the garden and heard a hiss as he passed through the edge of the building.

Outside, he glanced back at the building and saw a scintillating shield covering the room's face. Strange, was this some kind of a magical barrier protecting the room from the animals and insects outside? He heard monkeys chattering high in the trees and the chanting of birds and cackling of parrots as he followed a footpath through exotic orchids. Rounding a guava tree, he found another shield covering the room next to his. In a movement of curiosity, he raised his hand to the shield and found that it melt away at his touch, and to his relief, revealed Mara's sleeping form curled up inside.

He sat next to her and could see the gentle rise and fall of her chest as he admired her pretty, sleeping face. Her eyelids fluttered as if she were having a dream. She smacked her lips like she was nibbling on something delicious, and Talis stroked her long, auburn hair illuminated by the velvety, crystalline light, and was enraptured by the smooth silkiness of the feeling. He thought that she was the most beautiful girl in the whole world and worried whether she still cared for him as before.

She stirred from her sleep, and startled, he smiled and met her eyes as she squinted and glanced around the room.

"Where are we?" She pushed herself up and stared at the curved crystalline ceiling that arched down and around into walls. Her head swiveled around and she squealed in delight as she caught sight of a strange peacock flaring its beautiful, green feathers as two smaller females pecked around at the ground.

"I've never seen such beautiful feathers before!" she said, and stalked over towards the gardens, keeping herself low and her movements still to prevent them from being frightened. She lowered her voice to a whisper. "They're some completely different species, like we're on another world?"

"The Starwalkers must have mesmerized us and dragged us off through the star portal." Talis pointed at the gardens. "I found your room using the Surineda Map. It turns out they put us right next door. It's an amazingly beautiful jungle outside. Want to see?"

"I want one of those feathers." Mara chewed her lip in excitement and seized her daggers and went invisible as she stalked towards the shield. Soon the proud peacock shrieked and darted away, surprised at having one less feather in its plumage. Mara reappeared and smiled devilishly with the long feather in her hand. "It's so light and iridescent and green! Do you know how rare it is to find such a beautiful, green feather? Only in the south and I saw a few in the jungles of Lorello. But we were so rushed I didn't have the time to go feather hunting."

She narrowed her eyes as if remembering something morbid. "Where do you think the Starwalkers have taken Rikar?"

Talis pictured the horrified face of Rikar as Jared cast the spell that lulled his mind into submission. Were they torturing him for information? Conducting some strange experiment to understand how the Starwalker essence had been infused into his body? From Rikar's story of the blood magic spells the priest had cast over him to bring him back to life, Talis guessed the Starwalkers might be worried at the possibility of being vulnerable against the Nameless and his followers. But how could they ever follow them here?

Then the memory of Rikar following Talis through the worlds portal filled his mind. Was it possible for one of the sorcerers to sneak after them into the portal? Did the Jiserians possess the ability to cast spells of invisibility? From his memory of the Order of the Dawn, Talis never recalled such a spell. But Rikar had followed them through two worlds portals unseen, so it was highly likely that the Jiserians knew such a spell.

"I'm guessing they are examining him, maybe trying to understand how the priests cast the blood magic spell? I still don't know what it means for us, though. And I just want to go home." Talis sighed and scanned over the beautiful rainforest, wishing he could just enjoy his time here with Mara and ignore all the craziness surrounding Rikar and the Nameless. He wished he had more time with her like the time they'd spent together at the smuggler's cove.

"With the Surineda Map we have an advantage, right?" She ran her fingers through his hair and he shivered in response. "Don't worry, we'll find a way back home. At least it's likely that Naru is safe. With the Jiserians fighting, and the Nameless after the Starwalker's fragments, they'll be too busy to bother with Naru, don't you think?"

You've forgotten that you murdered Emperor Ghaalis and killed Princess Devonia's brother, Talis thought. It was better that Mara remained calm and believed that their city and families were safe.

"They'll be fine, I don't think we need to worry about Naru." He held her hand and strolled along the path towards the waterfall and pool, savoring the sweet scents of fruits and flowers in the air. "Wherever we are, this is a strange and beautiful place, and it feels very peaceful and safe. The Starwalkers have a really advanced civilization; I've never seen anything like how this building is constructed. Do you think those are diamonds?"

They stared at the edge of the crystalline building and Mara took in a deep inhalation and spread her arms wide in wonderment. "Whatever it is made of, it's truly amazing. And that magical shield that protects the rooms...how did it know who you were and allow you to enter my room? Really quite interesting. I'm dying to explore this place. The jungle is so fragrant and vibrant, and all the flowers everywhere. Look!" She pointed at a school of colorful fish swimming in the deep pool and giggled in excitement.

"We should be careful as well. Beauty is deceptive. If the Starwalkers think that we're the equivalent to insects, then the things on their planet that are of no concern to them might be very harmful to us. Likely this forest is protected by even more shields. This is probably like a secluded palace garden."

"Then let's explore and find the way out. There didn't seem to be a door inside the room, so maybe we follow a path?" She squeezed his hand and pulled him along, squealing at brilliant butterflies that bat their wings and danced from flower to flower. Little hordes of spider monkeys chased each other across the maze-like limbs and chattered and screamed as they approached. Mara sniffed so many strange varieties of orchids and colorful, sweet smelling flowers that she sneezed and flushed red as she wiped her nose from the outburst.

"I'm such a mess!" she said, and chuckled nervously at Talis. "This place is so huge and beautiful. Good thing you have your map, otherwise I doubt we could find our way back."

"Let's try over there." He pointed off to where the path widened and the light seemed stronger than the soothing coolness of the jungle shade. They passed strange banana trees with small, red fruits, and around the corner, the path reached a river that stretched almost twenty feet across. Looking for a way over, Talis noticed that Mara had discovered an invisible bridge that spanned the width of the river, and she motioned for him to join her.

"Seems like they don't want anything to upset the naturalness of the rainforest." He stared down at the peaceful river and remembered the crystalline bridge in Vellia. "There's definitely a connection between the aesthetic tastes of those of Vellia and the Starwalker's world—if this is indeed the home planet of the Starwalkers."

"I suspect it is." Mara studied an orchid the size of an elephant's head. "Jared mentioned that they would discuss this with their high council. Surely such a body of Starwalkers could only exist on their home planet?"

"But aren't they travelers and transients by nature? Any home planet would likely just be a temporary place of rest and reflection and meditation—"

"And perhaps discourse and debate," Mara said, interrupting him. "The high council is certainly not permanent, but reserved for those tired in their long journeys abroad and returning home to share what they've found."

"Imagine what their archives must contain!" As Talis spoke, Mara's face brightened and her eyes seemed to share in his excitement. "All those collections from their journeys across the vast universe, here on one planet? Their world must have the most amazing museum collection…"

Through the thinning foliage they could see a tall, expansive shield shimmering in a rippling silver light. This was definitely different than their rooms, and from the broad pathway that led up to the entrance, was likely well traveled. As they strode up to the building, the ground seemed to sense their arrival and the shield vanished and revealed a huge, cavernous chamber that looked out over the blackness of space splattered with the milky wash of millions of stars. Talis stumbled forward in wonderment

301

and Mara gasped and exclaimed praises to the gods. What was this place? *Gods are we floating in the stars? Am I dreaming?*

Talis glanced around and spied Jared staring down at something hidden from where Talis stood. The Starwalker's amused eyes caught his and the man beckoned them over to where he stood. Mara squeezed Talis's hand even tighter as they ambled over, still gawking at the stars shining brightly outside the glass. Was it glass or crystal or a diamond? He almost bumped into Jared because Talis stared up instead of watching where he was walking, and the Starwalker chuckled and told him he wanted to show him something.

At first he caught Jared's beaming gaze, then glanced back to Mara, and out of the corner of his eye he spotted something round and blue covering the sky down below.

His chin fell down to his chest and he gaped at a view he'd only seen in visions and dreams.

A massive blue planet, an entire world filling up half the sky, the oceans and clouds far below, the continents and islands, the mountains and deserts and green swaths of teeming life.

This was same world that the Surineda Map had first shown him inside the Order of the Dawn.

His world. The Planet Yorek. They were floating in space over his world.

This was no dream, it was real.

CPSIA information can be obtained at www.ICGtesting.com
Printed in the USA
LVOW10s1306310315

432729LV00005B/398/P